# NO WAY OUT

Lynda Page

**headline**

First published in 2008 by
HEADLINE PUBLISHING GROUP

First published in paperback in 2009 by
HEADLINE PUBLISHING GROUP

1

Cataloguing in Publication Data is available from the British Library

Typeset in StempelGaramond by Palimpsest Book Production Limited,
Grangemouth, Stirlingshire

Printed and bound in Great Britain by
Clays Ltd, St Ives plc

Headline's policy is to use papers that are natural, renewable and
recyclable products and made from wood grown in sustainable forests.
The logging and manufacturing processes are expected to conform to the
environmental regulations of the country of origin.

HEADLINE PUBLISHING GROUP
An Hachette Livre UK Company
338 Euston Road
London NW1 3BH

www.headline.co.uk
www.hachettelivre.co.uk

# CHAPTER ONE

To the rest of the gathering, the grief-stricken young woman looked every inch the devastated fiancée of the man they'd all gathered together to bury.

Appearances in this case, though, were deceiving.

Stephanie Mortimer was deeply distressed by his sudden death, but wasn't experiencing the all-consuming physical pain felt by someone who had lost the love of their life. Steph hadn't loved William Normanton in the way she believed she should love the man she was planning to marry. He had, in fact, been a hard man to love.

A lardy, round-faced, twenty-five-year-old account-ant, fussed over by his doting mother, William had been pompous, obstinate, opinionated; of the firm belief that his caustic sarcasm was in fact wit; never hiding the fact that he'd perceived all women as naturally subservient to him. Stephanie had been very aware that as his wife she would have spent her every

1

waking moment aiming to please him, while all the time being expected to feel eternally grateful that it was her he had chosen to spend his life with. But so desperate was Steph to escape her own intolerable existence, she'd been willing to accept what life with William would have brought her.

William, though, had turned out not to be her saviour, having accidentally killed himself two weeks before. After investigating, the police had been in no doubt that in an inebriated state after a heavy session down at the local pub he had stumbled getting out of his car, falling and smashing his head on a large stone in the rockery. His lifeless corpse had been discovered at six the next morning by the Normantons' hysterical daily as she had arrived for work.

Through wet lashes Steph cast a discreet glance around the rest of the sorrowful-looking congregation and wondered how many of them were genuinely grieving for his loss, and how many were only attending the funeral as it would have looked bad not to do so. She was prepared to bet that many of them were wishing the formalities would soon be over so they could be anywhere else but here.

Her gaze then settled on the only person she knew to be genuinely mourning: William's widowed mother. Her stick-thin figure was dressed from head to toe in black, and she was sobbing uncontrollably into an already sodden handkerchief. A surge of deep guilt swept through Steph for all the lies she had told Jessica Normanton and her son in order to cover up her background. Judging from past experience, though, if they had discovered the truth about her, the marriage would never have taken place.

She felt a gentle nudge in her side. She was being offered a box containing earth for her to scatter over William's coffin.

As she trickled it through her fingers and into the grave, she spoke a last goodbye to him in her mind. I might not have loved you the way a future wife should, but you'd never have known that. I'd have done my very best to make sure you never regretted settling for me. Rest in peace now, William.

The small crowd began to disperse. Comforted by her elder sister, Jessica Normanton was being led towards the waiting funeral car. Steph knew she would be expected to follow. She was dreading the wake and having to keep up the part she was playing of bereaved fiancée. She'd have to listen to more praise of William's virtues, regret for the unfillable void in their lives his death was going to leave, while all the time she knew that apart from his mother they were lying. In reality their lives would become far pleasanter now that William was no longer around to blight them.

She sensed a presence by her side and turned her head. William's cousin Sonia, girlishly pretty and gamine at twenty years old, was looking sympathetically at her. 'Aunt Jessica asked me to fetch you, but if you want a few more minutes to say your goodbyes . . .'

Steph was touched that in the circumstances William's mother was giving any thought to her. 'I'm ready to go,' she responded.

Silently they began to make their way over to join the rest of the family who were travelling back to the Normantons' home for the wake. Sonia herself was looking thoughtful. She cast several sideways glances at the attractive, shapely blonde beside her before she took a deep breath and said, 'I know it's not the done thing to speak ill of the dead but I . . . well, not just me but the rest of the family too, apart from Aunt Jessica, of course . . . none of us could really understand why you were seriously considering marrying William.

'Even on a good day he wasn't a very nice person. I've lost count of the number of nights I've cried myself to sleep over a vile comment he's made to me, and I know I'm not on my own in that respect. I've yet to meet anyone more conceited and obnoxious than he is . . . was. I can't remember him ever having a good word to say about anyone. We all privately joked that any woman would have to be absolutely desperate to consider putting up with the likes of him, so you can imagine the shock we all got when we heard he was getting engaged, and even more so when you were introduced to us. We weren't expecting someone like you, that's for certain.'

A fleeting look of guilt crossing her face, Sonia quickly added, 'It's not entirely William's fault that he was the way he was. After Aunt Jessica suffered three miscarriages before he came along, neither she nor Uncle Maurice could be blamed for treating him like the most precious thing in the world to them. And then, when Uncle Maurice died so unexpectedly fifteen years ago, it's understandable that in her grief Aunt Jessica concentrated on looking after William but, in doing so, my mother says she helped make him the . . . er . . . well, how he was.'

Steph knew Sonia had been going to say 'the spoiled brat' he was, but in consideration of his fiancée had thought better of it. It would describe him perfectly, though. William would often throw childish tantrums if it looked like he wasn't going to get his own way, usually over inconsequential matters. His mother just couldn't bear to say no to him, and he hadn't liked it at all when anyone else had. Steph was keenly aware that her relationship with him had been the subject of much curiosity amongst his extended family, but they'd all been far too diplomatic to bluntly ask her any questions. Now William was dead there seemed no reason any longer for them to hold back.

Steph's conscience began to prick her. She had felt justified in lying about her background while preparing to become the wife it was doubtful William would ever have acquired for himself otherwise. Now he was dead, though, she couldn't justify deceiving his family any longer. They had all shown her such an enthusiastic welcome when she had first been introduced to them. In fact, their manner towards her had been the deciding factor when she had accepted William's proposal. Having such pleasant relatives around her would have enabled her to endure his behaviour, she had felt.

Lies, though, had a habit of catching out the teller, and usually when they were least expecting it. Steph had vehemently hoped that should hers ever be discovered, it would be well into the future and hopefully by then William and his family would be understanding of her reasons and forgiving of her. But his death had seen to it that she was no longer going to become a bona fide member of this family so she no longer had any valid reason to conceal her background. Oh, but to come clean now would be too much, just after his funeral. Better just to absent herself and leave his family to do their best to mourn him.

Grabbing Sonia's arm, Steph announced, 'I really

don't feel at all well.' She pressed her fingertips to her temple. 'I've a blinding headache.'

A look of remorse flooded her companion's face and she said, 'Oh, I've been so thoughtless, speaking to you like I was just now! When all's said and done you've just lost the man you loved.' She laid a hand on Steph's arm and said in concern, 'You poor, thing. Aunt Jessica is bound to have something in her medicine cabinet that will sort you out. My mother jokes that her sister has a pill for every occasion. She kept a bottle of everything in, just in case William was ever in need.'

Steph pulled a pained face and said, 'I don't think a couple of pills are going to take this headache away. I need to go to bed and sleep it off.'

Knowing William's mother as she did, she realised that her prospective daughter-in-law's absence would not cause much anxiety. Jessica was too immersed in her own grief.

'Could I trouble you to make my excuses to your Aunt Jessica and the rest of the family, please? And tell Mrs Normanton I will call on her soon.'

Then, before Sonia could respond in any way, Steph planted a quick kiss on her cheek, spun on her heel and hurried off in the opposite direction, very mindful that Sonia must be wondering why she was making her way out of the back entrance of the cemetery. It was a long walk around the perimeter to get to the bus stop which would take her back to where William's family were under the impression she lived, in cheap lodgings, under the watchful eye of a strict landlady.

# CHAPTER TWO

A while later Steph came to an abrupt halt before the entrance to a shrub-lined driveway, staring at the detached, three-storey redbrick Victorian villa at the end of it. The gracious home was surrounded by immaculately kept gardens and situated in an affluent suburb of the city. The August sunlight danced off the second-floor windows. To her it seemed that the house was sneering at her failed attempt to leave its walls. It seemed to tell her then there could be no escape, its insidious influence reaching out to draw her back in. Instinctively, she fought to resist it by grabbing hold of a brick-built gate-post. As she stood clutching it a feeling of utter foolishness flooded Steph. The house was just bricks and mortar after all, it had no hold on her, posed no threat to her. It was the people residing inside it who had made her life so miserable that she had been prepared to saddle herself with a difficult man like William, purely to escape them.

Releasing her hold on the gate-post, she took several deep breaths then walked up the drive.

The house was deathly quiet when she let herself into the spacious, well-equipped kitchen by the back door. As Steph took off her coat, laying it temporarily on the back of a pine kitchen chair, a troubled expression appeared on her face. In her present mood she was thankful her mother was not up yet so she hadn't to contend with her – but then, it was only just after twelve so Steph would have been shocked if she had been about. What was more disconcerting was the fact that there seemed to be no sign of Irene Jordan going about her business either. Their daily had been bustling around when Steph herself had left this morning, but from what she was observing now it appeared the elderly woman, for whatever reason, had departed in a hurry. The sink was piled with dirty dishes, food items used for breakfast still out on the work surface.

Steph jumped then as a thumping sound resounded on the ceiling. Her heart dropped like a stone. It was her mother summoning her, and Ursula Mortimer was not the type to appreciate being ignored. Steph couldn't cope with an altercation just now so it was best she responded.

Forty-two-year-old Ursula lay propped up on ivory satin-covered pillows, wearing a silk and lace nightdress over a once shapely body that was now thickening as middle age advanced. She had a black eye mask pushed up on her forehead. Once she had been a stunningly beautiful woman with long, naturally waving titian tresses. The steadily creeping grey was kept at bay through the intervention of her hairdresser, but years of heavy drinking, smoking and late nights were markedly taking their toll. Ursula, though, refused to accept what the reflection in the mirror was showing her, still seeing herself as the beauty she had been years ago.

She fixed bloodshot, black-ringed eyes on her daughter when Steph arrived in the close-curtained room. Noticing she was empty handed, Ursula petulantly demanded, 'Where is it?'

Steph frowned, bemused. 'Where's what, Mother?'

'The bottle of vodka I told that despicable little man where you work to get you to bring home. He was insisting you weren't in today, but where else would you be? I warned him he'd better pass on my message to you or I'd be speaking to his superiors and *he'd* be seeking a new position himself.'

Steph was wide eyed with horror. 'Oh, Mother, I begged you not to telephone me at work again. I told you what would happen to me if you did.'

Ursula waved one shaking hand dismissively. 'Oh, stop being so melodramatic, Stephanie. Jobs for filing clerks are two a penny. How else was I supposed to get hold of you in an emergency?'

Tears pricked Steph's eyes, her already low spirits sinking to rock bottom. There was no point in her going into work tomorrow or ever again. Mr Damson, her boss, had warned her only yesterday what the outcome would be should her mother's demands to speak to her on the most trivial pretext continue. In most cases it was to order her home at once because Ursula couldn't find her gloves and was late for a lunch appointment; or an item of clothing she wanted to wear had not been collected from the dry cleaner's; or she just wanted to chat – ceaselessly. Steph had lost count of the number of jobs her mother had lost her through such selfish behaviour. No matter how much she pleaded with Ursula not to bother her while she was at work, or not unless it was a matter of life or death, she paid absolutely no attention. Jobs for clerical staff might be plentiful, but due to her mother's constant interference such lowly positions were all Steph was qualified to take because she was never long enough in any job to gain promotion, let alone to build a relationship with her fellow employees.

Steph sighed heavily. It wouldn't enter her mother's head to get herself up, dressed and down to the off licence to fetch what she needed for herself. 'Mother, I begged you never to disturb me at work again unless it was a matter of life or death. I daren't imagine what Mr Damson must think of my own mother demanding I come home because she needs a bottle of vodka!'

Ursula glared darkly at her. 'You, you, you! Have you no space in that selfish mind of yours for a single thought for others? After that insolent woman waking me up so early with that dreadful noise she was making, I needed a drink to soothe my nerves. She had the gall to call it singing – but to liken it to a cats' chorus would be an insult to cats! I had to bang on the floor three times before she bothered to come and enquire what I was summoning her for. And when I asked her to fetch me the bottle of vodka and a glass from downstairs, she had the cheek to tell me that she was employed to clean, not to fetch and carry for me. When I finally got her to do what I was asking, she said she couldn't find the bottle, and I *know* she was lying because it was at least a quarter full when I had a drink from it before I went out last night.' Ursula gave a haughty sniff. 'Anyway, the awful woman won't dare treat me like that again, after the dressing down I gave her.'

Steph spotted the empty bottle and glass on the bedside cabinet. Her mother had obviously finished it off before falling into comatose sleep in the early hours of the morning, and forgotten. Sighing heavily, she asked, 'Just what did you say to Mrs Jordan, Mother?'

'I told her what I thought of her disrespect towards her employer, and that she'd better mend her ways or she'd be seeking new employment.'

Steph issued another deep sigh. 'And she's responded by showing you what she thinks of you as an employer. She's walked out.'

With shaking hands, Ursula was reaching over for a packet of cigarettes on her bedside cabinet. Selecting one, she fixed it into a long black holder and lit it with a gold lighter while drawling, 'How very inconsiderate of her to leave without giving notice. Well, if that's her attitude then good riddance to her! She'll be easily replaced.'

Steph sighed again. 'No, she won't. Getting reliable domestic help is almost impossible these days. It took me weeks to find Mrs Jordan. Just, please, don't upset Cook, Mother, because the likes of Mrs Sanders would be the devil's own job to replace.' She was the longest-serving member of the household they had managed to keep, thanks to Ursula's drink-fuelled temper tantrums. But Mrs Sanders' husband had been a drunken bully whose violent rages and the physical harm he'd inflicted on his wife made her employer's antics pale into insignificance as far as she was concerned. The job suited her as it was only a bus ride away from where she lived in a tiny rented terraced house, and the Mortimers paid her a shilling an hour more than she could expect to get for the same duties elsewhere, so she wasn't about to give the job up lightly.

Ursula drew hungrily on her cigarette and blew a plume of smoke into the air. 'Do make sure the next daily you take on knows her place.' Then, belatedly, she looked her daughter over. 'You're dressed very soberly for work, aren't you? You never listen to me, do you? If anyone knows about dress sense, I do. All black is purely for funerals . . . with the exception of the little black cocktail dress. No wonder you can't get yourself a man, going around like that!'

Steph stopped herself from reminding her that the reason she was manless was nothing to do with her dress sense but down to the kind of family she had. Ursula had absolutely no idea where her daughter had been that morning. If she had, she would have insisted on accompanying Steph, acutely embarrassing her daughter in the process. But then, her mother had no idea Steph had even met William, let alone become engaged and planned to marry him. If she had, she would soon have put an end to the relationship, like she had to other relationships that had showed promise, before Ursula had entered the picture.

Now she was demanding, 'Are you going to bring me up that bottle or—'

She was cut short when the bedroom door opened. The man who entered was over six foot tall, powerfully built, with a head of dark hair, beginning to grey at the temples, and a full beard. In his smart suit, he had a commanding air about him and was brandishing a newspaper.

Gerald Mortimer glared at his wife. 'I suppose it would have been too much to expect you to be up and about before midday? And look at the state of you! How much did you drink last night? One bottle . . . two?'

'How much I drink has absolutely nothing to do with you,' Ursula sneered at him.

'I'll make it my business should your drinking start to affect my reputation in any way. Be warned, Ursula.'

She was well aware he meant it, too. But up to now, no matter how drunk she got, there had always been a warning bell inside her head that sounded in time to stop her doing something that could seriously annoy her husband.

Now Gerald was wrinkling up his nose in disgust as the smell of her cigarette smoke wafted into his nostrils. 'And when are you going to kick that disgusting habit too?'

Taking a long draw from her cigarette, smoke billowing from her mouth, she responded, *'I'll give up my nasty little habits when you give up yours.'*

The look he flashed her was one of pure contempt.

Satisfied her reply had had the effect on her husband she had intended, she took another draw from her cigarette, purposely blowing the smoke in his direction before adding, 'To what do I owe this pleasure of a visit from you? And in my boudoir, of all places.'

Striding purposefully to the opposite side of the bed from Steph, he thrust the newspaper under Ursula's nose. Stabbing his finger at a particular heading, he snarled, 'How dare you publicly disgrace me like this? How humiliating do you think it was for me to find several of my registrars poring over this article in the common room before rounds this morning? We have an agreement to be discreet.'

Steph held her breath. Arguments between her parents had a tendency to turn ugly thanks to her mother's habit of throwing things when she lost her temper, and Steph did not feel like being caught up in the middle of one today. To make her excuses and leave, though, could result in her being dragged into the fray, by reminding them both she was there. Best she kept quiet.

Ursula was blank faced. 'I haven't a clue what you're talking about, Gerald.' She snatched the paper from him and looked at it. A photograph of herself, seemingly on very good terms with a good-looking young man at the event she'd attended the previous evening, was prominently displayed. A smug smile lit her face. 'I was right to choose that dress, it really does suit me, and those accessories . . . inspired!' Arching one perfectly tweezed eyebrow, she met her husband's furious gaze. 'Your underlings were most probably in awe of you for having such a beautiful wife.' A malicious spark dancing in her tawny eyes, her voice once again laden with innuendo, she added, 'The young man is rather handsome, don't you think, dear?'

Steph stiffened as she witnessed the red tinge of anger in her father's face, and waited for the explosion to come.

As it did, full force.

Striding away, Gerald roared over his shoulder, 'You're beneath contempt.'

Ursula grabbed up the empty glass from her bedside cabinet and threw it at him as she thundered back, 'No, you are! How dare you insinuate I'm desperate enough for male company to be availing myself of a boy young enough to be my son . . . who just so happens to be my godson! *Our* godson, Gerald.' She thrust the newspaper back at him. 'Don't you recognise Clara and Frederick's son, Damien?'

Steph stiffened. The heavy crystal glass had struck her father's shoulder hard before it smashed to smithereens around his feet. He wasn't a violent man so she knew he wouldn't respond in like manner. His preferred path to retribution was to hurt Ursula where it mattered most to her, financially. But he was suddenly too engrossed in the photograph to be aware of any physical damage the blow had caused him.

'Huh . . . Damien, you say? Well, he's changed since the last time I saw him.' It was clear he felt he'd made a fool of himself.

Ursula's tone was sardonic when she replied to this. 'Hardly that much since his eighteenth birthday party two months ago. I trust I'm allowed to be affectionate towards my own godson without being accused of having a flagrant affair with him? Now, haven't you any lives you need to be off saving? I don't appreciate being interrupted when I'm in the middle of a matter of utmost importance.'

'That being you've not had your morning fix yet, I presume,' her husband hissed, through clenched teeth. 'Just make sure you're ready to leave promptly at seven this evening.'

Ursula pulled a face. 'For what?'

Steph inwardly cringed. She knew her mother was well aware of the reason, having divulged to her yesterday that she wasn't at all looking forward to an evening spent playing the dutiful wife amongst people she knew would be utterly boring.

Gerald's eyes darkened dangerously. 'Do you deliberately set out to goad me, Ursula?'

'It's the only fun I have with you these days, Gerald.'

'You're pathetic,' he snarled. 'And I haven't time to play stupid games with you now.' He prepared to take his leave then a thought seemed to occur to him and he addressed his daughter. 'Make sure your mother is sober and behaves herself tonight, Stephanie. I shall be holding you personally responsible for that.'

Steph inwardly groaned. She should have realised she would be expected to chaperone her mother at tonight's event. She usually was when her mother and father were out in public together. But William's death, and what it meant for her, had been so all-consuming it had not registered with her when her mother had been voicing her displeasure about the event the previous day that Steph herself would need to attend too. She didn't have the energy to conduct polite chit-chat with strangers to keep one eye constantly on her errant mother. All she craved was time on her own, to take in her loss and come to terms with the fact that she was stuck where she was, unless another saviour came along.

'Well, I . . .' she began, but the look her father gave her stopped her mid-sentence. As far as he was concerned her own plans came second to whatever he had in mind. He was the head of the house and expected to be obeyed.

Meekly Steph said, 'Yes, Father.'

Once again he made to depart but stopped to give his wife a last warning. 'If I could have avoided your being there tonight, I would have. But the Derwents are religious people with strong family values. They only deal with similar people and so wish to meet my family and confirm we're solid. Michael Derwent is on the verge of making a sizeable donation to my latest research project, without that it's doubtful it'll go ahead, so believe me, I won't be at all happy if you do or say anything this evening to jeopardise things for me. There are other people going to be there tonight who are similarly placed to make donations, so you'd better be polite to them too.'

Ursula scowled murderously at his back as her husband strode from the room, shutting the door with a bang behind him. 'Insufferable man,' she hissed.

Steph sighed. If outsiders had any idea of the lives her parents lived, they'd want to know why they stayed together. The truth was, they both needed each other. Ursula needed Gerald to provide her with the standard of living she would not be able to afford should they part; Gerald needed Ursula to give him the cover of respectable family man, when in truth he was anything but.

Gerald Mortimer was homosexual.

Since Ursula too believed appearances were all-important, she would sooner die than allow her husband's secret to be discovered. Steph couldn't comprehend what it must have felt like for her finally to find out the truth about the man she'd married. She'd spent years feeling bewildered and hurt by the fact that as soon as she became pregnant, only weeks after they had married, with what was to be their only child, her husband lost all interest in her sexually. Despite the many furious rows they'd had on the subject, on each occasion he'd managed to fob her off as to the real reason. For years Ursula could only conclude that other women were satisfying her husband's needs, and sought solace for this slight in alcohol; what had started off as a tipple to help her get off to sleep, gradually built into the bottle a day it was now. Convinced Gerald met other women through work, she'd made numerous unannounced visits there in the hope of catching him out, but never did. This sent her spiralling into despair, not able to understand why her husband didn't find her desirable when it was readily apparent to her that other men did.

Unable to stand it any longer, she finally hired a private detective and, to her absolute horror, learned through the photographs he provided that her husband's sexual preference was in fact for men. His deviance had never become common knowledge because he had been so careful never to seek sexual gratification on his home turf. After periodically informing his wife he was off on a medical conference for the weekend, he would in fact be in another town, trawling red-light districts or visiting venues where it was known men like himself could be found.

At this revelation, Ursula's whole world disintegrated around her. She had been expecting a string of women . . . that she'd have been able to handle . . . but not a succession of men! But rising beyond her feeling of utter disgust and devastation at Gerald's deceit, was the terror of what this becoming common knowledge would mean for her.

There were parts of her past that Ursula flatly refused to discuss with her daughter, but Steph was aware that her mother's family had once been wealthy, with considerable holdings in investments and property. But their money had virtually disappeared overnight in the 1930 Crash. Her weak-minded father used the last of his cash to buy one-way tickets for himself and Ursula's four-year-old brother to Australia, never to be heard from again, leaving her mother to fend for herself and their then two-year-old daughter. A notice for eviction from their comfortable home looming, other creditors warning of bailiffs descending, Ursula's mother went cap in hand to her last remaining relative, who was in fact only related by marriage, intending to beg her husband's elderly aunt to take them in.

The aunt was a dear old lady, renowned for her kindly ways and generosity, so the outlook was hopeful. But, to her horror, Ursula's mother arrived at the house only to find the aunt's body being loaded into a hearse. She had been discovered dead in her chair earlier that day by a close neighbour. Her estate, the neighbour told her, had been bequeathed to the local church. So traumatised was she by this turn of events, her one avenue of help gone, that Ursula's mother never made it home. She collapsed in the street and died on the way to hospital, from a massive heart attack.

Ursula was taken in by the Council who thankfully managed to find her loving and financially comfortable adoptive parents whose own plans for a large family had been crushed by complications during the birth of their son who was a year older than Ursula. They doted on the new addition and, under their care and protection, Ursula blossomed into a beautiful, confident young woman. But at the age of sixteen, in her first year at finishing school, for some reason which Ursula would never divulge to her daughter, she was suddenly cast out by her adoptive parents and warned never to darken their doors again.

That night a young war widow found her huddled in her doorway, sheltering from the rain, when she went to put out the milk bottles before going to bed. Taking pity on her, she offered the girl a roof over her head and help in getting on to her feet.

According to Ursula, her young benefactress had been annoyed when, eighteen months later, Ursula told her that she had found a man who could keep her in the style to which she was accustomed. She left the Good Samaritan's house and the two of them never spoke again.

Ursula enjoyed the trappings of Gerald's medical success, along with his substantial inheritance from his parents. Socially, she enjoyed the prestige of being the wife of such a well-respected doctor, who was continually rising in rank. She could not bear it if the truth got out and everyone thought she had connived at his deceit, which was the opposite of the truth. On the other hand, if it did, she could equally well be labelled as that poor woman who was married for years to a queer and never knew, and from then on viewed as an object of curiosity and pity, which was a similarly appalling prospect.

Gerald himself was terrified once his dark secret had been discovered by her. He had a high reputation as a top consultant, as Professor of General Surgery at the Leicester Royal Infirmary, with an ever-growing list of private patients, too, whom he saw in his plush consulting rooms in Queens Road. If his sexuality ever became public knowledge, his life would be ruined.

It was the only time Ursula was to see her normally controlled husband an emotional wreck. Gerald begged her to strike an agreement with him; admitted it had been unforgivable of him to have taken a wife, knowing he could never be a proper husband to her. At the time his own family had been putting pressure on him to marry, and he had convinced himself he could make a go of it. But then, in turn, he had known Ursula hadn't loved him with the sort of passion most women felt for a future husband; it was more his inheritance and the kind of lifestyle he could give her that she was in love with. That being the case, why could they not continue as they had been doing? They would lead separate lives, careful not to embarrass each other, and she would retain every comfort.

Ursula accepted his terms, of course, with conditions. He must regularly replenish her wardrobe and not quibble over funding her social activities.

Like all women, though, she'd needed a confidante, someone with whom to discuss her appalling secret. Knowing only too well how other women loved to gossip, especially about such a juicy topic as this, it was her own daughter she chose to confide in.

Stephanie was twelve years old at the time, and at a stage in her life where she was struggling with the transition from child to woman, plus contending with adjusting to a new school and making friends there, as well as beginning to realise that her own parents were not exactly the loving, nurturing types most of her school friends had.

Having been cared for by a succession of nannies up until this time, Stephanie regarded her mother as a glamorous creature of the type who adorned magazine covers, flitting in and out of her life when she had a little time to spare, usually in between readying herself for another round of social engagements – or sleeping them off.

Her father Stephanie saw even less of as he had invariably left for the hospital by the time she came down from the nursery in the morning, and at least three times a week he didn't come home at all but stayed at his club. Or so he told his wife. On the few occasions she did come into contact with him, their communication was brief. Her father always seemed to be uncomfortable around Stephanie, and she realised as she reached adulthood and understood human nature better that this was more than likely through guilt on his part, because of the lie he was living. In consequence she never felt truly comfortable with him, and the only affection he ever showed her was an occasional pat on the head in praise of an achievement at school. She never ate with her parents and they never took her on any family outings unless, she realised later, it was to put on a show of being a happy family, for the benefit of others.

Through playground gossip, Steph at twelve years old was only just beginning to grasp what sex was all about. That it took a man to put his penis . . . whatever that was . . . inside the opening between a woman's legs for a baby to be made, and if you didn't want to end up pregnant before marriage then you definitely didn't sit on a toilet seat after a man had! She had heard words like 'poof', 'gay' and 'queer' used in respect of a man but had no idea what they actually meant, and didn't want to make herself look an unworldly fool by asking.

Suddenly finding her mother frequently requesting her company, and being forced to listen to her rage and weep interminably about the horrors of being married to a homosexual, had totally bewildered Stephanie. Her already strained relationship with her father grew even more so, her mother having made her believe he was someone to distance herself from, as if she was in danger of catching a deadly disease.

As she grew older and learned what the word

meant, as well as how others perceived and treated those who did not conform to society's norm, Stephanie realised how trapped she was by her mother's misplaced confidences. She was forced to collude in the front they both put on while bitterly regretting the fact that she had never been allowed to think of Gerald as a man who might have been a loving father to her, despite his sexual preferences.

On discovering her husband's true nature, Ursula became very dependent on her daughter, expecting Steph to be available to her whenever she wanted company, at whatever time of day or night. Prior to this any friends of her daughter were only allowed to play with her in her nursery where her nanny was in attendance. Now, when she knew her daughter had visitors, a drink-fuelled Ursula would pay them visits and mortify her daughter by her drunken antics. As a consequence, Steph stopped inviting other girls to her house, consequently they stopped inviting her to theirs, and gradually she found herself without any friends. Many of them had in any case perceived her to be a spoiled rich bitch since she was always dressed in the best of clothes and lived in a large, lavishly furnished house in its own half-acre of grounds. Little did they know! Steph would gladly have lived in a hovel, with rags on her back and no shoes on her feet, if it had meant she had parents who cared for her and enjoyed doing family things with her, like most other children. Even now Steph was aware that less well-off outsiders would be envious of the life they assumed she was living, but doubted very much they'd swap places with her if they learned the shameful truth.

Considering that her social life was barely existent thanks to her mother's intrusions on it, Steph knew she had done well to have several boyfriends to her credit, and at least two of whom she felt could have developed into something special, had they been allowed to. But as soon as she'd introduced them to her mother, Ursula – whether she'd had a drink or not – was all over them, commandeering their attention as if she assumed that all men were completely unable to resist her charms. The two men had beaten a hasty retreat, unable to contemplate a future with the likes of Ursula for a mother-in-law, no matter how much they thought of Steph.

She knew that the only way she was ever going to be able to live her own life, something she was so desperate to do, was to make a complete break from her parents. But she couldn't fund a home of her own due to the fact that she had never been in a job long enough to enable her to earn good wages. Besides that, her father had spiked her guns by making it plain to her from a very early age that he expected her to be responsible for overseeing his household.

Ursula had stopped doing so as part of her retaliation against him for the mental pain and suffering he'd caused her by his secret way of life. The only way Gerald could ensure that Ursula stuck to her bargain with him, as well as making sure she didn't eventually bankrupt him, was to keep tight control of her finances. Consequently, apart from a small allowance in cash which he gave Steph each week, everything was charged and he paid only the bills from suppliers with whom he had opened an account.

Life under her parents' roof was intolerable for Steph. If she wasn't enduring the long stony silences between them, then she was caught up in the middle of ferocious arguments. Their selfishness towards her left her no opportunity to forge a fulfilling life for herself. She had racked her brains for a way out, but her lack of money brought her to the conclusion that the only way out for her was to marry – and she fully intended to do it secretly, so that her parents could not intervene and ruin her chances.

She wasn't the mercenary type. She didn't go all out to capture herself a wealthy husband. She told herself that if a man paid her some attention and she felt she could get on well enough with him, then that was good enough for her. Though William had been far from the man of her dreams, she'd believed that life with him would still be a damn' sight better than the one she was having to endure at home.

She had met him when he had come to the place where she was working at the time, to conduct an audit of the firm's books. It was apparent from the start that he was attracted to the pretty young receptionist and conceited enough to be of the opinion that, should he ask her out, she would jump at the chance. For Steph, dealing with William's conceitedness was child's play compared to assuaging her mother's all-consuming neediness. William wasn't really interested in Steph's background as he was too wrapped up in himself: he'd seemed happy when she led him to believe she had no family, and she took this to mean that he'd prefer to have her all to himself. His family were a little more inquisitive, but had no reason to doubt the humble background Steph had invented for herself.

Now William's fatal accident had shattered all her hopes of escape, and due to her limited social life there was no telling when she'd have a second chance. To add to her woes, thanks to her mother she had lost another job.

Could life for her get any worse!

Ursula was barking at her, 'For Christ's sake, get

me a drink, will you? I need something to wash the nasty taste of *that man's* visit out of my mouth.'

Steph sighed. Her father had warned her to make sure her mother was sober tonight, but how on earth she was going to achieve that was beyond her.

# CHAPTER THREE

With her back pressed against a wall covered in expensive flocked paper, half-drunk glass of Martini Bianco in hand, Steph cast her eyes anxiously around the room. Several waitresses fighting hard not to show their boredom were keeping the gathering supplied with drinks and canapés. Her father was deep in discussion with Michael Derwent and several other affluent-looking, middle-aged types over by the fireplace; a few dozen more smartly turned-out men and women were mingling, but it was her mother's whereabouts that she was forced to concentrate upon.

To Steph's surprise, Ursula had seemed sober and in a good mood when they had joined Gerald in the hall at seven, ready to depart, and Steph had prayed that this state of affairs would continue for the rest of the evening. Regardless, she had kept vigilant watch on her mother until, having taken her eyes off her for just a moment while she accepted a drink from one of the waitresses, about half an hour ago, Ursula had vanished. Steph had just returned from a discreet tour of the reception rooms and Ursula was nowhere to be found.

She was about to peel herself away from the wall and retrace her steps when a voice beside her whispered, 'Are you as bored as me?'

She turned her head to find a man standing by her side. He was older than herself, in his mid-thirties, she guessed, clean shaven and extremely good looking. She could tell by the look in his eyes that he found her attractive, too. But it was hardly the time for her to flirt. She had just buried a fiancé, after all.

'This sort of thing isn't my cup of tea,' Steph replied primly.

He took a sip of his drink. 'Wouldn't be so bad if they played a bit of music, then we could have had a dance. Do you like dancing?'

'I doubt I'd win any competitions, but yes, I do.'

'Me too. You should see my "Hippy Hippy Shake", but my party piece is "The Twist". You should see me go! I could give Chubby Checker something to worry about.'

He was a bit out of date, she thought. Steph herself preferred The Walker Brothers, Dusty Springfield and Aretha Franklin.

He was tapping the side of his glass and continuing,

'Mind you, I need to have had a few of these to give me courage first so there's no chance of seeing me in action tonight. I'm on a strict warning to be on my best behaviour. One drink and no more.'

Steph gave him a knowing look. 'From your wife, I assume?'

He shook his head. 'I haven't been so lucky as to find myself a good woman yet who'll put up with me and my demanding lifestyle as a doctor.' He grinned winningly at her. 'Unless tonight is my lucky night. No, my warning was from my boss.' Much to her surprise, a look of alarm crossed his face then and he unexpectedly dropped down on one knee – careful not to spill his drink – and pretended to be searching for something on the floor. He lifted his head cautiously to look through the crowd, then, seeming satisfied, stood up again. He said to a bemused Steph, 'I'm not mad, honestly. It's just I thought I saw him about to head over here and give me a rollicking for not doing what I was specifically invited here for.'

'Which is?' she asked, intrigued.

'To help sell the research project he is heading up, in the hope of prising more donations out of the Derwent's rich friends.'

Steph looked over at her father, still engrossed in his conversation. So this man worked for him? Gerald wasn't exactly the sort of parent she would have liked. She found herself suddenly intrigued to hear what sort of boss he made. 'Is he a decent man to work for?' she asked.

Her companion pulled a face. 'Depends what you call decent, I suppose. He's the best in the business and people fight to be accepted as one of his registrars. He's known to be a perfectionist, who doesn't suffer fools gladly. Personally I think he's a tyrant, and know I'm not alone in my view. He takes great delight in bullying his staff and watching them squirm. He's got absolutely no bedside manner either – woe betide any patient of his who dares question him about their condition. He's got all the nurses on his wards running scared of him, even Staff Nurse Frazier who we all reckon is Hitler's sister!

'He reminds me of James Robertson Justice playing Sir Lancelot Spratt in those old doctor films with Dirk Bogart. I used to watch them at Saturday matinees when I was a teenager. Ironically, they're what first stirred my ambitions to become a doctor myself. Little did I realise then that I would end up working for someone just like Spratt! Might have thought twice if I had.'

Steph had watched those films and many other black-and-white classics while curled up alone on the settee, her parents far too wrapped up in their own lives to consider spending any free time with her. It surprised her to find that she had not noted the resemblance between her father and the fictional consultant before, but now it was pointed out to her she could see they sported similar physiques, facial hair, and abrasive, no-nonsense personalities. She knew her father to be a difficult man, but regardless hadn't expected to hear a junior speak this way of him. She wished now she'd never asked. She really ought to put this young man wise as to who she was. It was going to embarrass him enough, before he said anything else.

She was about to when he continued, 'Mind you, I suppose I should count myself lucky I still have my job after what Morty . . . that's our nickname for him, by the way, not that we would ever dare call him to his face . . . caught me and a couple of colleagues doing this morning. We were poring over an article in the morning paper featuring his wife. She'd been at some do or other last night. None of us can believe she's such a stunner. We can only conclude she must have married Morty for his money. Apparently, his daughter is quite a looker, too.

'Anyway, the trouble was that Morty overheard us discussing his wife's attributes and our conclusions about why she'd married him. The upshot of it is that we've all been punished in Morty's own ineffable way. Osborne's been put on a fortnight of nights – and he only just finished a month's stint; Kitchen's been given a proper nerd of a junior doctor to accompany him around for the foreseeable future; and my penance is to help raise funds for his latest research, which means being here tonight when he was well aware I was supposed to be at a cousin's wedding.' He gave her a meaningful look and added, 'Though obviously it's not been without its compensations.' He held out his hand to her. 'I'm Adam Tennant – delighted to make your acquaintance. If you happen to be free on Friday night, maybe you'd like to . . .'

'Oh, thank God! There is intelligent life after all among all these boring relics. I was beginning to despair.' Hooking her arm through Adam's and staring meaningfully into his eyes, Ursula added, 'How about being my knight in shining armour and getting me a drink? Then we can find a secluded corner and you can tell me *all* about yourself.'

Steph had had to fight to keep her balance due to her mother's rudeness in squeezing in between Adam and herself. It was very apparent what her mother had been doing during her absence as she'd obviously consumed a good deal of alcohol recently. 'Be careful, Mother, you nearly made me spill my drink,' snapped Steph crossly.

Ursula spun her head to give her daughter an annoyed glance. 'Hark at you, calling me Mother.' She spun back to face Adam. Draping herself over him, she scoffed. 'As if I'm anywhere near old enough.

It's just my little sister's attempt at being humorous. Now, where were we?'

It never occurred to Ursula that any man could be more interested in her daughter than he was in her. Any other girl would have been extremely annoyed by such a flagrant display of bad behaviour, but this kind of situation had happened to her so many times that Steph took it in her stride. It was readily apparent to her, though, that Adam had recognised her mother from her photograph in the newspaper. His face had turned ashen, eyes darting towards her father over at the other side of the room. It was clear he was terrified of possible repercussions should his boss find him in such a compromising situation.

With a wrench he succeeded in freeing himself from Ursula's clutches, blurting, 'Excuse me, but I really should be mingling.'

With that he hurried off to introduce himself to a group of people nearby.

An annoyed Ursula shot at Steph, 'Now look what you've done. Lost me my only chance of having any fun here tonight.' Then, raising her voice, she continued, 'Go and tell our hostess to put some music on. At least that might help liven things up a bit.' She then thrust her empty glass at her daughter. 'Get me a refill first.'

In hushed tones, Steph said to her, 'Don't you think

you've had enough, Mother? We're representing Father, don't forget. He won't be pleased if we ruin this evening for him.'

Ursula looked across at her husband, her eyes holding open dislike. 'Just look at him, holding court! I doubt any of those men fawning around him would waste their spit on him if they knew the truth about him. I'd give anything to be the one to enlighten them.'

Steph paled. 'You wouldn't, though, would you, Mother?' she implored quietly.

Ursula fixed her daughter with her eyes. 'Only because I've got too much to lose. Anyway, I'll be the one to judge when I've had enough to drink and I've a long way to go yet, so fetch me another.'

'No, *I'll* be the judge,' another voice hissed.

Steph stiffened. It was her father.

Face thrust close to Ursula's, he snarled, 'I saw you draped all over my registar like a common tart! Have you no pride, woman? Thank goodness no one else seemed to have noticed.' He then glowered at his daughter. 'How could you stand by and watch your mother get into the state she's in? Take her home before she risks causing me embarrassment.'

'But I don't want to go home,' Ursula said defiantly. Her eyes sparkling maliciously, she added, 'Why should I when I'm enjoying myself so much?'

Just then their hostess appeared, an attractive, slim,

fifty year old, dressed becomingly in a simple black evening dress with her salon-blonded hair piled in loops and curls around her head. But, regardless, she paled into the background beside Ursula, who looked stunning in a clinging emerald green strapless cocktail gown, her thick titian locks waving gently to her slender shoulders. Simple diamond drop earrings and pendant necklace finished off the effect. It had been apparent to Steph on their first arriving that Davina Derwent hadn't been pleased to be upstaged by the younger, far more beautiful wife of their guest-of-honour. Simpering at Gerald now, she said to him, 'Is everything all right, Mr Mortimer?'

'My wife seems to have developed a migraine and I'm advising her to go home.'

'Oh, I'm so dreadfully sorry to hear that,' Davina responded sympathetically. Steph knew by the spark of delight that flashed in her eyes that she was lying. Ursula's departure would mean she could reclaim her status as most attractive woman at the party. 'Would you like me to arrange to have her driven home, so as not to spoil your evening? After all, it is being held specifically in your honour.'

'I'm sure that the young man I was just talking to would oblige,' said Ursula, a spark of devilment in her eyes. She then caught hold of her husband's arm and reached up on tiptoe to whisper in his ear, 'But, of course, if you have your eye on him yourself, I wouldn't dream of standing in your way . . . He is rather delicious, don't you think, dear?'

The purple hue of fury tinged Gerald's cheeks then. Gripping her arm tightly in response, he said through clenched teeth, 'I think it best you go home in a taxi. You're really not well at all, are you, *darling*?' He addressed his hostess again. 'Would you be kind enough to call a cab for my wife and daughter?'

She went off to do his bidding and Gerald hissed to Ursula, 'You're to go straight home, remember. I don't want to find my staff discussing your appearance in the morning papers again. And if you're considering defying me, then remember how keen you are to spend Christmas in Scotland with your friends. It won't come cheap.'

This was news to Steph, but then she wasn't surprised her mother was already planning to be away for the festive season as she couldn't remember the last Christmas she had spent at home. It would have been nice if her mother had shown her the courtesy of telling her herself, though. Her father was not religious or a family man, and Christmas was just an inconvenience to him inasmuch as it disrupted hospital routine and he had to manage with a skeleton staff. She would receive a gift from him, usually jewellery, which he would commission his secretary to purchase on his behalf. All the pieces she had received so far lay unworn in her jewellery box as they were a middle-aged spinster's preference and not at all the sort of thing Steph would have picked herself. He did at least bother, though. Her mother always gave her money, last year it was ten pounds, telling her to buy herself something nice. It was usually a parting gift before she headed off to wherever it was she had planned to escape to that year.

Ursula was glowering at her husband in pure hatred. How it infuriated her, not having the upper hand with him. The only way he could control her was with money, and she knew to her cost that he would not hesitate to spoil her Christmas if she defied him now. She didn't plan to spend her festive season staring at him over the dinner table.

Davina Derwent returned, accompanied by a waitress armed with Ursula's and Steph's coats. 'The taxi is on its way,' she said to Gerald, then to Ursula in a sickly sweet voice, 'I'm so sorry your evening has been cut short, Mrs Mortimer. I do hope you'll be feeling better soon.'

Steph stiffened, seeing her mother about to respond. Her father obviously realised it too because he snatched her coat off the waitress and, in a commanding voice, said to Ursula, 'Let me help you on with this, my dear.'

Steph herself was glad to accompany her mother home, desperately wanting some time alone after the way she had spent her morning.

The taxi had hardly turned the corner of the street when Ursula ordered the driver, 'Drop me off in Pockington's Walk.' Taking her compact and lipstick out of her handbag to touch up her make up, she said to Steph, 'Hopefully Harry's Place has more life in it tonight than that mausoleum we've just left.' Harry's Place was a private drinking club that was popular with the moneyed set at the moment. Naturally her mother was a member.

'But Father said I was to see you home,' Steph reminded her.

'Because the poor love is so worried about my safety?' she responded mockingly, as she peered into her compact, simultaneously puckering her lips to apply a fresh coat of lipstick. 'Only we both know the only thing he's really worried about is me doing something that could make people question that perfect family-man act of his.' Closing her compact and replacing it in her handbag, she said, 'Do you think I'd be stupid enough to do anything to jeopardise the life I've got? Not after all this time of putting up with it, I wouldn't. In truth, I have the perfect marriage. Most women eventually tire of having sex with their husband, you know. Whereas I can go out every night, having fun and sleeping with any man I choose, so long as I'm discreet about it.'

Steph was hardly in any position to question her

mother's ethics when she herself had been prepared to marry a man she wasn't in love with, in order to escape her parents' roof.

She was actually relieved her mother wasn't coming home with her because with Ursula out of the way she would get the peace and quiet she so desperately craved.

A while later, dressed for comfort in a pair of warm flannel pyjamas and a quilted dressing gown, and armed with a cup of milky hot chocolate, Steph was preparing to ascend the stairs to her room, when she heard a key scraping in the lock of the front door and, to her dismay, her mother entered.

Ursula didn't look pleased. Slamming the door behind her, she said bad-temperedly, 'Harry's Place was dead so I tried several others which were as bad. Oh, well, it looks like it's just me and you. Go and fetch me a large V and T and bring it up to my room. Then we can settle down for a long chat.' She draped her fur coat over her arm and made her way past her daughter on the stairs.

It was pointless Steph telling her mother she wanted to be on her own. Ursula had decided she wanted her company and wouldn't accept anything less. It wasn't as if Steph had a job to go to in the morning, either, although she would be seeking another urgently or it would mean she'd have the humiliating task of asking her father for financial assistance. And of course she'd have to pay it back, because there was no way her father was going to let her become independent. Sighing resignedly, she went off to do Ursula's bidding.

It was approaching three and her mother had demolished several more large vodka and tonics. She had been ranting incoherently for hours about people and places Steph hadn't a clue about or wasn't interested in before she allowed her daughter to leave – or rather, passed out. By this time Steph herself was having great difficulty keeping her eyes open and was desperate for sleep. She'd hardly snuggled under the covers when she heard a loud ringing on the doorbell. She sat bolt upright in bed. Who on earth could be calling at this time of night? Her mother wouldn't have heard it, comatose with drink, and even if she had wouldn't get up to answer it. As far as Steph was aware her father was still out as she hadn't heard him come home yet, so she knew it was up to her to do the honours.

A few moments later she stared stunned at the two policemen on the doorstep. Bewildered, she asked, 'Can I help you, officers?'

The elder of the two smiled kindly at her and asked, 'Sorry to disturb you but could we speak to Mrs Mortimer, please?'

It must be something important for them to be calling at this hour. Her mind whirling as to what it could possibly be, Steph politely stood aside. 'If you'd like to come in, I'll go and wake her for you.'

# CHAPTER FOUR

S teph swept her eyes around the gathering at the graveside. There must be at least two hundred people here, all of them appearing suitably mournful. She wondered how many were genuinely grieving for the loss of her father from their lives and how many were putting on a show. Would she ever attend a funeral where the departed was truly missed?

She knew for certain her mother wasn't remotely upset but revelling in all the attention she was receiving, sparkling in her assumed role of Gerald Mortimer's devastated widow.

Two weeks ago Ursula hadn't been at all pleased to have her sleep disturbed, and had risen only reluctantly to speak to the police, donning a flimsy silk robe over her matching nightdress, an outfit more in keeping with receiving a lover than officers of the law. As was her initial greeting to them: 'Well, hello, gentleman, to what do I owe the pleasure?'

Both policemen declined her offer of a drink as

they were on duty. As soon as Steph had handed her mother hers, the elder of the two constables informed them of the reason for the visit.

Gerald Mortimer was dead. His crumpled body had been discovered by a cyclist, on a dark stretch of road in the outskirts of the city. He was very clearly dead, the cyclist could tell even before he got off his bike to take a closer look. His injuries were appalling. It seemed that he'd been the victim of a hit and run. The police had later found Gerald's car parked at the side of the road with a puncture, so he was most likely hit by a careless motorist as he tried to flag down help. One of the constables admitted, grimly, that they were unlikely to find whoever did it; no one had owned up, no witnesses had come forward.

This shocking news had knocked the breath from Steph. Her legs started to buckle and she was only saved from falling by the quick action of the younger of the two policemen who leaped up from his seat to catch her. Gerald may not have been the kind of father she'd wished for, but he'd kept her clothed and fed and with a roof over her head, which was more than she'd been able to provide for herself. She did gather her senses enough to voice a query as to why he had been travelling down a quiet country road on the outskirts of the city, way off the route she would have thought he'd have taken to come home from the Derwents'. The police were as baffled as she was by this.

Steph did then have some difficulty in believing that in such a short space of time the two men in her life had met their end, their bodies to be buried in the same cemetery within feet of each other.

Ursula had appeared genuinely shocked by the news of her husband's death, but the tears that flowed then were purely for the benefit of the policemen, Steph knew. As soon as they had left, after making arrangements for her to formally identify her husband's body the next day, she had knocked back her drink, leaped to her feet and danced gleefully around the room, shouting out her joy that at long last she was free from the millstone around her neck. Now she'd be able to live her life the way she wanted – and she couldn't wait to find out how much she was worth!

On waking the next day, using the telephone at her bedside, she'd immediately set about booking herself appointments with her beautician and hair-stylist, and arranged for exclusive fashion retailers to bring around selections of discreetly flattering mourning wear. Despite secretly wishing she could have a hole dug in common wasteland and her husband's body dumped unceremoniously in it, she arranged for his funeral to be a grand affair. Gerald's body was to be transported by black coach and horses, the wake afterwards held at the Grand Hotel. She issued all her instructions to Steph and expected her to get on with it. Steph knew if she didn't the funeral would not happen, so she had no choice. But she was not at all happy with the elaborate plans. Her father may have been an important man in his particular field, and certainly they had received commiserations a plenty from his patients and colleagues, but the funeral her mother was demanding would be more in keeping with a minor aristocrat than a doctor, and neither would it come cheap.

Increasingly annoying as well was the influx of her mother's friends who arrived at the house to help her 'mourn'. They appeared sympathetic – gushingly so – and some of them may have belonged to Leicester's social elite, but it was glaringly apparent to Steph that all of them were nothing more than freeloaders. Between them they consumed enormous amounts of food and drink, all purchased and delivered by Simpkin & James, purveyors of the finest foodstuffs and wines to those who could afford their exorbitant prices.

Their daily having walked out meant that, until Steph could find another willing to work for them, it was up to her to tackle the household chores herself as her mother didn't do anything to risk chipping her immaculately manicured nails. Between keeping the house clean when it was constantly being disrupted by her mother's endless visitors and carrying out

Ursula's instructions for the funeral arrangements, Steph had managed to find time to put a card in the local shop window but as yet had received no enquiries from would-be cleaners.

She was mortally glad their cook hadn't yet decided she'd had enough, but feared she would if matters carried on the way they were. Mrs Sanders had already approached her and grumbled about the number of people that were invading her kitchen, demanding food. Her normal hours of employment were for an hour in the morning, which had been to see to Mr Mortimer and Steph's breakfast – Ursula's morning sustenance, whatever time she rose, being a pot of coffee accompanied by cigarettes – and three hours, from four until seven, for the evening meal. She also saw to all the ordering of the food. She hadn't a problem with working over the odds during this sad time, but she did expect to be paid for all the extra hours she was putting in.

Steph was deeply concerned over the rising costs of her mother's frivolous lifestyle when as yet they had no idea what financial state Gerald had left them in. A meeting with his solicitor had been arranged for the day after the funeral and therefore she felt they should be cautious until then. After she'd voiced her concerns to her mother, Ursula responded in no uncertain terms that she hadn't been at liberty to entertain her friends at home while her husband had been alive, and so now she was free to, she was going to make up for lost time and do it in style. And this conversation reminded her that she hadn't yet called back the travel agent's to inform them to go ahead and confirm the cruise she was going to take around the Mediterranean. It sailed the week after she returned from Christmas and Hogmanay in Scotland – first-class, of course – *and* she was taking a girl-friend with her and footing the bill herself.

Steph felt very much alone as she followed her mother towards the funeral cars. Ursula was flanked on either side by her friends, all busily fussing over her, which she was lapping up. How nice it would have been for Steph too to have had friends to lean on for support, but her mother had seen to it that she didn't.

In the throng she spotted Adam Tennant along with a couple of other smartly dressed men she assumed to be her father's current registrars. Adam must have sensed her looking at him because he turned his head and looked her way. For a brief moment their eyes met, but the instant they did a look of embarrassment filled Adam's face and he hurriedly glanced away, engrossing himself in conversation with his colleagues. He was either uncomfortable over the comments he had unwittingly made to her about her father at the Derwents' party or bothered that associating with her could result in his finding himself in a compromising situation with her mother again. Either way, it was obvious he didn't want to become involved. Steph felt hurt but supposed she couldn't blame him.

Then she felt a hand clasp her arm and a voice say, 'Steph dear, how lovely to see you. I was so sorry you were taken ill at William's funeral. Anyway, have you come to visit his grave? Well, so have I. We could go together, couldn't we?'

She gasped in shock to see Jessica Normanton. William's mother was holding a bunch of white chrysanthemums. Steph's mind raced frantically. She had led Jessica to believe that she was an orphan so as to avoid the families meeting and risking the end of the relationship. She couldn't very well now tell her that she wasn't visiting William's grave at all but was in fact attending her own father's funeral.

Then, to her horror, a middle-aged woman came up to Steph and said, 'I apologise for interrupting but I just wanted to express my sympathies for your loss, Miss Mortimer. I was your father's secretary at the Royal.'

The woman went on her way.

Jessica Normanton was staring at her, bewildered. 'Did that woman get you confused with someone else? You couldn't have just lost your father, could you, Steph dear, as you told William and me you were orphaned as a young girl?'

Steph gulped hard.

Then Mrs Sanders appeared and said to her, 'I think your mother's trying to catch your attention, Miss Mortimer. She's ready to leave but can't until you get in the car. She looks to be in a bit of a temper to me, so I'd hurry up if I was you.'

Steph gulped again. 'Er . . . thank you, Mrs Sanders.'

Jessica Normanton was staring at her darkly. 'So you lied to us about your orphan status? Why would you do something so despicable? And if you've lied to us about that, what else have you lied to us about . . .'

Steph looked at her imploringly. 'Oh, but, Mrs Normanton . . . I can explain why I wasn't truthful with you about my family. You see . . .'

The other woman held up her hand, her face distraught. 'And why should I believe anything you tell me? Is it not bad enough that I'm mourning my son, without finding out he was about to saddle himself with a liar for a wife? How could you deny the existence of your own mother and father? It takes a callous person to do such a thing. Did you really love my son, I wonder, or were you using him for some reason known only to yourself?' Her eyes were filled with hurt. 'I was so pleased when William brought you home. Delighted he'd found himself a lovely girl. I treated you like my own daughter!

'Since his funeral, I haven't been able to stop thinking about you, stuck in those miserable lodgings you described, with that stickler of a land-lady who wouldn't allow you any visitors. I was going to ask you to come and lodge with me, so that we'd be company for each other while we both got over William's death. And all the time . . . well, judging from this elaborate funeral, it's no miserable lodging you're living in, is it?' Jessica's eyes narrowed to slits and she hissed, 'Well, you won't be finding a welcome at my door ever again, so please don't even think of knocking on it.'

With that she walked away, leaving a devastated Steph staring helplessly after her. This was the very last thing she had wanted. William's family were all going to think the worst of her now, and even if she did brave it and go and see his mother, beg her at least to listen to why she'd lied to them about herself, she had badly damaged her credibility in their eyes. They'd never really trust her again after this. The loss of these people from her otherwise miserable life was something she felt acutely. This had taught her a very painful lesson. That it didn't pay to lie, whatever the reason.

Several hours later a mentally and physically exhausted Steph wandered outside to perch on the edge of the old well. It was situated on the periphery of a small copse at the bottom of the garden. There had been a dwelling on the land the Mortimers' house now occupied for hundreds of years and water from this deep well had been the only supply until the middle of the last century, when the old dwelling had been demolished and the present house built and connected to the mains water supply and sewerage system.

As a child, the well had been Steph's own private place. She liked to come and speak to the fairies who lived in the bottom of it – not that the bottom could be seen – but she would imagine them living there in mushroom houses in a fairy kingdom ruled over by a beautiful queen. It was this queen to whom she addressed her wishes. Would she please make her daddy and mummy like other mummies and daddies? And would they spend more time with her? She didn't want to be greedy, she'd be happy with an hour a day of them playing with her in her nursery or reading to her, and maybe they could take her out sometime instead of paying the nanny to. But the fairy queen obviously had not heard her as her wishes were never granted.

The sound of upbeat popular music and raucous laughter filtered down to her from the house. Steph gave a deep sigh. She felt it very disrespectful of her mother to be partying like this, considering they had buried Father only a few hours before. Even if her marriage had been difficult, Ursula had agreed to stay in it when she'd had the option of getting out.

Despite her mother knocking back at least three vodka and tonics before departing for the funeral, Steph was grateful that Ursula had conducted herself appropriately throughout the ceremony and afterwards at the wake, until the last of the hospital dignitaries and affluent acquaintances of her father's, such as Michael Derwent, had made their leave. Then she had suggested to the remainder, who were all her own friends, that they return to her house and continue there. It was now just after one in the morning, and from what Steph had observed of the merrymaking before she had sought solitude in the garden, it didn't seem like any of the guests were tiring. She was desperate for rest but there was no point in her going to bed. She didn't have a hope of sleeping with all the racket that was going on.

It was taking all her will-power not to go back into the house and order everyone to leave, but it was her mother's house now and Steph had no say in what happened in it. She did strongly suspect that the majority of the guests were the type who would move on once all the food and drink – especially the drink – ran out, but remembering the size of the stock in the pantry, it could last for days.

Steph's thoughts drifted. When she had her own place, she would be in charge of everything that went on inside her own four walls. She sighed heavily. That time couldn't come quickly enough for her. She peered down into the inky blackness of the well and whispered, 'Please, Fairy Queen, please let my father have remembered me in his Will.'

# CHAPTER FIVE

Gerald Mortimer had remembered his daughter, all right.

The next afternoon, at ten minutes past three, a furious Ursula let out a cry of: 'The bastard!'

Clarence Wilford, a pinched, wiry, middle-aged man of diminutive height, with strands of thin grey hair pulled across the top of his egg-shaped head in an effort to hide his baldness, gasped in shock at such an outburst from a respectable widow. 'Now, now, Mrs Mortimer, please calm down,' he tried to soothe her.

'Calm down?' she hurled at him. 'How would you feel, Mr Wilford, if you'd stood by your wife for years in order to cover up her nasty little . . .'

'Mother,' Steph interjected sharply. 'Don't say anything you might come to regret.'

Ursula glared at her. 'The only regret I have right this minute is staying in my hell of a marriage when I could have escaped from it years ago! How could Gerald do this to me? He's treating me like a child.'

'From my perspective, it seems to me to be Mr Mortimer's way of looking after you, Mrs Mortimer,' Clarence Wilford said diplomatically.

Ursula glared darkly at him. 'How dare you treat me in such a condescending, manner? My husband is trying to control me from the grave.' She ordered her daughter, 'I shall expect you to sign everything over to me once it is in your possession.'

But Steph was lost in a world of her own, thoughts whirling, heart racing excitedly. At long last the Fairy Queen had granted her wishes! She would now have the means at her disposal to make a bid for freedom. A jab in her side and her mother's angry voice brought her back to the present. 'Sorry, Mother?'

'Oh, for goodness' sake, you look like the village idiot with that face you're pulling,' Ursula snapped at her crossly. She said to Mr Wilford, 'Aren't we going to be shown the courtesy of being offered any refreshments?'

He stared blankly at her. He knew he had offered beverages when they first arrived but felt it best not to remind Ursula Mortimer of this in her present mood. He strongly suspected she had already had several drinks before she had arrived, and not the soft kind. He reached over, preparing to flick the switch on his desk intercom. 'I'll ask my secretary to bring in a tray of tea. Or would you prefer coffee?'

She looked down her nose at him. 'The news I'm hearing calls for something stronger than that. I'll have a large vodka and tonic.'

'Oh, er . . . I can't offer you any alcohol, I'm afraid.'

'You don't keep anything in, even for medicinal purposes?'

He shook his head. 'No, I'm afraid not.'

Ursula glared at him, appalled, as she put her handbag over her arm and rose to her feet. 'Then, if that's all, I've had enough of this. Just see to getting probate, will you?'

Without a word to Stephanie, she strode from the room, slamming the door shut behind her.

Steph gulped in embarrassment. 'I apologise for my mother, Mr Wiford. She's . . . er . . . very upset by my father's death, as you can appreciate.' She eyed him in confusion. 'So . . . er . . . if my father has left me the bulk of his estate, what provisions did he make for my mother?'

He stared at her as though she was stupid. 'Well, I would have thought that was obvious. He expected you yourself would do that.'

Stephanie's heart plummeted like a lead weight. How stupid of her not to have realised what was being expected of her, but instead become carried away with her dream of being able to live independently.

Mr Wilford had picked up a white envelope and

was holding it out to her. 'This is a letter to you from your father, explaining why he's done what he has.'

She accepted the envelope, opened it and took out the letter. Her father had never been a sentimental man and his last message to her was blunt and to the point.

*Stephanie,*
*Your mother is incapable of handling her own finances, hence the reason for my decision to entrust her welfare to your hands should I prede-cease her. My monies are to be held in trust for yourself until such time as your mother's death. In the meantime, I have allocated what I feel to be an adequate weekly amount for living expenses, to be signed for personally by yourself at the bank. The amount will increase yearly, at my executor's discretion, in line with inflation. The house is to be put into your name, with the proviso that Ursula has the right to reside in it for the rest of her life and that therefore the property cannot be sold until after her death.*
*Gerald Mortimer*

As she folded the letter up, hurt filled Steph's being. The fact that her father had eased his own conscience by leaving her to oversee the financial welfare of her mother was not what distressed her most. It was the way he'd signed that last letter to her. Could he not have signed it, *your loving father* . . . even *your father*? But then, he'd never shown her any real parental affection when alive so why was she expecting him to in a letter he'd meant her to read after his death?

Then the significance of what this would all mean for her hit her like a thunderbolt. So much for the future she had envisaged for herself. Being responsible for her mother was not part of her plan for future independence. She dreaded to think of Ursula's reaction when she discovered the full extent of her husband's plan. Her relationship with Steph was tenuous, to say the least. If Ursula had to come to her in future for money to fund her outlandish pursuits, and Steph had to send her away empty handed if she did not have enough to spare after settling their bills . . . She shuddered. Her life had been hard enough before but she had always retained a glimmer of hope for a better one, once she had engineered her escape from under her parents' roof, but on his death her father had seen to it that she was to remain her mother's keeper until the day Ursula joined him in the hereafter. A black cloud of doom settled upon Steph as a vision of turbulent times ahead flashed before her.

Seeing that she had finished reading the letter, Mr Wilford said, 'Well, if I could just resume relaying the details of your father's Will as I do have clients coming in at four . . .' Consulting the papers in front of him, he went on, 'The car is to be sold and the proceeds added to the rest of the monies. These monies, as matters stand at the moment, amount to eighty thousand, four hundred and twelve pounds, fourteen shillings and elevenpence.'

Steph was astonished. How much? To someone who, regardless of her father's financial state, had never had more than a few pounds to her name at any one time, that amount sounded phenomenal.

'. . . minus the funeral expenses and my charge, of course, and any outstanding debts yet to be settled. I assume that in his letter to you your father has advised you of his instructions for their administration? Now all that remains for me to tell you is that the flat at number 49a New Walk, together with the sum of ten thousand pounds, has been bequeathed to Mr Paul Fawkes.'

She was looking at him in confusion. Who was Paul Fawkes? And what was this about a flat on New Walk? Steph's thoughts whirled. For her father to have left this Paul Fawkes a flat, and judging from the exclusive area it was in it would be an expensive property, along with such a large sum of money, the man must have been a very special friend. But as far as her memory served her, she had never ever heard this name mentioned, nor had Paul Fawkes been a guest at the occasional dinner parties her father had held at home when he was entertaining people in the medical profession that he was out to impress, Ursula under threat to be on her best behaviour for the duration.

Then the truth struck her. This man must be a *very* special friend of her father's . . . his lover? The flat must be where they used to spend private time together. Thank goodness her mother hadn't heard this information. Steph dreaded to think how she would have reacted. She must keep it from her at all costs. But the thought of her father and this unknown man living as a couple upset her greatly.

'Oh, how nice of my father to remember his very good friend in the way he has,' she said weakly.

The solicitor adjusted his spectacles more comfortably on his high-bridged nose and stared at her fixedly. 'To apply for probate and tie matters up will take a month or six weeks at most, providing I don't meet any hitches which I don't anticipate doing. Mr Frobisher, your father's bank manager, will make separate contact with you in due course, to arrange for you to go and see him to sign the necessary documents, and for you to inform him of how you wish to collect your allowance. I'll have my secretary contact you to make an appointment for you to come in and sign the transfer of the house deeds to you when they're ready. That's it for now, Miss Mortimer.'

He rose, came around his desk and held out his

hand to her. Collecting her handbag, Stephanie stood up to shake his hand.

'May I again express my deepest sympathies for your loss, Miss Mortimer?'

She flashed him a wan smile and murmured, 'Thank you.'

As soon as Steph let herself in at the front door, Ursula came out of the lounge to accost her, glass in one hand, half-smoked cigarette in the other. It was apparent she was still furious at not being the sole beneficiary of her husband's Will, as she felt she should have been.

'When am I to go and sign the transfer papers so I can be handed what's rightfully mine?' she demanded.

Steph was taking off her coat. She really ought to enlighten her mother that that was never going to happen, but at this moment hadn't the strength to deal with the consequences. She fobbed her off with, 'Mr Wilford said he has to apply to the court for probate. It could take up to six weeks for Father's estate to be settled.' She hoped that during that time she could manage to muster the courage to tell her mother the truth.

'Six weeks!' spat Ursula. She took a long swallow of her drink before adding, sardonically, 'I've always been of the opinion that solicitors and such like sit on their backsides all day, pretending to be working on their clients' behalf, when in truth they're doing absolutely nothing in order to double the bills.'

Steph knew that by now her mother must have consumed at the very least half a bottle of vodka since rising, but she was still very much in control of her faculties. It took at least double that these days to render her comatose. A worrying thought struck Steph then. 'What are we supposed to do for money in the meantime? We're responsible for paying all the bills now.'

Ursula looked unconcerned. 'Well, I have an adequate amount to cover my immediate expenses.' Then a thought struck her and she did start to look concerned. 'But my trips to Scotland and the Med will need paying for. And I'll need some new clothes . . . Surely we'll get an interim payment mean-time, to keep us going. Didn't you ask the solicitor?'

Ursula was making her way back into the lounge and Steph followed her, dismayed to find there was still any number of dirty glasses and plates lying about that she hadn't had time to clear away after the revels of yesterday.

'Er . . . no, I never thought,' she said, brushing crumbs off the seat of the sofa and throwing them into the fireplace before sitting down, thinking her father would not have been pleased to see his house in such disorder. She frowned at her mother who was by now sitting in an armchair opposite her. 'You've money of your own? But I always understood that you were entirely dependent on Father for financial support, and according to you, you had to beg him for every penny.' Certainly that was what she'd understood from the constant rows her parents had on that subject.

'That's true, and didn't Gerald just love the power he wielded over me? But, thankfully, I knew he kept some money in his safe *and* where he hid the key, which was handy or else we'd have had to have it broken into now. Not that I dared help myself while he was alive, you understand. I knew he knew what he held in there down to the last penny, skinflint that he was.'

In fact, Steph felt her father had been very generous as far as her mother was concerned. He may have been constantly having a go at her over the ridiculous amount she got through, but in the end he'd had no choice but to cover her spending if he wanted his secret to remain that way.

'But you told the solicitor you found no cash in the safe, Mother?'

Ursula smirked as she took another sip of her drink. 'Well, there wasn't, not after I took it out.'

'How much was there?'

She shot her daughter a look of disgust that she should have the nerve to ask such a question. 'Not that it's any of your business but just a little over five hundred pounds. Good job I *did* raid the safe as it would have driven me mad being cooped up here while the estate was settled.'

'Well, you can't just squander all that money on clothes and going out, Mother.'

'What I spend my money on is none of your business.'

'But you'll need to give me some, so I can pay for food and cover bills until Father's money comes through.'

'You've your wages from your job, haven't you?'

'You lost me that job, Mother, remember? Besides, I doubt any wage I earned would go anywhere near covering the running costs of this house.'

Ursula looked most put out. 'Huh, well, we'll sort something out later.' Then an eager expression flooded her face. 'Did the solicitor tell you exactly how much I can expect to get? I was desperate to ask him but didn't want to appear vulgar.'

Keeping it all to herself until she was better able to deal with her mother's reaction was proving hard. Would it not be better just to get it over with? Taking a deep breath, Steph began, 'Er . . . well . . . Father's estate comes to just over eighty thousand pounds but . . .'

The amount obviously came as a tremendous shock to Ursula. Before Steph could continue with her explanation, she clapped her hands in delight and jubilantly exclaimed, 'Oh, how wonderful! I'd no idea your father was worth so much. Oh, it will be lovely, having all that dosh. All my years of suffering have been well worth it. No more second-rate champagne for me, it's the best vintage from now on. And I shall see about extending the Med cruise to two weeks instead of one. My life is going to be such fun in future.' Draining her glass, she got up. 'Starting tonight! I'm going for a lie down now. I've people coming in about eight for drinks before we leave and I don't want them to find the place looking like this. See to it, won't you? Oh, and run me a bath for six o'clock.'

Steph stared after Ursula as she swanned off. She ought to go after her, tell her what was what. It really wasn't fair of her to be allowing her mother to visualise her future as one long round of parties and holidays, when in truth they were going to be managing on an allowance. There was no telling how much she was going to be able to give her mother, but the moment for making that plain was gone. Tomorrow . . . she would do the deed then.

Her mother's parting instructions for her to tidy up ready for the arrival of her guests and to run her bath at six registered on Steph then. Onlookers would think her weak because she did her mother's bidding without question, but they had never been in the firing line of one of Ursula's tempers. Had they been they would be acting just the way she was now, dusting and tidying and clearing away so that the same people who had caused the mess could return and do it all over again.

# CHAPTER SIX

Steph was grateful that her mother's so-called friends only stayed long enough to have two drinks each and fill the ashtrays before all eight of them piled into three cabs, to take them to wherever it was they were off to party the night away. After once again clearing up after them, she dressed in her warm night attire, made herself a mug of milky cocoa and settled herself into a comfortable armchair in the firelight, glad of the peace and quiet so she could mull over today's unexpected events.

The sound of the doorbell made her jump. She nearly spilled her cup of cocoa down herself. Frowning, she set the cup down on the occasional table at the side of the chair, wondering who could be calling after nine at night.

When she opened the door she was most surprised to find a man facing her. He was a ruggedly good-looking sort in his mid- to late-thirties, Steph guessed, very well dressed but, judging by the puffiness of his eyes and the look of utter devastation on his face, obviously upset about something. He was a complete stranger to her.

'Can I help you?' she asked politely.

He looked at her uncertainly and Steph had the impression he was about to turn and rush off. Then he scraped his hand through his thick dark hair and confused her by blurting out, 'I'm so sorry but I had to come . . . I've no one I can talk to about him, no one at all. This is all such a shock to me. I'd no inkling until I found the letter from the solicitor yesterday evening . . . he asked me to telephone him and make an appointment to discuss a bequest made to me in a Will . . . and until then I'd no idea that Gerry had been killed. I never even got to say my goodbyes to him at his funeral. I didn't know about it.'

Gerry! Who was he? Then the truth struck her and her mouth fell open. 'Oh! Are you . . . Paul Fawkes?'

He looked startled. 'Gerry told you about me?'

It seemed strange to Steph, to hear her father being called Gerry. She had a memory as a child once of calling him 'Dad', to which he'd responded severely, *I'm your father and you will address me as such*. She'd never dared call him anything other than Father after that.

'I learned about you from our solicitor when he

informed me that my father had left a flat and a sum of money to you.'

'Oh, I see.' Paul Fawkes looked at her imploringly. 'We were just very good friends, your father and I,' he insisted.

Steph eyed him knowingly. 'I think you were a little bit more than that to each other, Mr Fawkes.'

He looked totally stunned. 'You knew that he was . . .'

'A homosexual?' she cut in. 'I've known since I was twelve.'

He gasped. 'And your mother too?'

She nodded.

Shocked, he uttered, 'You must both have loved Gerry very much, to be so understanding.' He pulled a large handkerchief out of his pocket, wiped his face and blew his nose, then uttered, 'I never knew he was married or had a daughter until the solicitor told me today.' He looked at her searchingly. 'I can see you're Gerry's daughter. You have his eyes.' His face puckered again and he muttered, 'Such lovely eyes he had. I can't believe I won't ever look into them again.'

A wave of revulsion swept through Steph then. Her own father and this man had been intimate; the thought revolted her. Clutching her dressing gown to her, she blurted, 'I need to go in. I've . . . milk on the stove.'

With that she leaped back inside and slammed shut the door before slumping back against it. Wasn't it bad enough that she was dealing with the fact she had lost the man who had fathered her, without being confronted by his homosexual lover? Then Paul's utterly bereft expression swam before her eyes and something he had said echoed in her ears. *I have no one I can talk to about him.* A picture of him sitting alone, nursing his pain, rose before her and, despite her outrage towards the man for showing up uninvited, her heart went out to him. He had so obviously loved her father, and due to society's views on homosexuality could not talk to anyone about his grief. She knew all about that as she had no one to talk over her bereavement with either, although she could hardly class what she was feeling anywhere close to what she suspected the man on the other side of the door was. Surely she could find it within herself to show him some compassion, as she would to any other human being who was so genuinely suffering over a death of a loved one.

Hurriedly righting herself, she wrenched open the door and stepped out on to the gravelled drive, her dressing gown billowing around her in the cool late-evening breeze.

Arriving at the end of the drive, she looked up and down the street and saw him highlighted by a lamp-post a few yards away. Although his back was to her, she could see how misery had caused his shoulders to slump and his head to hang.

Steph called out his name.

He stopped and turned, looking back at her warily.

'Would you like a cup of tea or maybe something stronger before you go home?' she called to him.

A look of surprise crossed his face. It was obvious this was the last thing he was expecting after having the door shut on him. He responded hesitantly, 'If you're sure?'

Steph flashed him a tight smile before she turned and made her way back to the house, the sound of his footsteps behind her letting her know that he was following.

Moments later they were seated in the lounge, he on the sofa nursing a neat whisky, she in an armchair clutching her now tepid mug of cocoa.

Taking a sip of his drink, he looked at her apologetically and said, 'It was wrong of me to come, I'm sorry I did, but I wasn't really thinking clearly.' His face crumpled then, pain-filled eyes cast down. Looking intently into the contents of the glass he was holding, he choked, 'It was such a shock, finding out that Gerry had been killed. I didn't know what to think when he didn't show up at the flat on the nights we always spent together. If something has kept him away in the past, he's always got a message to me because he knows I worry about him . . . I knew there was nothing wrong with our relationship, we hadn't had a tiff or anything. In fact, we never have, in all our years together, so I put it down to him being bedridden with some awful sickness wherever it was he spent his time when he wasn't with me. And to find out he actually had a family . . . I don't really know what to think. I believed *I* was Gerry's family, then to find out that he had another life I was completely unaware of . . . well, it just knocked me sideways and I found myself knocking on your door.'

Tears filled Paul's eyes and he stumbled over his next words. 'I can't believe he's gone . . . that I'll never see him again. Gerry was the love of my life, and he was always telling me that I was his. He was such a soft, gentle man. He opened my eyes to so many things. Classical music, opera, theatre. We've built up a huge record collection and a library of books between us. Our perfect night was cooking ourselves a meal . . . Gerry loved to cook . . . then after eating it and clearing away, settling down before a roaring fire to listen to music while we each read our book, just content in each other's company.'

Fury was building inside Steph as she listened to him ramble on. The man Paul was describing, the loving, gentle, caring man, was nothing like the one she had known. She had never witnessed her father cook himself a piece of toast, let alone prepare a full meal! He had been gruff and intolerant towards her, never showing any interest in helping her to develop her mind. She had never witnessed a soft side to him at all. How she wished she had never invited this man in, but it was too late. She had no choice but to hear him out.

Paul was continuing, 'I'd no idea Gerry was a doctor, and a prominent one at that. I was stunned when his solicitor told me, speaking to me like he assumed I must know. But then, Gerry never discussed my work with me, either. Our other lives weren't important. What we were when we were together, was.' His eyes glazed over. 'We met when we were both having a drink in the same public house after work one night. Our eyes met across the bar, and that was it for both of us. Apart from the three nights a week I spent with Gerry at the flat, I live with my mother. I assumed he either lived with his mother or on his own. My mother gave up badgering me to get married long ago. She's resigned herself to the fact that I'm too set in my ways and far too picky to find a woman who'll put up with me. It would kill her if she was aware of the real reason I'm a confirmed bachelor.

'It always grieved Gerry and me that we could never go out in public together as a couple, but at least we could be ourselves inside the flat.' The glint of tears sparkled in his eyes. 'Christmas was our best time . . . I don't know how I'm going to cope without Gerald. We always spent the day together. Since I met Gerry, I've always told my mother I was spending the day with friends in Derby. I wasn't leaving her on her own, she has her sister and family to entertain her. She'll be delighted when I tell her she'll have my company too this year. I just hope I can get through it.'

A brief smile touched his lips. 'I can't believe the sweet, dear man left me the flat and all that money. He left a letter, too, telling me to spend the money as I liked and either to keep the flat or sell it, the choice was mine. He said his life had been meaningless until I arrived in it and that he treasured every moment we'd spent together.' Paul paused to swallow the lump in his throat. 'I shall put the money in the bank until I decide what to do with it. I'll probably move into the flat . . . eventually. I can't go back there just yet. I know all I'll see is Gerry preparing meals in the kitchen, sitting in his chair with a book and glass of wine, lying in our bed . . .'

Steph's fury reached boiling point then. She had invited this man in as a gesture of compassion. What she hadn't invited him to do was to pour out all his intimate memories of time spent with her father, seemingly with no thought for the effect his selfishness was having on her.

'I don't want to be privy to this,' she cut in. 'You seem to have forgotten, it's my *father* you're talking so intimately about. I hate to burst your bubble but the man you're describing never existed for me. He was cold and aloof, and I stayed out of his way as much as I could because I was frightened of disturbing him. He never once, in living memory, made me a cup of tea let alone cooked a meal for me or even with me. He never once attempted to introduce me to music or books so we could appreciate them together. The only time I was out in his company was when we all put on a respectable happy family front for the benefit of people he was out to impress.

'While my father was spending his cosy Christmas Days with you, I was under the impression he was at the hospital tending to his patients. I was here on my own, you understand. His rejection of her turned my mother to drink, and when she finally discovered just why he wasn't interested in her as a woman and confronted him, he used his money to blackmail her into staying with him, to keep up a respectable front. He bullied and browbeat the staff under him at the hospital . . . I could go on. So, on Christmas Day, when you're about to lapse into depression because you've lost the love of your life, just remind yourself of the man he really was and be grateful you never saw that side of him.'

Steph got to her feet. 'Now, I'm very tired so if you don't mind . . .'

Paul Fawkes was looking at her agog, his mouth opening and closing. It was obvious he was aware that any apology he tried to make to his dead lover's daughter would fail to make any amends whatsoever for his thoughtlessness in coming here and speaking as he had. Head hanging in shame, he got up and hurried from the room. Seconds later Steph heard the front door shut behind him.

She sank back down on her chair, cradling her head in her hands, great choking sobs racking her body. She was weeping not for the father she had known but for the man she now knew could have been more to her, had he chosen to show her just some of the good side he had to his lover.

A bright fire was burning in the grate and Steph felt warm and content. The Christmas tree she was standing before looked magical, full of twinkling lights, colourful baubles, gold and silver tinsel. Stacked beneath it was an assortment of brightly wrapped parcels. An excited Steph could tell one was a dolly by the shape of it. She had asked the Fairy Queen at the bottom of the well in the garden for a dolly and she had granted the wish. She turned and looked around her, giggling with happiness to see her parents tightly embracing, then kissing each other lovingly, before her father spotted her spying on their intimacy and leaped across to scoop her up. She squealed in delight as he swung her round.

Then her squeals of delight turned to one of pain. Her father was pulling at her, hurting her. She suddenly felt icy cold. Then her mother's voice was booming in her ear.

'Stop pretending to be asleep. Come on, get up. I want some company.'

Steph forced open her eyes to see Ursula swaying at one side of her bed, cigarette in one hand, glass of vodka in the other, some of the contents of which were spilling on to the carpet. Ursula had pulled the covers off her daughter, and the pain Steph had felt whilst asleep was her mother pinching her, in her quest to wake her up. Grabbing the covers back up around her, Steph glanced at the clock on the bedside cabinet and gave a groan. 'Mother, it's after three in the morning.'

'Is that all? Still early then. I've got some great news to tell you.'

She stumbled out of the room, heedlessly dropping ash and slopping her drink as she went.

Steph groaned again as the sound of her mother calling her seemed to ricochet off the walls in the otherwise quiet night. This was typical of her. It didn't matter about anyone else, Ursula wanted company until she was ready to sleep and wouldn't settle for anything less.

Half an hour later, Ursula was lolling back on her pillows, drink and cigarette in hand, babbling on for the most part incoherently. Steph hadn't a clue what she was saying . . . nor did she care. What her mother's exciting news was, she still had no idea. It was probably something and nothing, just said to entice Steph out of bed. Sitting in the Lloyd Loom chair at Ursula's bedside, her dressing gown pulled tightly around her, she was having terrible difficulty keeping herself awake. That was until something her mother said jolted her fully awake, to stare at her thunderstruck.

'Did you just tell me you're getting married again?'

Ursula took a pull of her drink and a drag from her cigarette before answering, 'Well, eventually I intend to, but for now my aim is to have some serious fun with the man I met tonight.'

Steph gawped at her incredulously. 'Have you forgotten you've only just buried Father! Aren't you worried what people will think of you, taking up with another man so soon after his death?'

Ursula gave a dismissive shrug. 'No. Why should I be? Life goes on. My life is certainly going to. It was on hold long enough while your father was alive.' Her eyes glazed over. 'My new man is rather gorgeous. Now your father is no longer around, I'm free to do whatever I like without any fear of anyone seeing me and it damaging your father's reputation. I shall certainly enjoy showing this particular man off in public. My friends will be envious of me when they see what I've landed myself. They're already envious of me anyway for coming into all this lovely money.'

Steph groaned. Her mother had obviously been bragging about the size of the inheritance that she was under the illusion she was shortly coming into. She eyed her coldly. 'I'm disgusted with you, Mother, that you can even be contemplating taking up with someone else before Father's cold in his grave.'

'And you're just jealous that I can get men when you obviously can't,' she snapped back.

Steph would have liked to have pointed out to her mother then that men who were at first attracted to her, ran a mile when they'd had a taste of what life would be like for them *with* her. Curiosity was getting the better of her, though, and she couldn't help but enquire, 'What's so special about this new man of yours then?'

Ursula responded secretively, 'You'll see for yourself when he calls for me tomorrow.'

Then to Steph's surprise her mother's eyes drooped shut and she started snoring. The half-empty glass of vodka and tonic fell from her hand, emptying its contents over the counterpane; the half-smoked cigarette started sliding from between her fingers, and was only saved from burning a hole in the counterpane by Steph leaping up to grab it just in time.

# CHAPTER SEVEN

Having had her sleep disrupted by her self-centred mother, Steph had difficulty getting back off and consequently felt dreadful when she rose the next morning. Her head felt like hundreds of hot pins were being stabbed into it, her eyes gritty, and everything she did took extreme effort. As the day progressed, despite taking several painkillers at intervals, she did not feel at all improved. As a result her plan to look for a job was put on hold and instead she concentrated on giving the house a good going over in case any prospective dailies called enquiring after the job. While she was talking to them about their duties, she hoped her mother did not put in an appearance and send them scuttling with her superior manner.

As she busied herself, she had no idea that her mother had even risen, let alone was going out, until she heard the front door shutting and looked out of the lounge window to see Ursula being helped into a taxi by its driver which then immediately left, she had no idea where for. Steph sighed, annoyed. Her mother had not even shown her the courtesy of letting her know she was going out or asked if she needed anything bringing back. If the boot had been on the other foot Steph would never have heard the last of it.

It was after four when Ursula did return, again via taxi, laden down with shopping bags. Steph was just coming out of the kitchen, having been discussing with their cook meal plans for the forthcoming week so supplies could be bought. Considering what time her mother had gone to sleep and the fact that she had obviously been busily shopping, she looked very well. But then, she was wearing a layer of carefully applied make up.

Over the years Steph had instinctively known when her mother was having a secret assignation as she had had that certain sparkle in her eye, that spring in her step, but she could never remember having seen her with quite such an air of radiance about her. This new man in her life was obviously something special. There was a small twinge of envy in Steph's stomach then. She would have liked the company of someone to spend the evenings with, instead of always being left on her own.

Dumping the bags just inside the door, Ursula ordered her daughter, 'Get me a drink. A large one.'

She glanced at the grandfather clock nearby and gave a start when she saw the time. 'Oh, gosh, I meant to be home earlier, to give myself a good pampering.'

Steph was looking at the bulky bags, all six of them, and worrying how far the items inside had eaten into the five hundred pounds her mother had taken from the safe. The shops she frequented priced their cheapest items above the average weekly wage for a normal working man, and Steph guessed that her mother wouldn't have seen much change from a hundred pounds from this shopping expedition. In fairness to Ursula, her husband had taken care of financial matters previously so she had never had to concern herself with them and was more than likely of the opinion now that Steph would take on the responsibility. But unknown to her Steph didn't intend to live here after the money came through, so whether Ursula liked it or not she was going to have to learn to curtail her spending.

'I need to speak to you about money, Mother,' she ventured. 'There are bills to settle, and Mrs Sanders' and the gardener's wages to pay.' She took a deep breath and blurted out, 'In fact, there's something I really need to tell you . . .'

'I haven't time now,' she snapped at Steph, flashing her a look as though to say, How could you be so inconsiderate as to want to discuss such mundane matters when I have far more important things to do?'

She left Steph staring after her as she made her way up the stairs.

Steph went up to call her down for dinner at seven.

Ursula, clad in an oyster-coloured silk petticoat over matching lacy bra and French knickers, suspender belt holding up sheer silk stockings, was sitting at her dressing table, undoing her hair from large rollers. There was an air of nervous excitement about her.

'No time to eat,' she said breathlessly.

Steph looked in concern at the half-full glass of clear liquid on the dressing table, the half-smoked cigarette resting in the ashtray beside it. She knew this was far from her mother's first drink of the day, and the cigarette was at least her twentieth. Ursula had had no breakfast, to Steph's knowledge, and probably hadn't eaten while in town.

'Should you really be going for a night out on an empty stomach, Mother?' Steph asked her.

Ursula shot a glance of derision at her. 'If I wanted to eat, I would. I don't.' She picked up her glass and drained the contents, then handed it to her daughter. 'You can pour me another drink. Easy on the tonic.'

As Steph sat eating her solitary meal of stew and

dumplings, she was mulling something over in her mind. Since her mother hadn't eaten there was more than enough of the stew left over to feed them next day, so she could in fact give the cook the afternoon off tomorrow. In truth, though, did they really need the services of a twice-daily cook? The reason Mrs Sanders had been employed was to provide her father with a substantial cooked breakfast before he departed for the hospital. Ursula's breakfast time was around noon and usually she had black coffee and several cigarettes, for the most part washed down by a vodka and tonic. Tea and toast was all Steph ever had, not being able to face a heavy meal first thing in the morning, and she was quite capable of preparing that for herself. Maybe they only needed Mrs Sanders to come in for a couple of hours in the afternoon now, to take care of the evening meal. That was something that would need to be addressed once Steph had solved the problem of how to tell her mother that in future she was going to have to curtail her spending to within the limits of a weekly allowance.

Having had her fill, Steph was about to rise and clear the table when she heard a bang on the ceiling. Her mother was summoning her. Sighing, she went off to respond.

Normally chic and elegant, tonight Ursula was wearing a bright purple and yellow dress of the sort Steph herself would wear for a night out. She felt it was far too short for a woman of her mother's age, finishing as it did several inches above the knee.

Ursula was mistaking her daughter's look of utter astonishment for one of appreciation. 'I'm going to turn a few heads tonight, aren't I? Zip me up.'

Walking across to her, Steph did her bidding.

When she had finished Ursula turned around, adopting a model pose, and demanded, 'Well, aren't you going to tell me I look fabulous?'

Steph gulped. She had recently learned a very painful lesson: that it didn't pay to lie. Although to tell her mother what her own thoughts really were about that dress would be like putting her head inside a lion's cage, Steph didn't really like the thought of people sniggering behind her mother's back at her glaring attempt to present herself as younger than she was.

'Well . . . er . . . the dress looks great.' Which was true. Her mother might be in her forties but she had almost managed to retain the figure she had had as a young woman in her twenties, and one that other women of that age would give their eye teeth for. 'Do you . . . er . . . think it might be just a little short, though?'

Ursula glared at her, outraged. 'If I did, I wouldn't be wearing it, would I? I've got great legs so why shouldn't I be showing them off? Lots of women wear dresses these days much shorter than this. You do,' she said in an accusing tone.

The doorbell sounded then. A spark of excitement lit Ursula's eyes as she snatched up a Max Factor lipstick from her dressing table, taking off its top. 'That'll be my date. Show him into the lounge, offer him a drink, and tell him I'll be five minutes.'

Steph felt like a maid being given instructions by her mistress. As she made her way back down the stairs, she thought, Well, I'm about to meet the man who's tickled my mother's fancy. And then she wondered what he would be like. Tall, dark, handsome, suave and sophisticated? Her mother certainly had no trouble attracting that sort of man, but then Steph couldn't see a man of that type agreeing to escort her anywhere classy when she was dressed in such a teenage outfit. Then it struck her. Of course! Her mother was obviously off to a fancy dress party.

As Steph opened the door, though, and her eyes settled on the man on the doorstep, her mouth dropped open in shock. It wasn't the flamboyant way he was dressed, in a blue velvet suit worn with a frill-fronted white shirt, or the black Cuban-heeled shoes he wore, making him appear an inch or so taller than the six foot he was. Nor was it his thick blond hair, fashionably cut to collar-length, nor the fact that he was extremely good looking, the sort of man Steph had a penchant for herself, in fact. No, what flabbergasted her was his age. He couldn't be much older than she was herself, two or three years at most. This man couldn't possibly be her mother's date. He was probably selling something or had simply called at the wrong address.

'Can I help you?' Steph asked him politely.

He smiled at her, winningly. 'I've called to see Ursula.'

So he *was* her mother's date! What on earth was she playing at, dating a man young enough to be her son? And what was *he* doing, dating a woman old enough to be his mother? It wasn't as if either of them would have had any trouble finding willing partners from their own very different age groups.

Then suddenly Steph saw it all.

Her inebriated mother had obviously been bragging about all the lovely money she was under the impression she was coming into, and this individual must have heard it all and seen Ursula as easy prey. Full of conceit for having, as she thought, caught the eye of a much younger man with her looks and figure, Ursula couldn't see, like Steph could, that it was just her money he was after. Her youthful style of dressing tonight was not for any fancy dress party, it was for the benefit of this young con artist. Well, Steph wasn't going to stand by and let him fleece her own mother.

'You've picked the wrong target this time,' she hurled at him. 'You obviously overheard my mother bragging to her friends about her recent windfall and saw it as an opportunity to line your own pockets.

Why else would a man like you be going after a woman old enough to be your mother?' She saw a look flash into his eyes and could only conclude that it was of shock that his despicable plan had been sussed before he'd even had the chance to get it off the ground. She glared at him. 'Now, I suggest you go off and find another unsuspecting woman to fall for your charms because I'll be damned if I'm going to stand by and watch you wheedle a penny out of my mother!'

Without giving him a chance to respond in any way whatsoever, she made to shut the door in his face, but then a thought struck her. 'Oh, and should you still be thinking of going after her, as a matter of interest you'd be wasting your time. My mother was mistaken about her windfall. She isn't the beneficiary of my father's Will, he left everything to me.'

With that she did shut the door in his face.

Steph pressed her back against it and took several deep breaths to calm herself. She wasn't naturally the confrontational sort and had surprised herself by what she had just done. She felt a strong need for a drink and, as she made her way into the lounge and over to the cocktail cabinet, also a sense of satisfaction that she had stopped that young man's ploy at the starting post. She supposed she could appreciate why her mother had fallen under his spell. He certainly was very pleasing to look at, sexy too, and had he approached Steph herself for a date, she'd have been extremely flattered.

She had just poured herself a Campari and lemonade when she heard the sound of her mother making her way down the stairs. Steph froze. Oh dear. She had not considered how her mother would take her interference when she had dived in head first to save her from herself.

Ursula sashayed sexily into the room, stopping short when she didn't spot the young man she'd expected to see. 'Where is he? You haven't left him outside?' she accused Steph.

She took a gulp of her drink, then a deep breath before answering in a weak voice, 'No, I sent him away.'

Ursula looked stunned. 'You did what?' Then her eyes darkened with rage. 'Just who the hell do you think you are, sending my date away?'

Steph drained her glass and, while pouring herself another drink, said, 'I was looking out for you, Mother. Could you not see for yourself just what that man was up to?'

'What he was up to! What he was *up to* was showing me a good time. He couldn't believe his luck when I agreed to meet him.'

Steph shook her head at her mother incredulously. 'Oh, for goodness' sake, the only reason a man like him would show interest in a woman of your age is for what he could get out of her. He obviously thought he was on to a good thing with you, after hearing you bragging to your friends about how much money you were about to come into.'

Deeply insulted, Ursula slapped Steph's face hard. The blow sent her reeling backwards, to catch her side on the corner of the cocktail cabinet, the crystal tumbler in her hand flying against the wall from where it cascaded jagged chunks and sharp slivers of glass across the floor.

'How dare you interfere in my affairs, treating me like a stupid schoolgirl?' Ursula raged. Then she sneered knowingly, 'Jealous, were you, daughter dear? Couldn't stand the thought that your mother is capable of getting herself a handsome man when *you* can't seem to get anyone. Because it certainly looks that way to me. How many more chances are you going to ruin for me through your jealousy? This is the second time you've done this to me in the space of a couple of weeks! After all those years of having to be secretive about any affairs, for fear of embarrassing your father, I'm now free to go out with whom I want, when I want, and I was really looking forward to walking into the club tonight and seeing the envious looks on my friends' faces when they saw me with . . . Oh, now see what you've made me do. I've forgotten his name! Anyway, go after him and fetch him back,' she demanded.

Steph was rubbing her smarting cheek. Her mother had never physically struck her before, and the fact that she had now shocked Steph far more than the actual blow itself. Nevertheless she stared back at her mother defiantly. 'No, I won't. I won't be party to any of this.'

Ursula thrust her face into Steph's and hissed, 'And I will not be made a fool of, you silly bitch. I telephoned all my friends before I went out shopping this morning and told them to expect a surprise tonight with the new gentleman I was bringing with me. So go and fetch him back.' She gave Steph a push on the shoulder. 'Go on!' she screamed.

To avoid any further physical attack, Steph appeared to do her mother's bidding. She made her way to the end of the front garden then secreted herself by a gate-post where she knew she could not be seen from the house. After a good five minutes she made her way back, telling her mother she had searched high and low but could see no sign of the man.

A livid Ursula jabbed her hard in the shoulder, issuing a severe warning that she was never to dare undermine her again. Then, armed with a bottle of vodka, she stormed off upstairs, screaming that to save face she would have to tell her friends she had fallen ill and cancel her evening out.

Knowing her bad-tempered mother was closeted

in her bedroom, drinking herself into oblivion, Steph kept a low profile for the rest of the evening, creeping around the house and keeping the sound on the television set barely loud enough to hear so as not to attract her mother's attention.

# CHAPTER EIGHT

Steph didn't hear a peep out of Ursula for the rest of the evening. She herself rose early the next morning, fully intent on beginning the process of securing work for herself. She might now have the responsibility of eking out the weekly allowance her father had allocated them, making sure it was spent wisely and not all squandered by her mother on her own entertainment, but that didn't mean Steph had to be physically present in this house to do it. Gaining her own independence was just as much of a priority to her as it had always been. Trouble was, because she was going to have to use what little she had managed to save to settle household bills, she was starting out from scratch.

As she arrived downstairs, their elderly cook came out of the kitchen to greet her. 'Can I get you some breakfast, Miss Mortimer?'

Steph smiled warmly at her. 'I'd appreciate a slice of toast and a cup of tea, thank you, Mrs Sanders.'

Beryl Sanders made to retreat into the kitchen then paused and looked hesitantly at Steph. The older woman had always felt so sorry for this pretty young woman before her. Others might envy her for the affluent lifestyle she appeared to have, but they certainly wouldn't envy her the kind of parents she'd been dealt. It was all credit to Stephanie that she had turned out to be such a stable and pleasant young woman, considering what she'd had to put up with. Beryl might be just the cook who spent most of her time in the kitchen, but that didn't mean to say she was blind or deaf; it was surprising how voices carried in these old houses, plus she'd always been on very friendly terms with the dailies and it was surprising what could be learned from them over a cup of tea and a couple of her homemade biscuits.

The Mortimers had been a peculiar pair. They certainly didn't sleep together, occupying separate rooms at opposite ends of the house, and Mrs Mortimer was out most evenings, not coming home until the early hours, while Mr Mortimer had stayed out all night on a regular basis three times a week. She had been led to believe that he was at the hospital on those nights as he operated late, but it wouldn't have surprised her to find he never stayed there at all but in fact visited a mistress. He had, after all, been a fine figure of a man, and if he wasn't having his needs satisfied by his wife then a man in his prime like he'd been would have looked elsewhere.

Gerald Mortimer had proved a decent enough employer to her, always civil and paying her wages promptly each week, but as a father, from what she had observed and learned through gossip, he hadn't rated very highly. His approach to his daughter had been very austere and Steph had had as little to do with him as she could. In fact, Beryl would have gone so far as to say the girl had been a bit afraid of him.

As for Ursula Mortimer ... a beautiful woman, there was no denying that, albeit her lifestyle was beginning to show its effects on her face, but she was the most self-absorbed person Beryl had ever met. Whenever their paths had crossed, which thankfully for Beryl had not been often because, to the likes of Ursula Mortimer, a kitchen was no place to be seen, she'd acted very high-faluting. Mind you, Beryl wasn't stupid. If Ursula Mortimer was not already an alcoholic, she was working hard at becoming one.

To Beryl, herself the mother of two girls and two boys, all grown up and living away from home now, it was criminal the way Stephanie had been raised. There'd been a succession of nannies, none of whom had stayed long, and after that Stephanie more or less raised herself. And according to the dailies, Ursula had expected her daughter to be at her constant beck and call, demanding she drop whatever she was doing to look after her instead. Apparently Steph had lost countless jobs through her mother's selfishness, not to mention having at least two relationships scuppered through her interference.

Beryl still cringed to remember the two occasions when Steph had brought potentially serious boyfriends home for dinner to meet her parents. It had been shameful the way her mother had flirted outrageously with the young men, despite their obvious embarrassment, not to mention Steph's. Gerald Mortimer had remained oblivious to his wife's disgraceful behaviour. He certainly hadn't intervened in any way, but on both occasions, just as the meal was about to be served up, had announced he was needed at the hospital and made his escape. Beryl wasn't surprised never to have seen either young man again. It was obvious they'd both beaten a hasty retreat after seeing what life would be like with in-laws like that, no matter what they'd thought of Steph.

Still, at least she hadn't to be pussy-footing around her grouchy father like a scared cat any longer, but it was Beryl's opinon that Steph had been left with the worse of her parents to contend with. That girl would never have a life to call her own until she got well away from her mother.

'I really don't like to bother you with this but I was just wondering, Miss Mortimer, about me wages?

Only I haven't been paid since Mr Mortimer died. I appreciate Mrs Mortimer has had a lot on her mind but . . . well . . . I've my own bills to pay. Also Percy the gardener was grumbling to me that he's not been paid either, and the milkman, and if we don't settle our accounts with the grocer and butcher too they'll stop delivering until we do.'

'I'll speak to my mother urgently about it.'

'Thank you, Miss Mortimer.' Again Beryl made to return to the kitchen, Steph to make her way into the dining room, but something else was bothering the cook and this was as good a time as any to address it.

'Er . . . Miss Mortimer. I'm not trying to do meself out of work, but now I'm not seeing to breakfast for Mr Mortimer, and with you yourself not eating what I'd call a substantial meal, and Mrs Mortimer . . . well, I've never once seen her come down for breakfast in all the ten years I've worked for the family. So, I was wondering . . . the nursing home where me sister cleans is in need of a breakfast cook. It's for two and a half hours in the morning, more money for me which wouldn't go amiss with another grandchild on the way . . .'

Steph gave her arm a reassuring pat. 'I understand perfectly, Mrs Sanders. Please feel free to apply for the job in the nursing home, and I hope you're successful.'

The older woman gave her a gratified smile. 'Thanks, Miss Mortimer. I'll go and see to your tea and toast. It'll be with you in a jiffy.'

Well, that was one problem that had resolved itself, and very amicably for all concerned, thought Steph, as she went into the dining room to await her breakfast.

A couple of hours later the young woman dealing with her at the employment agency stifled a yawn as she handed Steph an introductory letter to hand to the boss of a plumbing company. They were looking for a clerk, apparently. Steph had lived with her mother long enough to recognise the signs of someone suffering from a hangover and the woman before her certainly was. She had never tried this particular agency before and was surprised not to have been quizzed as to why she had abruptly left her last job, and why she had had so many others since she'd left school. She had not even been asked for references. Maybe the woman's hangover was making her lax, or maybe it was the fact that the owner of the plumber's was desperate to fill the vacancy.

Apparently, though, he had an important job to attend to so couldn't interview her until after two. It was now only eleven so she may as well go home meantime.

Steph had just walked out of the door and into the

street, about to turn in the direction of her bus stop, when someone coming the other way crashed into her and sent her flying backwards. She was only saved from toppling over by their quick actions, and felt a strong arm steady her round her waist. When she had recovered her senses enough to look at the person who had caused her to stumble, she frowned. She'd seen him somewhere before, though she couldn't quite . . . Then she did remember.

This was the man who had called to collect her mother last night. The man who she firmly believed had been out to extort money from her. Gone was his flamboyant attire of yesterday evening. Today he looked more casual in a pair of jeans and tee-shirt worn under a dark blue Crombie coat.

Steph was not at all pleased to be encountering him again, though judging by the look on his face he felt rather differently.

'I'm so sorry, I wasn't looking where I was going. Are you all right?' he enquired with a pleasant smile.

Tersely she responded, 'I'm fine, thank you. You can let go now.'

'Only if you agree to come and have a coffee with me? You shut the door on me last night before I had a chance to put you right. Would you at least allow me the chance to now?' He looked deep into her eyes and implored, 'Please?'

The last thing she wanted to do was spend a

moment longer in this man's company, but then she remembered how Jessica Normanton had refused to listen to the reason for her own actions. If she had, Steph might not have been ordered out of her life. And she was intrigued as to what tale this man was going to try and spin her, to get her to change her mind about him. She did wonder, though, why he was wasting his time bothering and not concentrating on securing his next victim.

He led her to the Silver Street Café, helped her into a seat at a table in a quiet corner, and ordered two coffees from a waitress. When she went off to see to it, he gave Steph his full attention. Looking at her earnestly he began, 'I was absolutely flabbergasted by what you accused me of last night. What on earth made you think I was out to rob your mother? Actually, it was your mother who robbed me.'

She stared at him. 'She stole from you?'

'I don't think she meant to, but she pocketed my lighter. It was a gift from a friend. That was why I came to your house last night – to get it back.'

She was looking at him cautiously. 'You weren't calling to take my mother out, then?'

He looked horrified at the very thought. 'Good God, no. She's a very attractive woman but, as you quite rightly pointed out, old enough to be my mother.'

The waitress returned with their order. Spooning

sugar into her steaming coffee and giving it a stir, Steph said to her companion, 'So why did she think you'd called to take her out?'

He shrugged. 'I can't imagine. She was very drunk, though. When I came across her, she was having a job to stand up.'

Steph frowned at him thoughtfully. There was no denying that her mother was what she would deem a heavy drinker, but Steph had never seen her lose control of her bodily functions before. It had been obvious that she'd been very inebriated the night before last, when she had woken Steph up demanding her company in the early hours, but she had been far from unable to stand and, although her speech had been slurred, she had been coherent enough for Steph to understand her. It seemed to her as though they were talking about two different women.

The young man was looking concerned. 'I can see you don't believe me, but why would I be lying to you? Look, if I had been out to con your mother out of her money then you've rumbled me anyway so why waste time trying to prove my innocence to you?'

That was what she had wondered, too. Could it be that she had jumped to completely the wrong conclusion about him? Had he been insulted rather than shocked when she'd accused him of being a fortune hunter? She wasn't quite ready to admit she'd

been wrong about him, though, not without satisfying herself completely that he was genuine. 'So just
how did you come to meet my mother?' Steph asked.

He took a sip of coffee before telling her, 'I was
on my way to the taxi rank after just leaving my
friends. We'd been in the Adam and Eve disco, celebrating one of my mates' birthday. I was about to
pass by that place where all the toffs go . . . can't
remember its name now . . . when this woman came
out. Well, I say came out . . . more stumbled. She was
weaving about all over the place. I think she must
have caught her heel on the pavement or something
because she suddenly collapsed in a heap in front of
me. I did what any chap would do, I went to help
her.'

He paused, looking uncomfortable then. 'She was
all over me like a rash! I couldn't get her off me. She
kept going on that I was her knight in shining armour
and she wanted to repay me by taking me for a drink.
I can assure you, I kept insisting to her that there
was no need. I did manage to get out of her that a
cab was supposed to be picking her up, which the
barman had ordered for her in the place she'd come
out of, but it hadn't arrived by this time so I offered
to make sure she got into a taxi and took her with
me to the rank. On the way I offered her a light for
her cigarette. It wasn't until after the taxi had gone
off that I realised she'd taken my lighter with her.

'As I said, it was a present from a friend and I really would like it back. That's why I came to your house and no other reason, believe me. I knew your address because I got it out of your mother so I could make sure the driver understood where she wanted to go.'

His explanation seemed so plausible, he himself so sincere, that Steph couldn't find any reason to disbelieve him. The only odd thing was the fact that her mother had been in such a state that night she was hardly capable of standing when this man had come across her, yet only a short while later she had been more or less in command of herself. Certainly of Steph. Regardless, Steph felt very stupid and humiliated for thinking the worst of this man, when it seemed he'd been acting very chivalrously towards her mother and had only called at their house to retrieve a personal item.

She shifted uncomfortably in her seat and eyed him in embarrassment. 'I apologise for my mistake. I can't imagine what you must think of me?'

He smiled at her. 'I'm just glad we've straightened it out.'

'I'll get your lighter off my mother. If you tell me where, I'll post it to you.'

He smiled at her. 'I've a better idea. You could give it back in person.'

Oh! She hadn't been expecting that. She blushed

at the way he was looking at her. He was definitely flirting. This was his way of asking her for a date. She wasn't averse to the idea of spending some time with him, she could sorely do with some light entertainment after all she'd been through recently. She was, though, in mourning for the man she had been going to marry, whatever the reason.

He obviously sensed she was about to make an excuse. Looking deep into her eyes, he said coaxingly, 'I really would like to take you out. What about tonight?'

Would it be so bad if she accepted his invitation? She was only meeting him for a drink. A night away from her mother sounded idyllic. Steph smiled. 'The clock tower at eight?'

'I'll be there.'

And hopefully she would have something to celebrate with him tonight. Like securing herself the job she was being interviewed for at two.

There *was* something he'd omitted to come clean to her about, though. 'Do you have a name?' she asked.

He laughed, holding out his hand to her across the table. 'Jason Connor. My friends call me Jay.'

She grasped his hand and shook it. 'Stephanie Mortimer. Steph,' she introduced herself.

It was after twelve when they parted and Steph didn't think it worth making the journey home where she'd hardly have time for a cup of tea before she would need to set off for her interview. She idled away her time, window shopping around town.

At half past two Harry Draper, a thickset, craggy-faced man, stood glaring at Steph.

'I'm paying through the nose for that bloody agency to get me a clerk typist to manage the office side, save me the bother of advertising and interviewing meself, and they're doing n'ote but waste my time by sending me people who just don't cut the mustard.'

Steph said remorsefully, 'I'm sorry, Mr Draper.'

'Did the agency know you couldn't type, gel?'

She nodded.

'Well, then, you ain't got n'ote to be sorry about, have yer? But them agency floozies will when I have words with 'em.' He looked at her regretfully. 'I really need someone who can type 'cos folks demand proper estimates, invoices and receipts. In the old days it was all done verbally and by cash, and everything was a damned sight easier. Anyway, shame you can't type. You seem a nice enough gel, and I'm sure we'd have rubbed along well together.'

On first meeting, Harry Draper had come across as the grumpy sort and Steph thought she didn't fancy working for such a misery. The premises themselves weren't exactly salubrious either. They were housed in a small ramshackle building accessed down a muddy lane by the canal. The cramped space was heated by a smelly paraffin heater. The tiny windows were so filthy they hardly let in any light. Almost buried under piles of paperwork on a heavily scarred desk with ill-fitting drawers was an Imperial 66 type-writer and black Bakelite telephone. Jostling for space in the remaining area and spilling out into the surrounding yard was a vast array of plumbing para-phernalia, from toilets and sinks to plastic pipes.

Harry Draper had explained that he'd delayed her interview in order to attend to an urgent job, only to find that his potential customer had managed to do it himself and did not after all need his services. Then, to make matters worse, he had discovered that his time had been wasted once again by the agency, who had built up his hopes then sent someone who did not fit the brief he had given them.

Steph decided she really couldn't blame Harry Draper for being surly with her after all that. As a result her first impression of him changed. She realised he was actually a kindly man, and agreed with him that they would both have rubbed along very nicely together, she being willing to turn a blind eye to these less-than-ideal working conditions, as having a job was far more important to her . . . if only she'd been able to type!

It was with regret that she took her leave.

She decided not to continue with that particular agency but to go back to a firm called Reed's who had placed her in the past. Although she hadn't been successful at every job they had sent her to interview for, at least she had been sent to suitable positions. She'd go tomorrow as it was getting on for four and she wanted to have plenty of time to get herself ready for her date with Jay, which she was feeling quite nervous about.

As she entered the back door of the house, something struck her. She needed to acquire Jay's lighter from her mother. In order to do that, she would have to divulge that she had come across him, and then her mother would want to know when and where, and if she had made amends for scuppering their evening, and if so when she could expect him to call for her again. Having already learned the hard way that it didn't pay to lie, Steph decided to be honest with her mother despite the fact she knew that Ursula was not going to like it, though she didn't intend to mention her own date with him.

Before she had even undone the top button of her coat there was a banging on the ceiling. Ursula had obviously been listening out for her. Steph sighed heavily. Wouldn't it be nice for once to be summoned by her mother because she wanted to know how she was, how her day had gone, if she'd any problems that needed a mother's wisdom to help resolve? Steph had never had a conversation of that sort with her mother.

When she arrived upstairs, her mother was lying propped up in bed, black eye mask sitting on her forehead, amid a dense cloud of cigarette smoke. Steph instantly saw she was in an ugly mood.

'I want that woman sacking immediately.'

Steph frowned at her, bemused. 'What woman?'

'The woman who cleans. I summoned her several times and she blatantly ignored me. I will not tolerate that.'

Steph gave a fed-up sigh. 'She ignored you, Mother, because she doesn't work here any longer.'

'Since when?'

'Since just before Father died. She walked out, remember, after you gave her a dressing down?'

'Oh! I've got such a blinding headache, I forgot. I need some pills for it, fetch them for me. And a pot of coffee.'

It was a hangover she was suffering from. Usually Ursula's cure for those was a hair of the dog, followed by several more, but as there was no evidence Steph could see that she had partaken of any alcohol yet today, she deduced that her mother must really have drowned her sorrows last night and was not able to face a drink yet.

She made to go and deal with her demands when she remembered Mrs Sanders' earlier request. 'Oh,

Mother, Mrs Sanders reminded me this morning that she hasn't been paid since Father died.'

Ursula looked blank. It was obvious she couldn't at this moment recall who Mrs Sanders was.

'Our cook, Mother,' Steph reminded her.

'Oh. Well, pay her then,' she snapped.

'If you give me the money. I'll need enough to pay the gardener, too, and to cover immediate bills from our suppliers or they'll stop delivering to us.'

Ursula looked irritated that her daughter was bothering her with such trivialities. 'They'll just have to wait until Gerald's estate is settled. Now, for God's sake, will you fetch me the pills and coffee? My head is splitting.'

Despite her own rising anger at her mother's attitude, Steph kept her voice even. 'They can't be expected to wait, Mother. Mrs Sanders is a widow with rent and such like to pay and—'

She was stopped short by the look Ursula shot her. She was not going to part with a penny of the money she'd taken from Gerald's safe, that much was very apparent. Steph would have no alternative but to pay them herself out of her savings. She hoped what was left would cover their outlay until her father's estate was settled and they started receiving the weekly allowance.

'Oh, stop bothering me with this, Stephanie. Deal with it yourself. Has that lawyer man given you a date yet when we're to go in and sign the papers? I want this all done and dusted. I've my own life to get on with. Violet Dickenson-Wilson has bought a house in the South of France. The idea of shooting off whenever I want to, to enjoy some warmth and sunshine, sounds just divine! Not to mention all those delicious Frenchmen . . .'

Her eyes glazed and Steph could see she was picturing herself lounging by a pool, having her every whim catered for by well-honed handsome waiters. She really ought to inform her mother of the impossibility of it.

Taking a deep breath, she opened her mouth but Ursula stopped her in her tracks. 'And I don't appreciate having my sleep disturbed by people telephoning for you when you're not home. Make sure you arrange with them in future that they're only to telephone you when you're going to be here.'

Her mother's selfish instruction was so ludicrous Steph didn't even bother making a response to it. But she hadn't been expecting anyone to telephone her and was intrigued to know who had. 'Who was it, Mother?'

Ursula frowned for a moment while she searched her memory. 'Oh, some man . . . very common sort. He apparently got our telephone number from the agency you used to help you find a job. He said that after thinking about it, he'd like to give you a try out, if you'd be willing to learn to use a typewriter. He asked you to let him know. I've made a note of his number in my book, so that if you do take the job I can get hold of you when I need you.'

Steph was both delighted and dismayed to hear this news. She was thrilled to hear she was being offered the job, albeit with provisos, but utterly dismayed that Ursula already had the number. Was there any point in accepting it now? Out of respect, she'd return Harry's call and hope he wouldn't be too disappointed when she turned the job down.

Having made Ursula a pot of coffee and taken it and two painkillers up to her, Steph positioned herself at a safe distance from the bed, anticipating possible projectiles considering the conversation they were about to have. She took a deep breath before casually venturing, 'Oh, I bumped into Jay today, Mother.'

Ursula, shuddering as she swallowed back the painkillers helped down by a long draught of water, was looking at her, bemused. Finally she snapped, 'Jay?'

'Jason.'

'Jason?'

Steph gave a sigh of irritation. 'The young man who was supposed to be taking you out last night. That Jason.'

Her mother was now pouring herself a cup of

coffee. 'There was no *supposed* about it. He *was* taking me out until your jealousy reared its ugly head and scared him away. You did own up and make a suitable apology to him for your deplorable behaviour, I take it? Is he calling for me tonight?'

Steph shifted uncomfortably on her feet. 'Er . . . you don't think you could have misunderstood anything he said to you that night, do you, Mother?'

Ursula sat bolt upright and hissed, 'You think I made it up that a much younger man was interested in me? Why would I need to do such a thing? It's not like I'm ever short of admirers, either younger, my age or older than I am. When I arrived in Harry's Place that night, I spotted him straight away, looking at me from by the bar. It was very apparent to everyone else who was there that he liked what he saw. It was he who approached me, offering to buy me a drink, and that led to several more. He was all over me! He told me he'd never met a woman like me before and it'd make him the proudest man alive to have me on his arm. He fixed a date with me there and then. I wrote down my address for him so he'd know where to come and collect me. That's the story he told you, isn't it? You're just checking because you can't cope with the fact that men your own age find your mother attractive.'

Steph said quietly, 'That's nothing like the story Jay told me.'

'Anything other than my version is a lie. So what is his version then?'

Steph swallowed hard. 'Jay said that he'd been out with his friends and was on his way to the taxi rank when he saw you . . . to use his words . . . stumbling out of Harry's Place. Then you fell right over and he went to help you up. He said you could hardly stand by yourself so he did the gentlemanly thing and offered to make sure you got safely into a taxi. On the way to the rank he offered you a light for a cigarette and you pocketed his lighter. It was a present from a friend. He called around last night to collect it from you, not to take you out.'

Next thing Steph knew she was ducking to avoid a multicoloured Venetian glass ashtray that was coming her way, offloading the stub ends of several cigarettes and accumulated ash en route. It just missed her head to crash against the wall behind her, making a large dent in it before it fell to the carpet below.

'That man is a liar!' Ursula was screaming in rage. 'What I told you happened. Pass me my handbag,' she demanded.

It was on the dressing table. Steph went over to collect it. As soon as she'd placed it on the bed within Ursula's reach she hurriedly retreated to her place by the wall.

Ursula grabbed the bag, unclipped it and tipped out its contents. Out came an expensive enamelled compact and matching lipstick case, a leather purse, unopened pack of Peter Stuyvesant cigarettes, gold cigarette case and matching lighter. She picked up the lighter, brandishing it at Steph. 'This is mine. So where is the one I was supposed to have pocketed?'

'Well, maybe it's in your coat.' He had said she 'pocketed it'.

'I wasn't wearing a coat, I was wearing my mink stole and that doesn't have pockets. The man is a liar. I tell you.' As if to emphasise her point Ursula snatched up the tumbler from the bedside cabinet and Steph found herself ducking that as it flew towards her, to crash against the wall and smash into pieces on the floor and around the ashtray.

She made a hasty getaway. The next missile might just find its target. As she made her way to her own room to fetch her savings book, though, she found herself feeling an unexpected rush of pity for Ursula. She firmly believed her mother had convinced herself Jay had fallen for her and asked her out. How desperate she must be for admiration from every man she came into contact with. Ursula clearly needed to seek help for her drinking, but Steph knew it was no good suggesting it to her.

# CHAPTER NINE

Steph spotted Jay anxiously surveying the other pedestrians at just on eight that evening. Immediately he saw her his face split into a broad grin and he dashed over to greet her. 'You look good enough to eat,' he said, admiring her off-white, sleeveless woollen mini dress worn with low-heeled white boots and a black and white dogtooth-check belted coat. Her shining natural blond hair was parted down the middle and just reached her shoulders.

Jay had obviously made an effort to look good, she liked to think for her benefit. He had on maroon tapered trousers and a black polo-neck sweater under a black leather jacket.

'Any preference where you'd like to go?' he asked her.

She appreciated his consulting her. 'I'll leave it to you.'

Steph didn't resist when he took her arm, hooking it through his, and they set off.

A while later they were seated beside each other on a bench in a corner of the Hansom Cab public house on Humberstone Gate, opposite the Palais-de-danse, their drinks before them, his a pint of Carlsberg lager, hers a Cherry B. He offered her a Number 6 from his packet.

Smiling warmly at him, Steph shook her head. 'I don't, thank you. Er . . . about your lighter. My mother insists she didn't keep hold of it. To prove her point, she emptied her handbag out and it wasn't in there. I know it won't be the exact one your friend bought you, but if you describe it to me, I'll see if I can replace it as near identically as I can.'

He struck a match and lit his cigarette, drawing the smoke deep into his lungs before looking into her eyes and saying, 'Forget about the lighter. Hopefully it will turn up, but if not I shall remember it as my lucky charm. It brought you into my life, didn't it?' He could not have missed the pink blush that flared in her cheeks but she appreciated the way he was considerate enough not to embarrass her by making any comment. With his eyes still fixed intently on hers, he continued, 'So what I want to know is, why a woman like you isn't already spoken for?'

Steph smiled coyly. 'I might be, for all you know.'

He grinned. 'That's true.' Then he looked at her meaningfully. 'Well, if you are, then put the man out of his misery and end it with him so he can find himself someone else. Because you're mine now.'

Not sure whether to feel honoured or annoyed by his arrogance, she said, 'You're sure of yourself?'

'Yes, I am. I knew the moment I set eyes on you that you were the one for me. I'm not going to let you go, so you might as well get used to the idea.' Then he grasped her hand and said earnestly, 'Give me the chance to prove to you that I'm everything you could ever want in a man.'

Most women had a secret fantasy about a good-looking man taking one look at them and being instantly besotted, proclaiming them as their woman, to whom no other would ever come close. Steph was no exception to that. She couldn't deny that she was extremely flattered by his declaration. A thrill of anticipation began to swirl in her stomach. Had she finally met the man she was going to spend the rest of her life with? The one who was going to pluck her away from her life of oppression and whisk her into a new world, one in which she had a say in how her life was run? More important even than that, for the first time in her life would she experience what it was like to have someone truly love her? She could fall in love with Jay, she had no doubt . . . if she wasn't in the process already.

For a brief instant she felt as though she was soaring amongst the clouds, basking in euphoria, but the spell was broken when a sudden terrible thought struck her and she came crashing back down to earth with a thud. Please don't let it be true, her mind screamed, but in her belief that Jay was after her mother purely for monetary reasons she had actually announced that *she* was the sole beneficiary of her father's estate! Had she been right about him after all? Upon discovering he was wasting his time pursuing her mother, had he set his sights on her?

She needed to put to rest her suspicions, one way or the other. But how to do that without deeply offending him should she be wrong?

Eyeing him warily, Steph ventured, 'I know nothing about you. You could be a murderer, for all I know.'

He stared at her blank faced for a moment before he laughed. 'Clever girl, you've sussed me! Seriously, I'm just a straightforward guy who can't believe his own luck. I've met the woman I always dreamed of meeting but never dared hope for.' Then he took a long draught from his drink, set his glass back on the table in front of them and told her all about himself.

'I'm twenty-five, free and single, in partnership in a delivery business with my friend which is doing very well, and with my own flat on Charles Street. We can continue living there after we're married or we'll get a house, I'll leave it to you to decide. My

Triumph Dolomite is in the garage at the moment, it's got a fault they can't seem to pinpoint, so that's why I can't offer to drive you anywhere. What else would you like to know?'

Steph's heart soared. He *wasn't* out to con her out of her inheritance! He'd no need to as he was doing very well for himself. He was clearly doing his utmost to sweep her off her feet and she was not going to stop him.

'Is there nothing else you'd like to know about me?' she asked.

He looked at her long and searchingly. 'I already know enough to realise how I feel about you. The rest I'll have fun finding out as we go along.'

Oh, God, this man really was Mr Wonderful! She had hardly touched her Cherry B but felt drunk with elation. She wanted to know everything about him, though. 'Do you have any family?' she enquired.

Jay took a deep breath before responding matter-of-factly, 'I never knew my father and my mother's dead.'

Despite his emotionless tone she had witnessed a flash of pain in his eyes at the mention of his mother. She realised that the death was obviously still very raw with him. 'I'm sorry about your mother,' she said softly. 'Did she die recently?'

His face tightened as he cast down his eyes and said gruffly, 'Six months ago. I didn't realise until

131

after her death how lucky I was to have had her. She died before her time, struggling to raise me, and she shouldn't have.'

Steph felt a bit puzzled. The words 'she shouldn't have' didn't quite make sense to her. But before she had a chance to quiz him on why he had said that, Jay was saying, 'You've lost a parent, you know how devastating it is.'

But it hadn't been for her. She looked at him for a moment, trying to pick her words so she didn't appear too heartless. 'My father and I weren't close.'

He was watching her carefully. 'Oh, I see. But your mother must have been distraught? Drowning her sorrows, wasn't she, the night I came across her?'

'Er . . . well, not really. It wasn't a happy marriage, you see.'

'Oh, right.' More to himself than to her, he mused, 'So his death really was a relief to you both then.' He changed the subject. 'I expect you've had lots of boyfriends. Anyone serious?'

'One. I was engaged to be married to him but he was accidentally killed.'

'Oh, I'm very sorry to hear that. His death must have devastated you, since you were going to marry him?'

What would Jay think of her should she truthfully state her reason for agreeing to marry William? Suddenly Steph couldn't bear the thought of him thinking badly of her and just said, 'I was very upset, of course I was.'

She couldn't read his expression. All he said was, 'I see.'

He knew, or strongly suspected, that she hadn't been in love with William. Steph felt the need to explain to him then, make him understand why she had been prepared to marry a man she hadn't loved. She opened her mouth, but before she could speak he asked her, 'What do you do for a job?'

'I'm in between at the moment.'

He looked at her knowingly. 'Well, of course, you wouldn't need to work really, would you?'

Oh, did he assume she lived off her father's money? She started to point out to him that he was wrong, but then he was asking her, 'Another drink?'

'Oh, er ... let me,' she offered, making to open her handbag and take out her purse.

He placed his hand on top of hers in order to stop her. 'I wouldn't dream of your putting your hand in your purse when you're out with me. I don't know what sort of men you've had dealings with in the past but this one believes in looking after a woman and you'd better get used to that.'

He rose and went off to the bar.

Oh, she could get used to being looked after, all right! A vision of William flashed before her then. She felt guilty for falling for another man so soon after his death but she was alive and being given the chance of a happy future, which if the roles were reversed she knew William wouldn't have hesitated in grabbing.

When Jay returned with their drinks he immediately stated he was keen to learn all about her likes and dislikes. Steph couldn't believe it when she discovered his taste in everything from music to food virtually mirrored her own, with only minor exceptions. She felt that with them both sharing so much in common, there was little chance of discord in their relationship.

She was telling him about several films that she was keen to see at the cinema. One in particular, *Dr Zhivago*, had received rave reviews and she was hoping he'd take the hint and offer to go. William had loved going to the cinema. Armed with his bags of sweets and bottles of fizzy drinks, he would chomp and slurp his way through the trailers, B-film then main feature, getting her to fetch ice creams during the interlude. He would guffaw loudly at anything that tickled his fancy in the film and loudly voice his disgust if he weren't enjoying it. And woe betide anyone who'd disrupted his viewing in any way, despite the fact that he was disrupting all the people seated around him. Steph had no doubt whatsoever that Jay would not embarrass her in that way. Going to the cinema with him would be an absolute pleasure.

Instinct told her that he was going to make the offer, when to her surprise his attention was suddenly distracted by a new arrival in the pub. Surely the look that fleetingly crossed his face couldn't be of horror? Why would Jay be afraid of the man who had just come in? He looked unremarkable to Steph, nothing sinister about him at all.

She realised his look wasn't one of horror but annoyance when he said, 'Quick, drink up and let's get out of here. That's one of my drivers just come in, and if he spots us we'll never get rid of him. He'll want to talk shop, probably see this as an opportunity to hassle me about pay rises . . . anyway, call me selfish but I want you to myself tonight.'

It warmed Steph to know that he didn't want to share her.

They hurriedly downed the remains of their drinks and collected their coats, slinking around the tables towards the door, hoping Jay's employee didn't spot them. Unfortunately for them he turned round just as they were about to open the door. Recognising Jay, he called over, 'Oi, Jay mate, ain't leaving, a'yer? Stay and have another.' It seemed then that a thought suddenly struck him. 'You weren't in today and you obviously ain't sick so what—'

Jay cut him short, calling over to him, in a warning tone, 'Remember who pays your wages, Fred. I've a special job for you first thing in the morning so, immediately you come in, come and see me.' He grabbed Steph's arm with one hand, pulling the outer door open with the other and guiding her through.

Steph couldn't believe that an employee was treating his boss like he would another workmate. If she had been so familiar with any of her employers, she would have been instantly dismissed for insubordination.

They were outside on the pavement by now and she made to query this with Jay but he got in first by explaining, 'I try to keep on friendly terms with my employees, makes for a better working environment, but it does have its downside. Sometimes the drivers forget I'm actually their boss, like Fred did just now, and I have to gently remind them. As he didn't see me at work today, he thinks, like some of the other drivers who can't see further than their noses, that I was lazing around when in fact I was working my backside off, drumming up new business to keep them all in work . . . well, I was doing that apart from the hour or so I spent with you, persuading you I wasn't the conniving monster you first took me for!'

Steph smiled up at him. 'You've more than convinced me of that.'

The look that filled Jay's face was that of a man who'd had his dearest wish granted. 'Good. Now, we could go to another pub or would you like to come back to my flat for coffee? You'll need to see it anyway to decide whether you'd like to live there with me after we're married. If it's not to your taste then we'll need to find something that is.'

Was this all really happening or was she just in the middle of a delicious dream? Steph bit down hard on her bottom lip. Ouch, that hurt! This was no dream, this was reality. She could never, ever remember a time when she'd felt like this . . . so glad to be alive, so very much looking forward to her future.

Jay's flat was on the top floor of a 1930s building that housed a row of shops beneath. It was situated on the corner of Charles Street and Belgrave Gate, only a stone's throw from the centre of Leicester, and was clearly a very desirable property.

Entering the flat, they arrived in a hallway which had four doors off it. Each stood ajar and, as she followed Jay towards the door which led into the lounge, Steph took a quick peek inside the other rooms. A bathroom, bedroom and kitchen, all of a good size. They were scrupulously tidy, and if it weren't for a few personal items dotted around it would have seemed that no one was actually in residence. Jay was certainly a very orderly person. The furniture and furnishings were all of the latest style and of top quality. His business must be doing more than just well to fund all this.

'Tea or coffee?' he asked as he helped her off with her coat.

Later that night Steph lay in bed, staring up at the night shadows that flickered across the Anaglypta-papered ceiling. Adrenaline was still pumping through her veins and sleep felt far away. Not that she wanted to sleep. There was a saying that things looked different in the morning, but she didn't want to view her evening any differently. She just wanted to relive every wonderful moment of it. In truth, she had been reckless, going home with a man she barely knew, but Jay had been a perfect gentleman towards her and she had never once felt the slightest unease.

Having made her a cup of coffee, he had put on a Moody Blues LP, sat beside her on the sofa and pulled her close. They had listened to it together, without a word passing between them. Steph marvelled at how relaxed and content she had felt in his company, although very conscious as the record neared its end that she would have to leave soon or miss the last bus home. Jay had stressed his remorse that he couldn't take her home himself, due to his lack of transport at the moment, and offered to pay for a taxi for her. Steph politely refused. He hadn't allowed her to pay towards anything that evening and she didn't want him to perceive her as taking advantage of his genorosity. He insisted on accompanying her to the bus station and, for the first time that she could remember, she willed the bus to be late. To her dismay, it was already waiting when they arrived, a queue of people jostling each other to board.

Just before they were about to join the end of the queue, Jay pulled her to a halt. He took her hands in his and smiled deep into her eyes. His voice low and husky, he said, 'Tomorrow night?'

For once Steph was glad she had no family or friends commandeering her time. She was blissfully free to accept. Smiling up at him, she vigorously nodded her agreement, not a thought for the fact that she was appearing very eager. 'Same time, same place?'

Beaming with delight, he bent his head and kissed her cheek. Acute disappointed filled her then. She had so wanted him to gather her in his arms and kiss her on the lips ... a long, slow, passionate kiss. It seemed she was going to have to be patient, for the moment. Meantime, she could envisage what it would be like ...

She had never had any reason to thank her mother before now. True, Ursula had given her the miracle of life itself, but her idea of parenting had resulted in very few moments of happiness for Steph during the last twenty-four years. But now, at long last, it did look as if she owed her mother a huge debt of gratitude for bringing Jay into her life.

Steph heard the faint sound of a key scraping in the lock below, and stiffened. Her mother was arriving home, obviously the worse for drink judging by the difficulty she seemed to be having getting the key in. Steph wasn't ready to stop basking in her memories of a wonderful evening and prayed her mother didn't demand her company.

She heard the front door open and shut and then Ursula's footsteps cross the hall and start to ascend the stairs. Her uneven tread confirmed that she was well oiled. It was her likely mood that bothered Steph. If she'd had a good night then she would be talkative but fairly amenable, as long as Steph said nothing to risk annoying her. If it was a bad night then her mood would be an argumentative one and whatever Steph said would be misconstrued and seen as an excuse for Ursula to have a temper tantrum. She sighed heavily, a feeling of doom settling upon her as her mother's stumbling footsteps moved closer to her bedroom door.

Then an idea struck her. If her mother couldn't find her, then she couldn't force Steph to bow to her wishes.

Quick as a flash she'd dived out of bed, straightened the cover then concealed herself underneath the bed, just as the door was flung open and her mother staggered in, proclaiming, 'Stephanie, get me a drink and bring it to my room.'

Under the bed Steph held her breath as she heard her mother make her way across the room. She saw the high-heeled shoes appear an inch or so from her face, then heard the swish of the bedclothes being drawn back. There was silence for a moment as it obviously registered with Ursula that she had in fact been addressing an empty bed, then a disgruntled outburst of, 'Oh, damnation. Where are you, Stephanie, when I need you? Bloody inconsiderate, that's what you are, off out enjoying yourself when I've just had a rotten night and need someone to talk to.'

She heard her mother stomping back across the room and then the bedroom door slamming none-too-gently shut.

Steph lay where she was for a moment, just in case her mother should return and catch her out, and wouldn't she have a lot of explaining to do then? She suddenly felt ridiculous to be cowering under her bed in order to avoid spending time with her own mother. But then, wasn't it sad that she had a mother who didn't consider her daughter's need for privacy, but always put her own desires first?

She heard another door open and shut, again none-too-gently, and judged it was safe for her to come out as her mother had reached her own room.

Steph climbed back into bed, rearranged the covers around her and returned her thoughts to the topic she had been lost in when her mother returned home. With her mind still fixed on Jay, she finally drifted off into a delicious, dream-filled sleep.

# CHAPTER TEN

'It seems I'm talking to myself!'

At these barked words Steph jumped and jerked round her head, to stare blankly across at her mother, framed in the doorway of the lounge, half-full crystal tumbler in one hand, cigarette in the other. She was dressed in a cream silk two-piece leisure suit, the sort of style American film stars relaxed in in the 1940s. To all intents and purposes her mother *had* been talking to herself as Steph hadn't heard a word she'd said. In fact, hadn't heard her arrive in the room. She had been completely lost in a world of her own.

She'd been seeing Jay for nearly two weeks now, every night, since he had stressed to her that every minute he was away from her was a minute in purgatory for him. She had to admit that at the end of each evening with him, it was becoming harder and harder for her to leave and go home alone. Jay had told her at the outset that he was out to prove he

143

was the man for her, and he'd been true to his word. Up to now there was nothing about him she could find fault with. He seemed to be perfect in every way.

She had never been held by a man the way he held her, as if he was afraid to let her go in case she disappeared; never been kissed the way he kissed her ... slowly, his tongue intimately exploring the inside of her mouth, she becoming so lost in him she was unaware of anything else around her. The only thing she hadn't shared with him as yet was her body, despite the fact that, unable to help herself, she had made it plain that she would not spurn his advances should he approach her in that way. Jay had made it clear in return that, despite his desire for her, he respected her far too much to have sex with her before he'd married her. This show of regard only served to deepen her feelings for him.

Last night as they had said their goodbyes at the bus stop – his car still in the process of being repaired – Jay had intimated to her that their date the following night was going to be something special. As they had already had several romantic meals in expensive restaurants, visited the cinema, theatre, museum, enjoyed a trip on the canal in a barge and walks in the park, Steph couldn't think just what he had in mind that would prove any more special. She'd been trying to guess when her mother started demanding attention.

Much to Steph's relief, so far she had managed to keep her relationship with Jay a secret from Ursula. But then, these days, with no husband to keep a rein on her activities, her mother was far too caught up in what was going on in her own life to wonder about her daughter's.

'I'm sorry, Mother, did you ask me something?'

Ursula issued an irritated sniff. 'How I hate repeating myself. Get Cook to make breakfast.'

Breakfast! It was getting on for two o'clock. Steph looked back at her, bemused. 'You don't eat breakfast, Mother.'

'My friend does.'

Her friend? Steph had been up since seven-thirty that morning, hadn't been out as she was waiting for news . . . nothing had arrived in the post today, so hopefully she would hear by telephone. She'd attended several job interviews over the past fortnight but had had little hope of landing any of them when at the end the interviewers all told her they were seeing several people. Should she prove the most suitable, they would be contacting her last employer for a reference and would then contact Steph herself with a start date. If only she hadn't had to turn down the job with the plumber's but, really, she'd had no choice. Her mother had found out about it, and Steph knew all too well that it would have only been a matter of time before she ruined it for her. But anyway, there'd been no callers to the house that morning, so just when did this friend arrive? Then she knew. Ursula had obviously brought the friend home with her last night – and the odds were that it was a man.

Steph wasn't sure how she felt about her mother entertaining a strange man in her bed while she herself was asleep in another room down the corridor. Besides, her father had hardly been dead any time and, whatever the circumstances, she felt her mother could have shown some decorum for a while longer. But Ursula had never taken any notice of her daughter's opinion before so there was absolutely no point in Steph expressing it now.

'Mrs Sanders no longer comes in in the morning, Mother. There didn't seem any point after Father died as you don't take breakfast and I'm capable of making tea and toast for myself.' By way of a dig at her mother for not noticing Mrs Sanders no longer did a morning shift, she added, 'She hasn't been coming in in the morning for two weeks.'

Her attempt to make her mother realise her own ignorance of the running of the house was totally wasted. Ursula didn't even bat an eyelid but just said, 'I didn't enquire whether my friend prefers tea or coffee but I want coffee, so make a pot of both. We'll be in the dining room.' She was about to leave but stopped to ask, 'Have you heard from the lawyer yet about the money coming through?'

Steph shook her head. 'He said a month to six weeks and it's only been two.' As her mother had a guest, this really wasn't the time to discuss personal matters. But her mother needed to know that Steph wasn't going to be in a position to hand over quantities of money to her. Steph wasn't being very fair, allowing her to make plans for expensive holidays and such like when it could well turn out that their allowance wasn't going to finance these. She really ought to get the deed over with. She prepared herself.

But, before she could open her mouth, her mother was ordering her, 'Get on to the man and instruct him to hurry up the proceedings. I've my trip to Scotland to pay for, and the travel agent's will be pressing me to settle the bill for my cruise in January before we know it.'

Despite not relishing the prospect of the possible aftermath from her one bit, Steph took a deep breath and began, 'About those trips, Mother. You see, there's something you really should . . .'

Rearing back her head, Ursula interjected, 'What *about* my trips?' Her lip curled in disgust. 'You're not going to be selfish enough to suggest I cancel them because you don't want to be left here on your own? Well, at twenty you're old enough to find your own entertainment, I hope.'

So her mother didn't even know that Steph was, in fact, twenty-four? And hadn't she been left to find her own entertainment practically from birth?

Before Steph could say this a man appeared behind her mother. He was younger than she, no more than thirty-five against her forty-two, tall and swarthy with a full head of black hair, dressed in a smart suit, albeit his shirt was slightly crumpled. He seemed to be taking a great interest in Steph.

'You never told me you had a daughter, and such a good-looking one at that,' he said to Ursula, without taking his eyes off Steph. She was already feeling unnerved by him.

Ursula spun round to face him, issuing a dismissive laugh. 'As if I'm old enough to have a daughter of her age! She's my niece, just paying me a visit. Cook has gone home until this evening so my *niece ...*' she reiterated '... has offered to cook breakfast.'

Dragging his eyes away from Steph, the man said, 'When I agreed to stay for breakfast, I didn't realise it was actually afternoon. I've things to see to so I'd best get off.' He looked back at Steph. 'Another time?'

Slimy toad, she thought. He was a lounge lizard

if ever she'd met one. She'd taken an instant dislike to the man. Regardless, she flashed him a tight smile.

'Will I see you tonight, to discuss joining you in your venture?' Ursula asked him.

He smiled seductively. 'You most certainly will, my sweet. I'll book us a table at eight at the Claremont and we can discuss things further.' He kissed her cheek. 'Until then.'

'What venture?' Steph asked her mother when her visitor had left.

Ursula arched an eyebrow at her. 'Not that my business is any of yours, but I'm trying to persuade Harvey to let me go in with him in a property deal. He let slip to me last night that he's on the verge of signing it. He doesn't really want a partner. According to him it stands to make thousands.'

According to him sounded right, thought Steph. There were pound signs visible in her mother's eyes. It was Steph's opinion that any money handed over to that man would be lost for good. She'd been very wrong about Jay trying to con money out of her mother, but knew she definitely wasn't about the smooth operator who had just left. Thank goodness Ursula wasn't in a position to give him anything. Which reminded Steph that she really ought to advise her mother of that fact.

Before she could try again her mother announced, 'Forget the coffee, I'm going back to bed. Looks like

I've another heavy night with Harvey ahead of me so I'd best get some proper rest.'

With that she turned and left the room.

Steph made to go after her. Now that she had built up the nerve to impart to her mother what she had to know, she was reluctant to let this moment pass. But the shrilling of the telephone stopped her.

Making her way up the stairs, Ursula instructed Steph, who was now in the hall, 'Take a message from whoever that is and tell them I'll call them back when it suits me. Oh, and telephone my beautician and make me an appointment for a facial for about two tomorrow afternoon, and my hairdresser after for a shampoo and set.'

Ursula never even considered that the call might be for her daughter. And Steph didn't appreciate the fact that her mother was taking advantage of the fact that she was at home at the moment, due to her lack of a job, to use her as her social secretary. Biting her tongue, she picked up the telephone. It was for her mother after all. The travel agent was informing her that Ursula's instructions for an upgrade to first-class for herself and her travelling companion had been arranged, and they looked forward to receiving payment in full for the trip no later than fourteen days before departure.

Steph realised her need to fill her mother in on the precise terms of the Will was paramount.

\* \* \*

It was apparent that Jay was bursting with excitement when he dashed across to greet her that night. After he'd hugged and kissed her, Steph looked at him expectantly.

He grinned. 'Have patience! I've booked us a table at the Sweet Garden. I remember you telling me you'd never tried Chinese food, so thought you might like to give it a go. Over dinner I'll tell you my news.'

She knew by his manner that whatever he had to tell her was good.

Her patience had been stretched to its limit by the time they had ordered, sweet and sour chicken and plain rice for her, beef in black bean sauce and chow mein for him, and waited while the waiter brought their drinks. As soon as he had departed Steph implored, 'Please put me out of my misery.'

Jay took a long draught from his glass of bottled beer, set it down in front of him, then said, 'You, my darling, are my lucky charm . . . but then, I knew you were special the moment I set eyes on you. Anyway, the morning after our first date, when I knew for certain I'd met the love of my life, my business partner asked if I'd buy him out. His brother and his family are emigrating to Australia, taking advantage of the government's ten-pound deal, and wanted my partner and his family to go with them and set up a business over there. Of course, I've jumped at his offer. I'm not even going to haggle over the price. He wants thirty thousand.

'The business is doing very well, and the icing on the cake is that last week I landed a contract with one of Leicester's biggest ... if not the biggest ... hosiery company, to handle all their deliveries. I'm in the process of adding six lorries to our fleet at the moment. Anyway, today I handed the money over to my partner and now the business is all mine! I've been dying to let you in on this but wanted to make sure it was a done deal first.'

'I'm so pleased for you,' Steph enthused.

'This will benefit both of us. Once I've paid off the loan I took out to buy my partner out, the profits will all be mine. You and our children will want for nothing. I've thought of a great way to celebrate.'

Champagne with their dinner, she guessed.

She was right. Jay summoned the waiter and ordered a bottle. Unfortunately the restaurant didn't stock it but to oblige his customer the owner of the establishment insisted on sending a waiter over to the Griffin across the road, to get a bottle from them.

After they had drunk a toast to the success of Jay's solo venture, he asked her casually, 'Are you doing anything tomorrow morning?'

Steph would have liked to have said that she'd be at work but so far she'd had no success. Clearly any prospective employer who'd taken up her references had been put off her.

She shrugged. 'I've nothing planned at the moment.'

Jay looked pleased to hear this. 'Fancy coming to a wedding with me? A friend of mine is getting married at eleven at the register office on Pocklington's Walk. It's just a very small affair, the bride and groom and me as a witness, and as I've told him about you, he asked if you'd like to be the other one.'

Steph looked positively thrilled. 'Oh, I'd be honoured to.'

'Then I'll meet you at about a quarter to outside the register office. Don't be late. Oh, and just as a precaution, you'd best bring your birth certificate in case the official wants proof you're over twenty-one and of age to be a witness.'

Like a typical woman, Steph's thoughts were already centred on going through her wardrobe, working out what she would wear. She wanted to look nice for Jay but definitely didn't want to upstage the bride. Absently, she responded, 'Yes, okay.'

He was looking at her. 'You seem worried?'

'Pardon? Oh, it's just I've no idea what to wear.'

He looked at her meaningfully. 'You'd be beautiful to me in a potato sack.'

Steph laughed. 'Better make sure I wash it first.'

The waiter arrived then with their meals and the

rest of the evening was spent very pleasantly. When it was time for them to part, Steph's reluctance to walk away from him was stronger than ever and she knew by Jay's manner that he was feeling just the same.

# CHAPTER ELEVEN

Steph crept around the house the next morning, readying herself for the wedding. The last thing she wanted to do was rouse her mother. Ursula would only demand to know why she was dressed as she was, then once she was aware there was a wedding in the offing, would insist on accompanying her daughter in the hope of a celebration where no doubt she would end up taking over the proceedings, showing herself up and mortally embarrassing Steph.

It was an honour indeed to be asked to be a witness at a wedding so this friend of Jay's must be a close one. She wanted to make a good impression on them as his girlfriend, and her mother's presence would ensure the opposite would be achieved. There was also the fact that there was a strong possibility that her friend Harvey the lounge lizard was sharing Ursula's bed again, and should Steph wake them she'd be commandeered to make breakfast, no doubt.

It was with great relief that she found herself ready

to depart. Weddings were such happy events, she felt privileged to have been invited to be part of Jay's friends' special day. Maybe sometime in the not-too-distant future she could return the compliment . . .

As she opened the front door to let herself out, Steph just stopped herself from yelping in shock on finding herself face to face with an elderly woman, her hand outstretched, about to grab the knocker. She was dressed in a shabby black coat. A chequered head square covered her iron-grey hair. The beige woollen stockings she wore were wrinkled and stout legs ended in black zip-up ankle boots. She was carrying a capacious handbag and a string bag full of shopping. Her small grey eyes eyed Steph sharply.

In a deep, loud voice she shouted, 'You looking for a char?'

Having placed adverts in several shop windows over two weeks ago and not received one response, Steph had practically given up on replacing their cleaner. She had been managing to keep the house clean and tidy herself, but if she did manage to land herself a job shortly then maintaining such a big property would have a severe impact on time available to spend with Jay. Each moment she spent with him had become so precious to her, the thought of having to turn down any date with him because of household tasks didn't sit well with Steph. She hadn't time to interview this woman at the moment, though, or she'd be late for the wedding.

Steph smiled at her warmly. 'That's right, we are, but unfortunately I'm late for an appointment so cannot interview you now. Is it possible for you to call back tomorrow at the same time?'

The woman was peering at her. Cupping her hand to her ear, she shouted at the top of her voice, 'What's that yer said, ducky?'

Steph groaned. The woman was deaf as a door post. Taking a breath, she raised her own voice and repeated herself.

Still cupping her ear, the woman shook her head and bellowed, 'You'll have ter speak up, lovey, I can't 'ear yer.'

Steph completely forgot about waking her mother, so conscious was she that time was swiftly passing. If she missed the next bus into town . . . She bellowed back, 'I said . . .'

Thankfully the woman understood her this time and shouted, 'Can't come back tomorrow, lovey, got a funeral, see.' Her prune-like face puckered and tears glinted in her aged eyes. 'I shall miss Ethel. Such good friends we was, me and her. We're giving her a good send—'

An annoyed voice called out, 'Who on earth is making all that noise?'

Steph spun round to see her tousled-haired,

bleary-faced mother, dressed in a pale pink silk house-coat with matching pyjamas underneath, making her way unsteadily down the stairs. She didn't look at all happy to have had her sleep disturbed.

Having caught sight of their caller, Ursula demanded with a look of disgust, 'Who is that creature?'

'What's she say?' the old dear shouted to Steph.

Steph said to her mother, 'This lady has come about the job as our daily.'

'And she has to shout so loudly about it?' Ursula looked the woman up and down and gave a superior sneer. 'I'll not have her type working for me. Get rid of her.'

She really had no idea how hard it was to get domestic staff these days. There was no telling when someone else would apply. Besides that, she had no cause to turn her nose up at a woman who might be shabbily dressed but otherwise seemed respectable enough. 'But, Mother, we really should give this lady a try as—'

A look of disgust stopped Steph. 'I said, get rid of her.' Ursula began to retrace her steps back upstairs, ordering, 'Bring us up a pot of coffee.'

Her mother hadn't even noticed she was dressed for going out! And she had said *us*. So Harvey had stayed again. And had no doubt been strongly hinting to Ursula that he needed to see concrete evidence in a monetary form that she was serious about putting in to his venture. And, in turn, she would be badgering Steph for news of when the money was coming through. Steph really needed to put her mother wise regarding her father's Will, but she was already running late.

'What's she say?' the old lady shouted.

Steph turned back to face her. Stepping out on to the doorstep, she pulled the door shut behind her and, forgetting to shout, responded, 'I'm sorry, the job's gone. Please excuse me, I'm late for an appointment.'

With that she hurried off down the drive, leaving the deaf old dear staring after her in bewilderment as she hadn't taken in a word of it.

Steph just managed to catch her bus and arrived outside the register office at ten minutes to eleven. Jay was already waiting for her, looking handsome and fashionably smart in the blue velvet suit and frilly shirt he had been wearing the night she had first met him.

He beamed when he spotted her and ran across, throwing his arms around her to pick her up and swing her round. Putting her back down, he stared at her intently. 'You look gorgeous,' he said, casting an appreciative glance over her pale blue wool minicoat and matching sleeveless shift dress. She wore white tights with it, navy and white platform shoes and a navy shoulder bag.

Worried she was going to be late, she'd been running and was still breathless, but she was overwhelmed by his obvious delight to see her. 'You don't look so bad yourself. Bride and groom not here yet? I can't wait to meet your friends. I feel so honoured to be part of their special day.'

'Yes, they're here,' he told her.

She looked around. Several pedestrians were passing by, a group of people were milling around on the front steps of the register office, but no one amongst them was dressed or acting like a bride and groom.

'They're already inside then?'

'No. You're looking at the hopeful groom, and hopefully I'm looking at the bride.'

She frowned. 'I don't understand.'

He reached inside his jacket pocket, pulling out an envelope which he handed to her.

Accepting it, she asked, 'What is it?'

'Only one way to find out.'

Intrigued, Steph slit open the envelope and took out the piece of paper inside. Then she gasped, 'It's a special marriage licence!'

Jay reached over to grab her hands, eyeing her intently. 'I love you, Steph. Will you do me the great honour of marrying me? I told you on our first date that I knew you were the one for me, and I can't see the point in waiting any longer. I don't even feel guilty that I told the biggest lie to the register office to get that special licence. Said I'd been unexpectedly sent abroad with my job for three years and the only way I could take you with me was for us to get married.'

Steph gazed at him, utterly stunned. She had thought she was being a witness at a wedding, not attending her own!

He mistook her shocked silence, tightening his grip on her hands and beseeching, 'I promise I'll be a good husband to you, Steph. I'll even promise to obey you in the ceremony, instead of you me. I'll agree to anything! I've a good income, somewhere for us to live . . . all you have to do is pack your clothes and move in. Like I told you before, if you don't like the flat I'll sell it and we can move somewhere else. Oh, Steph, please make me the happiest man alive by saying yes?'

So that was the real reason he'd wanted her to bring her birth certificate along with her! Steph was no different from most women. Secretly she had dreamed of a big white wedding in which she'd float up the aisle in a froth of lace, long train held up by several page-boys followed by a succession of bridesmaids, the man of her dreams waiting at the end of the aisle to make her his. When she'd agreed to marry William, she'd put such thoughts behind her.

Now it seemed she had got her dream man after all. Suddenly the big white wedding was unimportant: she would settle for marrying Jay anywhere. He had certainly convinced her that he would die of a broken heart if she refused him. She was soaring in the clouds again, aware of no one and nothing else, just Jay and herself. She couldn't believe that all her years of praying for a knight in shining armour to sweep her off her feet and save her from the miserable life she was living had at last been answered. Thank God she had never had to settle for a miserable second best like William.

Oh, yes, she would marry this man, with the greatest of pleasure.

'Yes, Jay, yes!' she cried.

He wrapped his arms around her and hugged her tight, then gave her a long, lingering kiss. When he reluctantly let go, he glanced to left and right, seeming worried by something. 'My former business partner Darren and his wife Suzy were over the moon when I asked them to be our witnesses. They should have been here by now. It'll be like a double celebration afterwards ... well, triple really ... our wedding, and me taking over the business, and Darren and Suzy and their kids moving to Australia to begin a new life. I suppose I was presuming a lot, thinking you'd say yes, but I've booked us a table at the White Hart Hotel for afterwards. Anyway, hopefully they'll arrive any minute. We'd best get inside and let the officials know we're here, at least.'

Twenty minutes later, back out on the pavement outside the register office, after profusely thanking the two strangers they had accosted and begged to be witnesses, Jay took Steph in his arms and looking at her lovingly.

'Well, Mrs Connor, how do you feel?'

She was no longer Miss Mortimer but Mrs Connor. Mrs Jason Connor. Stephanie Connor. It had a lovely ring to it.

Steph grinned. 'I think I'll get used to it. I'm sorry your friends didn't make it.'

His face clouded over. 'I'm worried something has happened to them. In all the years I've known Darren, he's never let me down – and especially not over something like this. I'm worried something awful has happened to them.'

'Had we better go and find out?'

'But our table at the White Hart . . .'

'Finding out about your friend and his wife is more important.' Steph hooked his arm with hers. 'Maybe it's just something as simple as oversleeping.'

He smiled at her. 'Yes, it's probably something and nothing.' He pulled away his arm. 'Look, I'll grab a taxi and go and pay them a visit. Meantime, you could go and wait at the White Hart so we don't lose the table? My friends don't live that far away so I shouldn't be long.' He looked at her apologetically. 'I'm so sorry about this. I don't want to ruin your day.'

Steph grabbed his hand and squeezed it tight. 'It's not your fault. And nothing could ruin this day for me, Jay. I'm just reeling from it all.'

He kissed her lips, then she watched him sprint off down the street and disappear around the corner. She didn't like the thought of sitting in the hotel dining room by herself, but hopefully it wouldn't be for long.

For the umpteenth time Steph looked anxiously towards the restaurant's door. It was approaching two o'clock. She had been waiting for over two and a half hours but there'd been no sign of Jay, and no waiter had approached her with a telephone message. She was really starting to worry. He must have discovered that something awful had happened to his friends or he'd have been back well before now.

A stiff-backed waiter approached her. 'We don't take any orders after two, madam. If the rest of your party doesn't arrive within the next five minutes . . .'

Even if they did, the meal would be hurried as the restaurant closed at three in order for the staff to prepare for the evening session. Steph was feeling very awkward, sitting here slowly sipping her orange juice – three of them she'd had now – other diners flashing her curious glances. She'd better wait outside.

'I'm sorry, I've no idea what's happened to the rest of my party. If you'd give me the bill for my drinks, please?'

Outside in the street, she looked up and down but could see no sign of Jay amongst the throng of afternoon shoppers. A bitter wind was gusting and the late-September afternoon was already beginning to draw in. She could stand here waiting and risk catching a chill or . . . what? She realised she had no idea where Jay's friends lived nor where his business premises were situated. She could go to his flat but had no key to let herself in with and there was no telling when he would be back. She could always leave a message with the concierge, informing him that she had returned to her own home to await him there. She needed to pack her belongings anyway. And . . . she had to tell her mother what had happened. Steph wondered how she would take this news. Probably be annoyed that she had been done out of a reception. And, of course, that she was going to have to arrange her own visits to the beautician in future. She wouldn't like that at all. Her mother would miss her, only for what Steph did for her.

A while later she paused on the doorstep to steel herself for the confrontation to come. It was with some relief that she remembered Ursula would be at the beautician's and then after that the hairdresser's so wouldn't be home until at least five. Thank goodness Steph could pack her belongings in peace.

It wasn't until she was in her bedroom that it struck her she hadn't got a suitcase of her own. She'd never needed one as she'd never been on holiday. Her parents had never taken her, and she'd never been able to keep friends long enough to get to know them well enough to go away with them. Outsiders would assume from her address and her father's position that trips away would be commonplace to her. How wrong they'd be! She'd have to borrow a case from her mother. Ursula had a selection of leather cases and trunks to choose from. They were kept in the cellar.

Jay still hadn't made an appearance and Steph was really worried by his lack of contact by the time she'd parked two heavy cases containing her worldly goods beside the front door. She was just about to go through to the kitchen and join Mrs Sanders, who had arrived a short while ago and was preparing supper, when she heard a key being inserted in the lock. The door opened and her mother walked in.

Immediately she spotted Steph, she snapped, 'Get me a drink. A large one. Those people do witter on incessantly about nothing. It's bad enough enduring that, but the fact that you can't even get a drink in those places . . . Did you contact the bank?' she asked

Steph as she slipped off her shoes and stripped off her gloves.

Steph looked bemused. 'I didn't know I was supposed to?'

'The insubordinate creature who rang wouldn't tell me what they wanted to see you for.' Now Ursula was taking off her fur coat, looking at Steph enquiringly. 'So why do they?'

'It'll be to make arrangements for collection of the weekly allowance as per Father's Will. Or signing some papers to open a bank account. Something like that, I expect.' It was now or never. Steph took a deep breath. 'Look, Mother, there's . . .'

But Ursula wasn't listening to her. Her eyes were dancing. 'Weekly allowance! On top of all that other lovely money! Well, I'm starting to remember your father more favourably.'

Steph cringed. She could tell her mother was already plotting what to spend the weekly allowance on. It was a certainty that paying bills didn't enter into the equation.

Having laid her coat over the end of the banister, Ursula was now making her way up the stairs, still calling out orders to Steph. 'Bring my drink up and then run me a bath. I'm meeting Harvey in Harry's tonight. Oh, that reminds me. Did you get a date from the solicitor yet about just when we're going to get our hands on the money as Harvey is pressing me to hand over my contribution? I had a job persuading him to let me in on this deal and if I don't hand over my share soon, he could change his mind and leave me out. And if that happens, I won't be happy, believe me.'

She had arrived at the top of the stairs now and was making her way down the landing towards her room. Steph needed to tell her face to face what she had to say, not shout it up to her for Mrs Sanders to hear.

Several moments later, armed with a glass brimming with vodka and tonic, she entered her mother's bedroom. Clad in just her underwear and stockings, a Turkish-style towel wrap protecting her hair, Ursula was removing her make up using cold cream on a pad of cotton wool. She greedily grasped the tumbler her daughter handed her and took a long swig from it. 'Ah, that's better,' she said, then took another before she set it down on her dressing table and resumed her task.

Steph meanwhile retreated to her position by the door in order to make a hurried escape if things turned ugly. 'Mother,' she began. When she received no response she said more loudly, 'Mother, I need to talk to you urgently.'

She turned her head and shot Steph a look of irritation. 'Not now, Stephanie. Can't you see I'm busy?'

Oh, how easy it would be to turn and go. But she was leaving for good as soon as Jay called for her. She couldn't begin her new life without putting her mother straight. 'It's about Father's money . . .'

The word 'money' was enough to get Ursula's attention. She stopped what she was doing and spun her head, glaring at her daughter. 'What about his money?' Her eyes darkened then. 'You are going to hand it all over! I will not stand for anything less. I don't care how your father left it, that money is *all mine*, do you hear me?'

Steph took a deep breath. 'Well, it's not actually, Mother, and it's not mine either . . . or only what's left after you die and it could be hardly anything by then. If you hadn't left the solicitor's office before he had finished then you would have heard how Father has had all the money put in trust. We're to live on a weekly allowance from the interest earned. I'm not sure how much that allowance is until I've had my interview with the bank manager. The solicitor couldn't tell me himself until all outstanding bills had been paid, funeral expenses and solicitor's costs, and it was calculated exactly how much money remained. You also need to know that this house is mine, but don't worry, you have the right to live here until you die. Only then am I free to do what I want with it. The solicitor will confirm everything I've told you.'

Ursula's face had paled to an ashen grey, her mouth

gaping wide enough to lodge a tennis ball. She stared wild eyed at Steph in the mirror for several long moments while she digested what she had just been told, then twisted around on the stool to face her. 'WHAT!' she screamed out. 'THAT BASTARD DID WHAT?'

'I'm positive Father was only worried about you ending up penniless, with him not around to keep an eye on your spending. By leaving his money the way he has, he was ensuring you wouldn't.'

Ursula looked ready to lash out. Wagging one finger at Steph, she shouted, 'You've known about this all this time and not told me? Allowed me to make plans for how I'm going to spend the money . . . watched me make a fool of myself!'

Steph stiffened, fearing the eruption to come. She glanced to one side, to make sure the door was open for her to dart through should she need to escape. She was relieved to see it was. 'I've tried to tell you so many times but you wouldn't allow me to, Mother. Always too busy doing something more important than listening to anything I have to tell you.'

Steph was surprised herself by the forthright way she had just spoken to her, but not as shocked as Ursula. She was glaring at her daughter, mouth opening and closing like a fish's. She picked up her tumbler and tossed back the contents, then pulled open a drawer in her dressing table to fumble frantically around in it. Not finding what she was seeking, she rammed it shut and yanked open the drawer beneath. Finally finding the half-full bottle of vodka she was after, she pulled it out, unscrewed the top and poured a generous measure into her empty glass, then knocked the lot straight back. Immediately, she poured herself another and drank that straight back too.

Then she ordered Steph: 'Get out.'

She would have liked nothing more but she had other news for her mother first. 'I've something else . . .' She jumped aside just in time to avoid being struck by the heavy tumbler which sent glass flying all around her.

'GET OUT!' Ursula screamed at her.

Steph was happy to comply. She had tried to tell her mother about her marriage and that she would be leaving, but Ursula had refused to listen to her.

She hurried down the stairs to the background sound of breaking glass and screamed obscenities, foul words Steph had never heard her mother use before. It was obvious that in her fury at learning what she had, Ursula was throwing anything to hand. Nothing in her bedroom was cheap. Her temper tantrum was going to prove costly if she meant to replace the items she was now mindlessly destroying.

As Steph arrived at the bottom of the stairs, Mrs Sanders, hands caked in flour, came out of the kitchen.

Her brow was creased. 'Everything all right, Miss Mortimer?'

From the commotion above, it was very apparent everything was far from all right.

Steph answered diplomatically, 'My mother has had a bit of an upset.'

Beryl Sanders looked back at her as though to say, More than a bit of one in my opinion. 'Dinner at the usual time?' was all she said aloud.

But Steph didn't plan to be here then. Surely Jay would have put in an appearance before that. In a slightly raised voice she responded, 'As matters stand at the moment, Mrs Sanders, it's only my mother who'll be eating tonight. Well, I presume so. She hasn't intimated otherwise to me.'

'Oh, going out to eat tonight then, Miss Mortimer?'

Beryl was fishing to learn if Steph had a date. She suddenly felt desperate to tell someone about her marriage, wanting so much to share the happy event. 'I shall be eating in my new home tonight.' She paused for a moment before adding, 'You see, I got married today, Mrs Sanders.'

The look on the other woman's face was a delight to behold. 'Married? Well bless my soul! Married, indeed. That was kept very quiet?'

'Yes, it was. Even from me. Jay . . . my husband . . .' My husband! she thought. I've got a husband and don't need to wish for one any longer. '. . . sprang the surprise on me this morning. I thought I was going to be a witness at the wedding of a friend of his. Little did I realise it was my own wedding I was attending.'

Steph could tell by the knowing look on Beryl Sanders' face that she was assuming Ursula's tantrum was over this news.

Beryl stepped over and placed a floury hand on Steph's. 'Well, congratulations, my dear. I hope you and your new hubby will be very happy together.' Then her face fell as a worrying thought struck her. 'Oh, dear, I suppose it means I'll be dealing with Mrs Mortimer in future instead of yourself. Oh, well, we'll have to see how that goes.'

Steph hoped her mother would behave herself or she'd shortly be looking for another cook as well as a daily.

'STEPHANIE, COME UP HERE NOW!'

The ferocity of Ursula's summons made them both jump.

Beryl Sanders looked at Steph as though to say, Well, aren't you going to jump to it, like you normally do?

Steph, though, had not the energy to subject herself to another confrontation with her mother today. She had more important matters occupying her mind. Her husband . . . Where was he? It must have been something very important to keep him away so long.

It might be dark now and cold outside but that was a far more tranquil place to wait for him. She would come back tomorrow when hopefully her mother would have calmed down enough to listen to the rest of her news.

Steph smiled at Beryl Sanders and held out her hand to her. 'Goodbye, Mrs Sanders.'

'What, you're off now, are you?' Giving her hand a quick wipe on her soiled apron, she grasped Steph's proffered one and they shook. 'It won't be the same around here without you.' Beryl cast her eyes upwards then fixed them back on Steph. 'Between you and me, I doubt I'll be long behind you unless your mother has a personality change. Best of luck, love.'

She made her way back into the kitchen and Steph took her coat off the hall stand and put it on. She then opened the front door, hauled one of her heavy suitcases outside, and repeated it with the other case. Shutting the door behind her, she lugged each case separately down to the end of the drive then sat herself down on them to wait for Jay.

# CHAPTER TWELVE

From her position at the end of the drive, Steph had a good view up and down the well-lit road. Several people walked by, each looking at her with curiosity. She smiled politely at them all, wishing them good evening, as if it was nothing unusual to be perched on a suitcase in the street at that time of night.

There was still no sign of Jay, though.

Her wristwatch was telling her it was approaching seven o'clock. Two hours she had been waiting, the icy nip in the night air having long ago seeped through her clothes to chill her bones. She'd been willing him to arrive and collect her, take her off to the warmth of his flat where they'd begin their life together. By now she couldn't imagine what had happened to keep him. She was concerned that he hadn't received the message she had left at the White Hart, informing him of her whereabouts. But then, Jay was an intelligent man. Even if he hadn't had the message, he would work out for himself where she would be waiting for him. What she was reluctant to consider was the fact that it might have hit him what a reckless thing he had done that morning, marrying a woman he'd known for barely a couple of weeks, and, unable to face her, had absconded. If he didn't arrive soon, however painful it would be, that was the conclusion she would have no choice but to draw.

She heard the swish of gravel behind her and turned her head to see the shadowy form of Beryl Sanders heading towards her down the drive.

The woman looked most surprised to see her. 'You look frozen to the marrow.'

'Yes, it is a bit chilly out tonight. I'm just waiting for a taxi.'

'But you left the house over two hours ago! Surely it should have arrived by now?'

'They're just busy. It's on its way,' said Steph dismissively. 'Er . . . how's my mother?'

Beryl pursed her lips. 'Well, after you left, Mrs Mortimer shouted several more times for you to go up then it went all quiet. I put dinner on the table for her at seven but she hasn't come down for it. I believe she's in her bedroom, drinking herself into a stupor.' She looked at Steph knowingly. 'Look, I'm not as green as I'm cabbage looking. I know Mrs Mortimer has a drink problem. You've been a saint to put up with the way she treats you for as long as you have. I'm really glad that you're finally breaking away. Pardon me for speaking so bluntly, but sometimes things have to be said. Hopefully I'll be seeing you when you visit. Ta-ra.'

Steph watched her walk off down the road. She felt a certain amount of embarrassment for the fact that the staff in their employ had noticed her mother's manner towards her and seen Steph as weak for not standing up to her, but then they didn't know that she had tried to lots of times but her wily mother always managed to come off the victor.

As the figure of Beryl Sanders was swallowed up by the night, another emerged. As it advanced towards her, Steph could make out it was definitely that of a male who was labouring under the weight of something heavy. Then the outline became clearer and her heart leaped. It was Jay!

She made to dash over and greet him but the hem of her coat was trapped in the lock of a case and, by the time she had freed it, Jay was at her side.

Steph was so overjoyed to see him that the fact that what he was carrying was a suitcase did not register with her. Nor did the expression on his face.

Flinging her arms around him, she cried, 'Oh, Jay. I've been so worried! What happened to your friends? You've been so long, I was starting to think you'd had second thoughts . . . Oh, well you're here now.' She peeled herself away and looked at him quizzically. 'So what did happen . . .' Her voice trailed off as the wretched expression on his face finally registered with her. Her own face paling, Steph clamped her hand to her mouth and uttered, 'Oh, dear God, it's bad, isn't it, Jay?'

Nodding miserably, he sank down on his upturned suitcase and cradled his head in his hands.

She sat down on her case next to his and laid one hand gently on his. 'You mean, one of them . . . both of them . . . are . . .' she swallowed hard before uttering '. . . dead?'

His hands dropped away and his head jerked up. 'I wish they were,' he hissed.

'You can't mean that! Darren is your best friend.'

'No friend would do to me what he has.'

Fear gripped Steph. 'Just what has he done to you?'

'Screwed me good and proper, that's what.' To her great distress Jay's face puckered, fat tears glistening in his eyes. 'It seems Darren wasn't happy with just the purchase price we agreed for his share of the business. He wanted the lot, all our assets, and he got it too. He's left me in a right old mess. I hadn't a clue what he was up to, not an inkling, and the worst of it is, it's all my own fault.'

Steph was reeling from this news but also trying to work out how Jay's partner had managed to fleece him out of the business. 'But how did he manage to hoodwink you?'

Jay wrung his hands. 'I trusted him implicitly, had absolutely no reason not to.' He gave a deep sigh and hung his head low as he told her, 'We started off the business with just an old Ford Transit that belonged to Darren's dad. We worked evenings and weekends at first, taking stuff to the rubbish dump, that sort of thing. It was really just a lark at the start, to make us both some extra cash on top of what we were earning from our jobs at the factory. Then we started being asked if we could do jobs during working hours and because it meant we'd earn more than we would have at the factory, we'd sometimes skive off to oblige. It wasn't long before we realised we could make a full-time living at it so we started putting all our delivery earnings aside. When we'd enough, we bought two half-decent vans and put word around about ourselves. Work started to pour in, far more than we had dared hope for. It wasn't long before we were in a position to upgrade our vans, buy another, and take a man on to drive it.

'Darren had always been good at figures and right from the start he handled what we then called our books, though it was nothing more than a jotter, if I'm honest, in those early days. All our jobs were for cash and we never declared anything to the tax man, but as we expanded we knew we'd have to operate the business properly or we'd land ourselves in trouble. It was always me that did all the negotiating with potential customers and worked out the best routes between places, so that's how it came about that I handled that side of things, and because Darren had been the one to take care of the financial side at the outset, it just automatically continued on that way. He took an evening course in book-keeping so he knew how to do the accounts properly.'

Jay heaved a great sigh and in a sad voice continued, 'I always thought me and Darren would be partners for ever. I was totally taken aback when out of the blue a month ago he told me about the proposition he'd had from his brother. He said he and his wife had discussed it at length and decided they liked the idea of a new life down under. They planned to sail on the same boat as his brother and his family, treat the six weeks they were at sea like a holiday for them all.

'Darren wanted thirty grand for his share of the business, a lot of money but actually quite reasonable considering how well we were doing and how much capital we'd tied up in our vehicles and office equipment. In fact, I was surprised he wasn't asking for at least ten more. Obviously I was bothered about how I'd handle the financial side in future as I hadn't the first clue how to, but Darren said he'd take someone on to see to all that for me, so I didn't need to worry. The chap he hired, Ian Jones, was a nice enough man. He'd worked in accounts departments all his working life for decent companies and had glowing references. I felt comfortable having him on board. Anyway, I wasted no time in making an application to the bank for a loan to pay Darren out. I was worried they might refuse but, after looking at the books, they didn't hesitate.

'I handed over the money to Darren yesterday, all in cash as that's how he'd asked me to get it for him so he could change it to Australian dollars when he arrived there. We had a glass of whisky to toast our future successes and that was our partnership over with. It wasn't goodbye for good, though, as I would see Darren and his wife again when they acted as witnesses for us. And I'd been told by Darren that there was a leaving party planned on Saturday night, that his parents were holding for the rest of the family and friends.

'Under the impression they weren't leaving for Southampton until Sunday evening, travelling down on the overnight train, I couldn't understand why I arrived at the house to find it deserted. I learned from a neighbour that they'd actually moved out the day before and travelled down to Southampton on the overnight train last night. They set sail for Australia around eleven this morning, same time as we were expecting them to arrive at the register office to act as our witnesses. I thought the neighbour must have got her wires crossed somehow because I believed Darren would never go off to the other side of the world without saying a proper goodbye to me. So I went to see his mother. I caught her on the way to the shops. She said she was so glad to see me up and about after my dose of the influenza, and was sorry I hadn't managed to come to the party last Saturday night. I asked her who'd told her I was ill, and she said Darren had. She assumed I was paying a visit on her to check that he and the rest of them had all boarded the boat safely. She told me they had as she'd had a message via the corner shop 'cos she isn't on the telephone. They said they'd be in touch again as soon as they could after they'd landed.'

Jay heaved a great sigh. 'By this time I was wondering if I'd had a brain seizure or something and it was me who was getting all my facts wrong. I was also anxious to get back to you because I knew you'd be starting to worry what had happened to me. I don't know what made me decide to detour by the firm on the way to the White Hart. I'd left Chris Baker in charge today to cover my side of things; he's a good man and completely trustworthy, and when I spoke to him yesterday about me taking today off, Ian Jones said he didn't envisage any problems on the administration side, so I felt confident about leaving them to it.' He paused for a moment. It was apparent that this was all very painful and bewildering to him. In a shaking voice he added, 'I still can't believe what I arrived to find.'

Steph was left wondering while he took a cigarette packet out of his pocket. He lit one, drawing deeply on the smoke. He seemed to have lapsed into a world of his own. Desperate to find out what he had arrived to find, she urged, 'Just what did you find, Jay?'

He jumped, exclaiming, 'Eh?' Then he rubbed his hands wearily over his face. 'Oh, I'm sorry, Steph. I keep hoping I'm in the middle of a nightmare and I'm going to wake up and find it's all a dream. It's really still this morning and I'm going to be surprising you at the register office with my proposal . . .' He took a deep breath before continuing. 'What I found was bailiffs sent on behalf of the landlord and other suppliers, removing our office equipment and pricing up vehicles ready to auction off to recoup money it seems we owe.

'It all sounded like nonsense as far as I was concerned. Darren had assured me when I handed him his payout that everything was all up to date. I told the bailiffs a mistake had been made and they were to stop what they were doing while I went to see the landlord myself, to clear up his oversight. But the landlord confirmed to me that the rent on the premises hadn't been paid for three months, despite reminders and threats of court action being sent. I still felt it was a mistake somehow and shot off to the bank to take out the cash to pay it. Meantime I got Ian Jones to check back over the accounts and find out where the mistake was, and also to check with other creditors who were saying their bills hadn't been settled.'

He paused, taking another long draw from his cigarette before gruffly adding, 'That's when I discovered Darren had cleared out all but a couple of pounds from the firm's bank account three days before. He hasn't even left me enough to pay the wages this week. I can't believe he's done this to me!'

Steph was grappling with what this all meant for Jay. She had no idea how businesses were operated but surely what Darren had done was illegal? Even though she wondered just what they could do since he'd left the country now, she asked, 'You are going to get the police involved?'

'I went straight to the station from the bank but I knew I was wasting my time. There's nothing they can do. You see, our partnership was never formalised so Darren was at liberty to do what he did, same as I could have done at any time.'

She gasped, 'Oh, my God. So where does this leave you?'

He looked at her. 'In Queer Street, Steph, that's where it leaves me.' She could tell he was fighting back tears when he lowered his head and uttered, 'All that hard work in building the firm up, believing

I was financially stable enough to be able to support my wife and the family we would have . . .

'The worst thing I've ever had to do in my life was lay the staff off this afternoon. They're all good men and I've no doubt they'll get jobs, but with Christmas in a few months it's not the best time to secure work. I felt most sorry for poor Ian as he left a good job with Standard Engineering to come to us, under the impression we were offering better prospects.'

Jay threw the stub end of his cigarette on the pavement and ground it out with his Cuban-heeled boot, then immediately withdrew another cigarette from the packet and lit that.

'The only hope I have is that I can sell the remains of the business and my flat for enough to settle the loan I had from the bank and cover the debts. Or else I'll be left to pay them off, for however long it takes me.'

She gasped again. 'Sell the business! Surely there must be another alternative?'

He exhaled smoke into the cold evening air to hang above his head like a cloud. 'Unless you know someone who'd be willing to lend me roughly fifty thousand pounds and bear with me while I pay it back, then there's no other alternative I can come up with.' He lifted his head and eyed her hopefully. 'Do you know anyone who would be willing to back me?'

Steph would willingly have helped out her husband, as any wife worth her salt would, if only she'd had free access to her inheritance. But as matters stood, since Darren hadn't completely cleared out the firm's bank account but had left a few pounds in it, Jay could actually lay his hands on more cash than she could. If only her father hadn't left his money the way he had, then she could have come to his rescue.

'I would without question . . .' she began.

His face lit up and he cut her short, exclaiming, 'You would!' Then his face fell. 'But you haven't that kind of money . . .' Then his face lit up again. 'Oh, of course, your inheritance from your father. I'd completely forgotten about that until now.' He flicked his half-smoked cigarette into the gutter and grasped both her hands in his, looking earnestly into her eyes. 'I won't take a penny of the money until we agree on a proper rate of interest. Well, obviously it'll be lower than the bank would charge as we're husband and wife, but it's only fair I give you some return on it. When do you think you can get it for me? Because as soon as you do, I can pay off my debts and put a stop to the interest that's accruing on those *and* the threatened court action. And I can pay off the bank loan and save the interest on that too.'

His face then screwed up thoughtfully. 'Actually,

if you could make it sixty thousand I could still honour the contract I won to deliver goods for that hosiery company. I was paying for the extra vans needed out of the profits Darren helped himself to.' He smiled at her lovingly. 'But the main thing to me, Steph, is that I'll be able to take the men back on and pay them their wages this week. I was worried sick, wondering how they and their families were going to cope. Well, thanks to you, my darling, they won't have to hide from the rent man and go without food on their tables until they've got themselves new jobs, will they?'

He grabbed her to him and hugged her fiercely. 'I am such a lucky man! You won't ever regret marrying me, Steph, never. I'll work day and night to pay back that money, I'll go back to driving the vans myself, if necessary. You don't know how much I was dreading breaking all this to you. I'd promised to look after you properly, and how could I after my partner had embezzled me out of a business, not to mention the embarrassment of him having done it under my nose. I worried you'd want to have our marriage annulled, but with you coming to my aid I will still be able to give you the life I promised you.'

He loosened his arms around her just enough to step back so he could look at her. 'So how soon do you think you'll be able to get me the funds? Oh, but thinking about it . . .' he paused, rapidly making some mental calculations before continuing '. . . better make it seventy thousand. You see, the landlord we . . . well, *I* now . . . rent the business premises off approached me the other day, giving me first refusal on the property as he needs to raise some money. He wants eleven grand for it but I reckon he'll settle for ten as I happened to hear a rumour that he's got himself into financial trouble. It would be a great investment for us, it's in a fine location. The place is perfect for the firm's needs. The office building is in a good state of repair and there are several rooms we don't use at the moment so when the need arises to take more staff on in the future, we've the space to accommodate them. The yard is plenty big enough to park twice as many vans as we have just now, so plenty of room for expansion.

'As we were ploughing our last year's profits back into the business by expanding our fleet of vans, I told the landlord that the answer was no, though I was worried about maybe having to find the equivalent space should the new owners want us out for any reason, and then all the rigmarole that goes with relocating, et cetera. But by buying the premises, I'll never have to worry about that or the yearly rent rises.' An excited expression filled his face. 'So you'll go and make arrangements with the bank tomorrow?'

Steph gulped hard and her whole body sagged in despair. 'Oh, Jay, I would give you the money, not loan it to you to save your business, but I can't! My father left his money and the house in trust. I'll come into sole possession of the house and whatever is left of the money on my mother's death, if there is any then, that is, as she's only in her early-forties. In the meantime we're to receive a weekly allowance out of the trust. Just what the amount is I'm not sure until after I've spoken with the bank. Actually Mother told me they had called today about making an appointment to go in and see them.'

He stood looking at her, frozen faced, for what seemed like an age. Finally he uttered, 'Oh, I see.'

Her heart broke for him then. What his so-called friend had done to him was despicable. She desperately fought for something to say to give him some encouragement. 'Look, Jay, hopefully you'll manage to sell the business and your flat for enough to clear what's owed, and still have a bit left over so you can start again. I'll help you in whatever way I can.'

He shook his head forlornly. 'I wish it could be that simple. We did well because we started up at the right time, when neither of us had wives or homes of our own to keep. Now there are lots of men with vans doing small haulage jobs and I'd be fighting with them for what's on offer. It's a dog-eat-dog business, Steph. I'd be having to cut my profit to the bare minimum to get jobs over the others, in some cases slash it altogether, just in the hope that people will ask for my services next time. I'd be lucky to make enough to live on with just the one van, let alone be putting money aside to expand the business.'

He withdrew another cigarette from his rapidly emptying packet, drawing hungrily on the smoke.

'I have to accept that my days of being my own boss are over, thanks to Darren. After receiving the news I did at the bank, all I could think of was how to raise as much money as I could, as quickly as I could, to cut my losses. I knew a couple of the big firms, Pickford's in particular, have been interested in buying us out for quite a while, especially after me landing the contract with the hosiery company, so I went back to the office and called them. Trouble is, though, although I didn't tell them why I was suddenly interested in selling up, word will soon spread, if it hasn't already in the trade, about the situation I'm in. Then they'll be out to screw me down to get the firm as cheaply as possible, and they can afford to hold out whereas I can't. The first offer I get, I'll have to go for.

'I then telephoned an estate agent to get an idea of how much my flat is worth. I'm in luck. I was told that properties in my block are much sought after. They had a man on their books who's been waiting for one to come up for a while. They kept me on hold while they telephoned him and he's really interested. Even expressed his keenness to buy the furniture, too, and has the cash to do it. The estate agent is showing him around as we speak. I'm hoping I'll get word that he's put in an offer tomorrow when I telephone them. If he wants to move in straight away, he can. In hope of a quick sale, I went to the flat and packed up my stuff . . . well, it seemed pointless you moving all your belongings in tonight only to have to pack them up if a buyer does decide to take the place and wants to move in straightaway.'

Steph was so impressed by him. He'd suffered the most dreadful blow today but instead of wallowing in self-pity he had immersed himself in trying to find a way out of the mess as best he could.

He was saying to her, 'I've got enough to cover the cost of a room for us in an inexpensive hotel for a couple of weeks while I secure a job. When we know how much I'm earning, we'll know what rent we can pay on a place. I'm sorry it won't be up to the standard of the flat. Anyway, we'd better make a move or we'll be too late tonight to get ourselves a room.'

He made to get up but she stopped him by grabbing his hands and squeezing them tightly. For years now . . . as long as she could remember . . . she had been desperate to make her escape from under her parents' roof and this morning she had thought she had finally done so, but due to the selfish actions of others it seemed she wasn't going to gain her freedom just yet. She really didn't want to make the offer she was about to but it was madness to pay for a room in a hotel when she had the means to house them both more than adequately, for however long they needed, and rent-free.

'Jay, we don't need to pay for a room. We can stay in my room back in the house, for as long as we need to.'

His relief at this news was apparent. He tenderly stroked his hand down the side of her face and told her, 'Staying temporarily at your place will certainly solve our problem short-term, but I mean to get us a place of our own as a matter of urgency.' He then asked tentatively, 'Will your mother have a problem with me living with you?'

Oh, God, Steph had forgotten about that complication. She hadn't even told Ursula yet that she was married, but that wasn't her fault as she had tried. Her mother, though, was going to have to get used to the idea that she was married to Jay and, due to circumstances beyond their control, the young couple had no choice but to live under the same roof as her for the time being, and that was that. All Steph said to her husband was: 'I bet you haven't eaten since breakfast? You must be famished. Let's get inside and see what's in the pantry.' She remembered their suitcases. 'We can put these inside the gate for now and collect them later.'

As she inserted her key into the front door Steph mentally prepared herself to face her mother. She secretly hoped Ursula had drunk herself into a coma which would mean she wouldn't have to speak to her until at least midday tomorrow.

She wasn't to be that fortunate.

As soon as she opened the door she heard her mother's alcohol-slurred voice boom out from the lounge, 'Returned from wherever it was you slunk off to? Come in here *now*. I want words with you.'

Steph inwardly cringed. Her mother was still fuming from learning that no huge lump sum of money was coming her way and was obviously looking to carry on where she'd left off earlier, venting her anger on Steph. She turned and looked anxiously at Jay. 'If you want to wait here . . .'

He pressed his finger to her lips. 'I'm your husband, Steph. Where you go, so do I.'

She felt a warm glow rush through her then. In future it seemed that her mother wasn't going to get away with treating her with such flagrant lack of respect. Steph had a husband to champion her now.

With Jay following behind, she arrived in the lounge to see an obviously drunken Ursula sprawled on the sofa, her silk negligee riding up to expose her thighs, full breasts bulging out of her matching low-cut nightdress. Steph was mortally embarrassed, her immediate thought that her mother looked sluttish.

'Mother, cover yourself up, we have a guest,' she hissed urgently. Though 'guest' was actually the wrong word because in fact Jay was now a member of the family. She hoped she had not upset him by her use of it.

Ursula's back was to them. Without even turning her head to look at the new arrivals, she snapped, 'I'm not in the mood for guests, so tell whoever it is to go.' Then she raised the glass she was holding to her lips, tossed back the remaining contents and held it out. 'Fill this up, and don't stint on the vodka.'

Automatically Steph obeyed her mother, refilling the glass from the bottles of vodka and tonic already out on the cocktail cabinet. Grabbing the refilled glass without saying thank you, Ursula took a large gulp from it then immediately went on the attack. 'Gave you pleasure, did it, allowing me to make a fool—'

Steph interjected, 'Mother, there's something I need to tell you.'

This was the second time in one day that her daughter had interrupted her and Ursula was as shocked by what she deemed her insolence this time as she had been the last. With a look of contempt on her face, she glared at Steph for a moment before snapping, 'I asked if you got pleasure out of—'

Steph once again interjected: 'Mother, I tried many

times to tell you what the solicitor explained after you left, but you wouldn't allow me to.' She saw Ursula's mouth open to contradict her and knew that if she didn't speak now she would never get the opportunity to impart her important news. 'I got married today,' she blurted out.

Ursula looked taken aback for a moment before she gave a disdainful click of her tongue and said sharply, 'I know there is nothing wrong with my hearing so you have obviously lost your mind.'

'There is nothing wrong with me, Mother. You heard what I said.'

Ursula laughed sardonically. 'I couldn't possibly have heard you correctly. I categorically refuse to be the mother of a married daughter. I'm nowhere near the age to have a marriageable daughter.' A terrible thought suddenly struck her then and she shot at Steph, 'You'd better not be pregnant? I will not be a grandmother. I WILL NOT!'

'I'm not pregnant, Mother.'

Ursula's relief on hearing that was most apparent. She took a long swallow from her glass then lit a cigarette before looking suspiciously at Steph and saying, 'So if you're not pregnant, why all this secrecy?' Then she smiled knowingly. 'Oh, no need to explain, I know why. You kept your man secret from me because you knew he'd take one look at me and prefer mother to daughter. Does this new husband of yours not wonder why you haven't introduced your mother to him?'

And then Jay was standing next to Steph, smiling charmingly down at Ursula. 'We've already met as it happens, and I'm delighted to meet you again, Mrs Mortimer.' He held out his hand to her. 'Or may I call you Mother?'

Ursula's face turned red with anger. 'No, you may not!' she fumed. Her eyes narrowed then and she peered at him closely. 'We've met previously, haven't we?'

Steph told her, 'Jay was the young man who made sure you were put safely in a taxi home that night.'

Ursula gazed at him wide eyed. 'You're *that* young man! The one who came on strong to me in Harry's. Told me you'd always dreamed of meeting a woman like me and thought it would never happen for you. You were buying me drinks all night. You asked me out and we made arrangements for you to call only—'

'Whoever that young man was, Mother, it wasn't Jay,' Steph said resolutely. 'You fell over outside Harry's and Jay came to your rescue, then he escorted you to the taxi rank to see you safely on your way home.'

Ursula glared icily at him. 'What web of lies have you been weaving for my daughter?' She wagged her cigarette at him in a warning manner. 'Tell her the truth. You were coming on to me that night. You *did* say all that. You *did* make arrangements to take me out. You're after something, I can tell.' She smirked then. 'Oh, of course, you learned I wasn't rich after all . . . but hasn't my dear daughter told you that neither is she? Not so you can get your hands on it anyway. So if you've married her thinking you're going to be living a life of luxury, then you're badly mistaken.'

Jay said quietly, 'I married your daughter because I love her and for no other reason, Mrs Mortimer.' Then he turned his attention to Steph. 'Darling, what I told you about the night I met your mother is the truth.'

Ursula jumped up from the sofa, slopping the contents of her drink down herself in the process. She leaned forward and stabbed Jay in the shoulder with one pointed nail. 'LIAR!' she cried. Then she turned on Steph. 'You're to get this farce of a marriage annulled. Now get this man out of my house! Do you hear me? When you've got rid of him, come up and see me in my room.'

With that she stumbled her way out, but not before grabbing the bottle of vodka from the cocktail cabinet on her way.

Steph felt utterly humiliated. 'I'm so sorry for my mother's behaviour. She's got it firmly into her head that you were the young man who was propositioning her that night.'

He took her in his arms and hugged her to him. 'Your mother was very drunk then, it's easy to see how her memory could be distorted.'

She felt she really ought to warn him that her mother became similarly intoxicated most nights, but thought that as he was going to be living under the same roof as her for the foreseeable future he would quickly learn for himself.

Steph gave a sigh. 'I must go and tell her that we'll both be living here for the time being. Will you fetch the cases in the meantime?'

'Of course, my love,' he responded, giving her cheek an affectionate peck.

Ursula was lounging on her bed, full glass of neat vodka in one hand, cigarette in the other, apparently watching a programme on the television nearby, but whether her drink-fuddled brain was actually registering what she was seeing was debatable.

'He's gone, I hope,' she snapped at Steph. 'You're responsible for your own mistakes. It's up to you to meet the cost of the annulment.'

Steph stood by the door, on the alert as ever. Sounding far braver than she actually felt, she announced, 'There isn't going to be an annulment, Mother. I'm here to tell you that Jay will be living here with us until we have the money to get a place of our own.'

Ursula's contempt for her daughter was clear. With

a sneer on her face, she said, 'Not only have you been fool enough to marry a liar, you've married a penniless one.'

'He's not a liar,' she snapped back defensively. 'But what happened that night and with whom are two different things. And for your information, until today Jay was in partnership in a very successful business, though he found out this afternoon that his partner has embezzled him out of his share. That's why we have to stay here while he gets back on his feet again.'

Ursula knocked back her drink and picked up the bottle from her bedside cabinet to refill it, gulping half the contents before she said, 'Mark my words, that man you've been foolish enough to tie yourself to is up to no good. Just what he's up to I can't work out, because it's not like we've any money to spare, is it? I'd prepare yourself, daughter dear, because it's a hard lesson you're going to be learning. And don't say I didn't try to warn you or come crying to me when he shows you his true colours.'

Fury was building up inside Steph. Why couldn't her mother just be happy for her, like other mothers would be when their daughter found happiness? Before she could check herself she blurted, 'You've never been there for me before when I've needed a mother to turn to. Why should I expect you to be there for me now?' She held her head high and said defiantly, 'I'm not going to be needing anyone's shoulder to cry on, ever, because Jay and I are going to grow old together. And I should remind you, Mother, that this is now my house, and although you have a right to live here for as long as you wish, it's my decision who else resides here.'

She jumped aside just in time to avoid the heavy glass vase the Ursula had grabbed and thrown at her. Her mother looked most annoyed that it had missed its intended target.

'Get that man out of *my* house, and yourself out of *my* room!'

Steph didn't need telling twice.

She ran down the stairs to the accompaniment of her mother's ravings. As she arrived at the bottom Jay entered the front door, lugging the last of their three suitcases. Placing it next to the other two by the coat stand, he said to Steph, 'Your mother didn't take the news of me moving in for the time being very well then?'

'She'll have to get used to the idea.'

'In the meantime, we'll live in a strained atmosphere. It's not how I planned the start of our lives together.' He stepped over to his new wife and took her in his arms. 'Let me go and speak to her.'

Steph vehemently shook her head. 'I wouldn't advise that. When she's like this, it's best to give her a wide berth. Mind you, there is no best time to speak to my mother. If she doesn't like what you've got to say, she doesn't hold back in letting you know.' In fairness Ursula was also having to deal with the shock of learning about their future finances, which for a spendthrift like her must seem like a living hell.

'I don't like the thought of living here under a cloud, Steph. Please, let me just make an attempt at making peace with her? You were going to get me something to eat. Why don't you go and make a start in the kitchen?'

There was no harm in his trying to make peace with her mother, Steph supposed. If he could make even the slightest inroad, then living in a more harmonious atmosphere was certainly preferable.

She watched him make his way up the stairs then went off to the kitchen.

In the fridge and well-stocked larder, she found the remains of the chicken casserole which Mrs Sanders had prepared that day and had been left uneaten by her mother and herself. The simplest thing for Steph to have done would have been to heat it up and boil a few potatoes to go with it, but she wanted to impress Jay by cooking him a meal she had prepared herself. As she searched around the larder and fridge she couldn't help but strain her ears for sounds of argument coming from above.

She heard a purposeful rap on a door. The sound of it opening then shutting. Whether he'd been invited in or not, Jay was now inside her mother's bedroom. Armed with her selection of two pork chops, several potatoes and a tin of garden peas – an easily cooked meal that even an inexperienced cook like she was could surely make a success of – she made her way out of the pantry and back into the main kitchen to the muffled sound of a raised voice, its tone angry. Her mother was shouting again.

Having put the items down on the work surface, Steph stood staring anxiously upwards. By the sound of it Ursula was in full flight. She debated whether she should go up and lend her support to Jay, present a united front before her mother, but that could be seen by her husband as showing no faith in his abilities. He had asked her to give him a chance to ingratiate himself with Ursula and she should leave him to it. Steph did her best to shut out the sound of shouting by forcing herself to concentrate on what she was doing.

The frying pan was on the stove heating fat ready for the chops to be added, potatoes had just come to the boil, when suddenly everything went quiet upstairs. She hadn't heard any door opening and shutting so Jay was still inside her mother's bedroom. Her hopes soared. He must have managed to calm Ursula down enough to listen to him. That was such a good sign. Five minutes passed, then ten, then twenty, and by this time Steph was confident – not to say amazed – that Jay must have worked his magic on her mother or else the shouting and the thudding of missiles would have started up long since.

Humming happily to herself Steph turned the sizzling chops in the pan and then put the heat down a fraction to reduce the risk of them burning – then she almost leaped out of her skin at the sound of a single blood-curdling scream. By sheer luck she had just managed to grab the handle of the pan and stop it falling off the stove after jolting it as she had jumped in fright.

Steph stood frozen to the spot. That scream had sounded like a mortally wounded animal. But it had been Ursula's scream, she knew. She sounded like she was being murdered. What on earth was going on?

Panic stricken, Steph made a dash for the hallway. As she arrived, she heard the sound of a sash window being thrust up, then another frenzied shriek, then sudden silence but for a dull thud resounding from outside at the front of the house. Next thing she knew Jay was racing down the stairs towards her. His face looked deathly.

'Jay, what . . .'

He grabbed her by her arms and blurted out, 'It's your mother . . . I tried to stop her. I did try, honestly!'

'Stop her! Stop her doing what, Jay?'

'Throwing herself out of the window.'

'She did *what*?'

Without further ado Steph pulled herself free from Jay's grip and raced over to the front door, which she yanked open. She immediately saw the outline of a figure sprawled in the shrubbery under the front window, the light from inside eerily illuminating it. A cry of anguish escaped her as she dashed over and threw herself down beside her mother's still body.

'Mother?'

Jay arrived by her side. He stood staring at the crumpled figure, as if transfixed.

Steph looked wildly up at him. 'Do something, Jay,' she beseeched him. When he didn't respond, she bellowed, 'Jay!'

He jumped and exclaimed, 'What?'

'Please do something. You're supposed to check for a pulse, aren't you, but I don't know how to do that, do you?'

He gave a helpless shrug. 'No, I don't.'

'Then telephone for an ambulance. Tell them to hurry!' He seemed not to hear her, again just staring at her mother. Steph shouted at him, 'NOW, JAY!'

He stared at her blankly for a moment more until what she'd said sunk in. He ran off down the path, then disappeared through the open door.

Steph could barely see her mother for the tears filling her eyes. She might not have anything like the sort of close, loving relationship with her she'd have liked, but she had never wished any harm to come to her either. She picked up Ursula's hand and tenderly stroked it.

'Mother? Wake up. Come on, Mother, wake up!'

# CHAPTER THIRTEEN

Steph's face was puffy, eyes red and swollen from crying. 'I don't understand, Jay,' she was saying. She paused while a hospital porter walked by pushing a wheelchair with an old man in it, his newly plastered arm in a sling. 'What made my mother throw herself out of the window?' she continued.

They had been sitting side by side on a bench against a wall in a long corridor in the Accident and Emergency department of the Leicester Royal Infirmary for over two hours now, waiting for news of Ursula's condition. As the minutes ticked by Steph became more worried. She knew her mother had regained consciousness in the ambulance on the way here so wasn't dead, but that was all.

A look of utter bewilderment on his face, Jay put his arm around her, pulling her close. 'I really have no idea. As I've already told you, I went into her room and she started ranting and raving at me, accusing me of tricking you into marrying me and demanding to know what my real motive was. I told her that I married you because I loved you and wanted to spend the rest of my life with you. I'd known it from the moment I met you and couldn't see any point in a long-drawn-out courtship. I thought my way of proposing was romantic. Thankfully for me you thought so, too, else I'd have felt a right fool.

'She wouldn't believe me, though, was still screaming at me that I was a liar, insisting I was the man who'd chatted her up in the club that night. Then she made a grab for a heavy glass ashtray and I knew her intention was to throw it at me, so before she could, I dived over, grabbed her arm and took it off her. She was screaming even louder now and trying to hit me with the empty tumbler she was holding in her other hand, so I grabbed that wrist and held it firmly while I pleaded with her to calm down, at least do me the courtesy of hearing me out. To my surprise, she did.

'I repeated what I'd already told her and asked her to give me a chance to prove my sincerity. She told me that she would if I let go of her. So I did. What happened next is a blur it happened so quickly. Before I could stop her, she had leaped off the bed, run over to the window, opened it, and I saw her dive out head first. I couldn't believe my own eyes but that's exactly how it happened, Steph.'

She rubbed her hands wearily over her face. Her

mother had been as inebriated on many other occasions and had never done anything remotely as reckless. At the moment, though, all Steph cared about was that Ursula would not suffer any lasting effects from her fall.

A door opened further down the corridor and a young doctor came out and made his way over to them. They rose to greet him and Steph, despite her desperation to find out about her mother, noticed how tired the doctor looked and felt remorseful that he'd probably had his much-needed sleep disturbed, being summoned to attend to her mother's self-inflicted injuries.

He addressed Steph. 'Miss Mortimer . . .'

'Mrs Connor,' Jay corrected him.

'Mrs Connor,' he began again. 'I'm glad to say that Mrs Mortimer is a very fortunate woman. Her fall could have been fatal but, thanks to the thick shrubbery that broke it, all she's sustained is a nasty bump on her head and a few minor cuts and bruises. She's still in shock over what's happened to her, not really saying anything at all, but we have managed to coax out of her what led up to the fall.'

Jay blurted, 'Well, she's obviously very confused so you can't really trust anything she's saying, can you?'

The doctor looked at him strangely. 'It is our medical opinion that Mrs Mortimer is in full possession of her faculities, despite her actions. She told us that she'd been celebrating a little too much over some good fortune she'd had, went to open the window and lost her balance.' With a twinkle in his eyes, he added, 'I've advised her to keep away from windows in future, if she's celebrating any more good fortune. Next time she might not be so lucky.'

Jay looked relieved. 'Yes, that's exactly what did happen. It's just that she was angry at the time and already saying things that weren't true, so I was bothered she might make up a story she was pushed out.'

Steph looked at him strangely then. 'Mother wouldn't do that.' She was, however, mortally relieved to hear her mother wasn't going to be suffering any long-term damage and decided not to argue with Jay. 'So we can take her home, Doctor?'

'We're going to keep her in overnight for observation in case she's suffering from concussion. Come back at twelve tomorrow. Provided she's spent a comfortable night, you can take her home then.'

Steph smiled appreciatively at him. 'Thank you for everything you've done for her, Doctor. May I see her before I go?'

He shook his head. 'I asked Mrs Mortimer if she'd like me to send you in but she said she wasn't feeling up to seeing anyone tonight.' He noticed the small case, coat and handbag on the bench where they'd been sitting. 'I trust those are for your mother? If you give them to the nurse in the office on your way out, she'll make sure Mrs Mortimer gets them.'

Steph had been surprised that even while her mother was still unconscious and she herself desperately wondering how much damage the fall had caused, as the ambulance men were getting Ursula on to the stretcher, she had had the presence of mind to rush indoors and pack a small case for her mother, containing basic toiletries and a set of clothes plus top coat and handbag. She smiled again at the young doctor. 'I'll do that, Doctor.'

As he walked away, Steph said to Jay, 'So it was an accident after all? Drunk or not, I should have known Mother would never do anything that might mar her good looks.' Hopefully, the shock of this could be the catalyst that would make her cut down on her consumption of alcohol.

By the time they arrived home it was approaching eleven o'clock and their appetites had long since left them but a cup of tea would not go amiss. Leaving Jay to take their suitcases up to her room, Steph went into the kitchen.

Thankfully she'd also had the presence of mind to switch off the hot plates under the pans before she had left in the ambulance to accompany her mother to hospital. The meal she had been in the process of cooking her new husband was ruined during the half-hour it took the ambulance to arrive and the pans were going to be a devil to clean, but she had no mind to tackle that job now. After scraping out the blackened mess in each of them, she put them into soak until the morning.

As she put on the kettle and collected cups and saucers, she heard the rhythmical thudding of a case hitting the steps as Jay hauled it upstairs. Then, like a thunderbolt, a memory struck her. She had got married today! Tonight was her wedding night. The fright of her mother's fall had made her temporarily forget it, but now she was able to concentrate her thoughts on herself.

A nervous knot tightened in her stomach. Normally a bride would have had time to prepare herself for such a momentous event, but Steph hadn't had any idea when she had risen from her bed this morning, a single woman, that she would be married by the time she got back into it that night. Her nervousness turned to worry then. The sheets on her bed needed changing for fresh ones, and she hadn't the sort of nightwear she would have liked to have worn for her husband on this most special of nights. She had a cute baby doll set that was still in its tissue paper but she would have preferred something a little more womanly. Did her legs need shaving? Oh, thank goodness she had done that this morning when she had taken a bath before readying herself for what she had thought would be someone else's wedding. Her thoughts then turned to the act itself. She wasn't a virgin but wasn't what she would call sexually experienced gained through having a string of lovers and she was suddenly so afraid that Jay, who for all she knew being the attractive man he was, could be very experienced and she might disappoint him.

Jay came into the room then and immediately noticed the worried look on her face. His own clouded over. 'Anything wrong?'

Steph blushed and stuttered, 'Oh, er . . . no. I was just . . . er . . . well, I need to change the sheets on the bed before . . . before . . .'

'We get in it together?' With a twinkle in his eyes Jay finished her sentence for her. Then he walked across, gathered her in his arms and whispered seductively, 'What side of the bed do you prefer?'

She gulped and responded lightly, 'Oh, the opposite side from you.'

A short while later, a highly charged Steph made her way from the bathroom to the bedroom to join her new husband, after making herself look as desirable as she could. He was already in bed, propped up against the pillows, and as soon as she appeared in the doorway the unmistakable look in his eyes reassured her. Jay wanted her! It would be all right. There was no hesitation at all on Steph's part as she rushed to join him under the covers.

\* \* \*

It was with mixed feelings that she lay beside him after they had consummated their marriage. She couldn't deny that she had enjoyed his very apparent desire for her but she would have liked them to have spent more time before the actual act, kissing and caressing, exploring each other's bodies. Still, they had the rest of their lives together for that.

Jay turned away from her and gave a loud snore. His shallow breathing told her he was already asleep. Steph turned to nestle against him. Sheer exhaustion caused by the emotional roller-coaster of the day she'd had overcame her as quickly as switching off a light.

# CHAPTER FOURTEEN

'What do you mean, Mrs Mortimer discharged herself at ten this morning?' Jay demanded of a middle-aged staff nurse the next day at just before noon.

Steph stared at him, taken aback. She had been surprised when he had insisted on accompanying her to the hospital as she'd assumed he would still have much to do, tidying up his own business affairs. But he had assured her that he had done all he could yesterday and there was nothing urgent that needed his attention. He felt that in view of the way Ursula had taken the news of their marriage it was important they both show a united front, by collecting her together.

Steph felt he had a point and happily went along with his suggestion, but what she couldn't understand was his reaction to Ursula's departure before they reached the ward. On the face of it, it appeared Jay was just put out by the fact that they'd had a wasted journey when he could have been better occupied elsewhere, but Steph sensed that inside he was frantic about Ursula's whereabouts. Why?

The nurse responded matter of factly, 'Mrs Mortimer was advised it was in her own best interests to wait until she got the all clear from the doctor, but she was adamant she was feeling fine and wanted to go home.'

'And you let her?' Jay snapped.

The nurse looked askance at him. 'This isn't a prison. Now, if you'll excuse me, I have sick people who need my attention.'

'We'd better get back to the house, make sure your mother's got back safely,' Jay suggested.

Steph smiled warmly at him. 'The way she's treated you, she's lucky you're so concerned.' She hooked her arm through his. In the past the place where she'd resided had never been somewhere to which she looked forward to returning; it had never felt like a sanctuary from the outside world to her, because the two other people who had resided in it alongside her had not done anything to make it feel warm and welcoming. But now that she had Jay beside her, for the first time ever she felt the house could become a home to her and Steph was looking forward to getting back there.

Jay practically raced back from the hospital and seemed very agitated to find no sign of Ursula having returned meantime. Now he was pacing the kitchen, trying to decide what to do. He suddenly stopped and said to Steph, 'You'll need to telephone all your mother's friends, see if she's gone to any of them, and then we can go and bring her back.'

Steph had been watching him in bewilderment, unable to understand such apparent desperation to get her mother back under this roof. He already knew that his new mother-in-law was not an easy woman so she would have thought he'd be more concerned with keeping Ursula from under their feet, giving the newly marrieds time to be alone together, than the opposite.

'My mother has always been a law unto herself, Jay. She'll be back soon enough.' And believe me, won't we know about it? thought Steph.

'I still think we should go and look for her,' insisted Jay.

'I wouldn't know where to start. She's more than likely taken herself off shopping for a new outfit to wear tonight when she goes out. If anything had happened to her since she left the hospital, the police would have informed us by now.' She was about to ask him if he'd like something to eat when a memory struck her. The pantry might be well stocked at the moment but the grocer and butcher weren't going to keep supplying them if their bills weren't settled, and the gas and electricity would be cut off without prompt payment. 'I need to go out this afternoon and visit the bank, to arrange for our weekly collection of the allowance.' Hopefully the payment would start immediately. Steph's purse contained only a few coppers.

'Take as long as you need. Someone ought to stay here and make sure your mother doesn't need anything when she gets home, a doctor fetching or something.' He saw the worried expression cloud Steph's face and stepped over to her, putting his arms around her to pull her close. 'Darling, I'm not trying to alarm you but your mother had a lucky escape yesterday, she could go into delayed shock, that's all I was thinking.'

A warm glow filled her. Jay was such a caring man, she was so lucky to have him.

He was saying to her, 'Now I'm quite capable of getting myself something to eat, so you get yourself off to the bank. And when you come back, I'm going to go down to the works and see what has happened today.' He heaved a deep sigh and in an emotional tone added, 'Keep your fingers crossed that one of the bigger firms has made an offer, and that the man who viewed the flat yesterday has decided to buy it. Part of me wants this all over with quickly so I can put Darren's betrayal behind me and get on with something new. But I helped build that company up from scratch, it was like watching a baby grow. It's not going to be easy for me, signing it away.'

How Steph wished she were in a position to help him, but she wasn't. All she could do was be a supportive wife and see him through this traumatic time. 'If I can do anything to help in any way. I will, Jay. If you need to make any telephone calls or . . .'

'I appreciate the offer to feel free to use the telephone,' he cut in. 'But business is business, home is home. I've always lived by that rule.'

She could understand why. Her father had constantly been telephoned by the hospital and, having been privy to some of the conversations, she'd realised by his tone of voice and response that they'd often been about trivial matters that could have been resolved without the need to disturb him at home.

She felt she ought to try to advise Jay on how to handle her mother should she come home while Steph wasn't there, however. 'Jay, about my mother. It's best . . .'

He pressed his fingers to her lips. 'Leave her to me.' He grinned. 'I shall dazzle her with my charm and soon have her eating out of my hand.' He gave Steph a playful tap on her bottom. 'Now you get off and do what you have to.'

She was just about to leave when the telephone rang. Answering it, she found it was the solicitor's secretary, asking her to come in as the papers were all ready for her to sign, to finalise the distribution of her late father's estate. Thankfully the solicitor could see her that afternoon so Steph could go straight round there after she'd dealt with the bank.

It was with a jaunty step that she made her way to the bus stop a short time later. Life was far from perfect, what with Jay's worrying business situation and her own convoluted ties to her mother; the fact was that the last thing a newly married couple needed, and especially ones who didn't know each other as intimately as they would have done after a long courtship, was to be living under the same roof as someone as selfish and demanding as Ursula. But, regardless of that, Steph felt happy.

Feeling glad to be alive and looking forward to a bright future was not something she was used to. She had never before experienced the way her own inward sense of well-being affected her view of everything around her. The heavy grey sky above, threatening to shed its load of rain, looked blue to her; the chilly wind whipping through her felt like a warm summer breeze; the grumpy faces of the passers-by all seemed to be smiling at Steph. She owed it to Jay. And once again she blessed her mother for the only positive thing she had ever done, albeit unintentionally, bringing this young man into her daughter's life and transforming her miserable existence to the joyous one it now looked set to be.

Much to her relief, she came away from the bank with their first weekly allowance of twenty-five pounds. A very generous amount, she felt, considering that an average working man's wage was around fifteen pounds. The Mortimers had no rent to find, after all. Steph was not too worried about their household expenses as Jay would soon be seeking work, and if necessary she would find some herself to contribute further. The allowance should prove sufficient to provide her mother with a reasonable standard of living, albeit not on the lavish scale she had previously enjoyed.

Jay pounced on her as soon as she opened the front door.

'Your mother's not back, Steph. No word or anything. I've not been over to the office 'cos I thought someone should wait in.'

She felt warmed that he was showing such concern. Unbuttoning her coat, she said to him matter of factly, 'Jay, my mother goes off for days at a time on a whim and never thinks to tell me, so this is hardly unusual. She's probably still out shopping or else has gone to see one of her friends.' She hung her coat on the hall stand and with a quizzical look on her face, said, 'You hardly know my mother. She could be yours, the concern you're showing for her.'

He stared at her blankly for a moment before saying, 'Well, it's just that I consider her my own family now. Naturally I won't rest until I know she's all right.'

Steph's heart swelled with love for him then. Oh, he was such a considerate man! Whether her mother deserved such consideration was another matter. They had spent all day consumed with worry over her, and she probably hadn't given them a second thought.

'Let's give it at least until I know the shops are shut. If she still hasn't come back, I'll fetch her telephone book from her room and start to call around her friends.' And suffer the consequences of Ursula returning meantime, not at all happy that her daughter had dared to enter her inner sanctum.

'I trust your visit to the bank was successful?' Jay asked her.

She smiled. 'It was, thank you. Everything is organised for me to collect the allowance every Friday from today. My father has been very generous. Twenty-five pounds he's allotted my mother each week.'

Jay looked impressed. 'That much? And your visit to the solicitor went smoothly too?'

She nodded.

He looked gratified she'd had no trouble. 'Oh, a woman arrived here at four, said she was the cook.' He grinned. 'She thought I was a burglar until I explained who I was and that I was living here with you for the time being. She's in the kitchen.'

'That's Mrs Sanders. She comes in from four until seven to see to our evening meal. I can always cook your breakfast . . . if you like a cooked breakfast, that is? We had a daily until just before my father died, but she left and I haven't found a replacement for her yet.'

Steph went off into the kitchen to inform Mrs Sanders that her new husband and herself would not now be taking up residence in his place after all, but had decided to stay here for the time being. And that her mother would not be taking dinner with them tonight as she was out.

At just before eight o'clock Steph replaced the telephone in its cradle, closed her mother's address book and went to rejoin her husband who had been waiting anxiously for news, perched on the stairs.

'Well, as you heard, my mother isn't with any of the friends I called and none of them has any idea where she could be. She's not been admitted back into hospital either. She would never go on an extended visit without taking most of her wardrobe with her, and certainly all her creams and lotions, and as she hasn't then I can rule that out. There's nothing else we can do now but wait until she decides to come home.'

Jay sat in silence, apparently lost in thought. Eventually he turned to look at her and, patting her hand, said, 'Well, your mother will have to come home sooner or later won't she? Silly for us to worry.' He then took hold of both her hands and looked deep into her eyes. 'How about we take advantage of having the house to ourselves and get an early night?'

# CHAPTER FIFTEEN

Steph was so distressed she thought her heart would break. It was late afternoon the next day and Jay was sitting beside her on the sofa, holding his head in his hands in despair. In a voice choked with emotion, he was saying to her, 'I suppose I should be grateful that the business, flat and my car sold so quickly. With the money I raised I can settle my debts, though I walk away without a bean. I was used to having the car, but public transport did me before so it will again. And I don't care about the flat. I mean, I loved living there and was looking forward to sharing it with you, us making a home together, but it's just four walls at the end of the day. But the business . . .'

His voice trailed away and he gave a violent shudder, then raised his head and looked at her with remorse. 'I was hoping that there'd be enough left over when I'd settled everything for us to have a deposit to buy a small house, or at the very least the

225

deposit on a rented place. This means I can't give you the kind of future I promised you, Steph. Not on the money I'll be earning, working for someone else. I've let you down so badly . . .'

'No, you haven't,' she assured him. 'It's your partner that let *you* down and made it impossible for you to keep your promise to me.' She laid one hand tenderly on his arm and said softly, 'I'll be working too, Jay, so between us we'll soon be able to afford the rent on a small place of our own. I'll start looking again tomorrow. Meantime, I know it's not ideal living here with my mother, but at least we have a roof over our head and . . . we have each other, don't we?'

He flashed her a weak smile. 'I'm being selfish, I know.' There was a hopeful look in his eye when he asked, 'Is your mother back now?'

A worried look crossed her face and Steph shook her head. 'No, she's not. I've heard nothing from her or any of her friends, and they did promise to call if she turned up. I haven't left the house since you went out this morning to attend to your business. I called all the hospitals again and she hasn't been admitted. It's like she's disappeared off the face of the earth.

'I know she has some money on her but there can't be much of it left. Anyway, like I said yesterday, my mother doesn't go anywhere without a trunkful of clothes and all her creams and lotions. Jay, do you think I should telephone the police to report her as a missing person?'

He was staring over her shoulder into space, a dark, angry expression in his eyes. Thinking of the treachery of his so-called friend, she guessed. She supposed she had to expect this reaction, at least until he came to terms with what had happened to him. 'Jay?' she prompted him.

He jumped. 'Sorry? What?'

'I was asking your opinion on whether I should report my mother to the police as a missing person?'

He shook his head. 'You'd be wasting their time. She's over the age of consent. She can come and go as she likes, for as long as she likes. They won't do anything.'

Steph looked at him for a moment before admitting, 'Yes, you've got a point.' She couldn't imagine Ursula not returning home soon, though, as she only had the one set of clothes that Steph had taken up to the hospital for her. Ursula was fastidious about her appearance, never wore anything without its being washed or dry cleaned, and cleansed and creamed her face religiously at least twice a day. This wasn't in character, vanishing without luggage.

Jay had taken Steph's hands, and was biting his lip. It was obvious to her something was troubling him apart from what he'd already told her, which was bad enough. 'What is it, Jay?' she asked.

He took a deep breath. 'Well . . . this is difficult for me to ask of you, darling, but . . . I wondered if you could see your way to helping me out with some money? I've only the loose change in my pocket as things stand.'

Steph was having trouble stemming her tears, so distressed did she feel for him in his plight. 'Of course, I'll gladly give you what I can.'

It was a godsend, in a way, that Ursula wasn't here demanding more than her fair share of the allowance, so Steph could help her husband instead.

At just after six the next evening, Steph was humming happily to herself as she alighted from the bus and jauntily headed down the road for home. She had some good news to tell her husband. She had got herself a job! It was only temporary, but she had started immediately as a receptionist for a shoe factory, covering for their permanent receptionist who had suddenly been taken ill. It was uncertain how long she'd be away. They seemed nice people and Steph had enjoyed her afternoon there, and was looking forward to returning in the morning. Meanwhile the agency who had placed her would be seeking her a suitable permanent position, but until then assured her they had plenty of temporary work to keep her going.

She wondered how Jay had fared on his own job

quest today? He had said he was going to tout around local businesses for a start, see what was on offer there before he ventured further afield. She wondered if he'd spotted the position of van driver for a local firm, advertised in the shop window by the bus stop. She'd seen it there herself that morning.

Steph felt sure that between them they'd soon be in a position to fund a place of their own. Starting up his business again from scratch was out of the question, Jay had told her, as competition was now fierce. But she had assured him she would be prepared to make sacrifices if it meant he would be his own boss again.

She found him fast asleep, sprawled on the settee in the lounge. She tiptoed across and gazed lovingly down at him. What he had done today had obviously tired him out. Steph's heart went out to him. It must have proved so demeaning for him, explaining to potential employers over and over again that he had once owned his own transport business. She vehemently hoped he'd been offered a position by every firm he had visited and could choose which job to accept.

Steph tiptoed back into the hall. From what she had observed on arriving home, there was still no evidence of her mother's return, but that didn't mean to say she hadn't gone straight upstairs to her room. She went up and pressed her ear to the closed door.

She couldn't hear any movement coming from inside, but that still didn't mean her mother wasn't in there. She tapped on the door. No response. She turned the door handle and opened the door wide enough to put her head around. To her dismay, she saw the room looked just as Ursula had left it. Well that wasn't quite true. It was just as she herself had left it after she had tidied up and changed the bedclothes the morning Jay and she had wasted going to the hospital to fetch Ursula home.

Steph's face clouded with worry. Where was her mother? She must be holed up with a friend some-where, it was the only thing that made sense.

She was just about to step back and shut the door when something struck her. Steph pushed the door further open and stepped inside. The room wasn't quite as she had left it. The pale pink satin counterpane that completely covered the bed down to the floor had a kink in it to one side at the bottom, as if someone had lifted it up to look underneath the bed and not smoothed it back into place properly.

She went across and gave it a shake to smooth it down. Then she took a slow glance around. Her eyes settled on her mother's dressing table. All her jars and bottles of creams, lotions and perfumes were still neatly arranged; her silver and mother-of-pearl brush and comb set sitting on its silver tray; her mahogany jewellery box beside that. But Steph felt sure that all the drawers running down the side had been perfectly in line after she had cleaned the room ready for her mother's return. Now the bottom one was slightly protruding. She looked across at the bedside cabinet next. When she had replaced her mother's address book after calling round all her friends, she was positive she had put it back beside the lamp, replacing her mother's fountain pen on top, just as she had found it. The book was now in front of the lamp and the fountain pen to one side of the book.

Steph frowned. Someone had either been poking around in here or else her own mind was playing tricks on her and she hadn't left the room as she'd thought.

Shutting the door after herself, she returned downstairs. Jay was awake, sitting up and stretching himself after his snooze. He jerked his head around when he sensed someone entering the room.

Steph felt it must be her imagination that she fancied she saw a flash of disappointment in his eyes when he saw who was joining him. But then, who else could he have been hoping to see?

Then she knew her mind had been playing tricks on her. He smiled over at her and said, 'I wondered what had happened to you. I thought you'd have been back long before now.'

'Well, I would have been only the agency I went

to register with had a temp job that was right up my street. I started immediately. Meantime the agency are going to put me forward for anything permanent they think I'm suitable for. Did you have a good day too?'

His tone was flat when he responded, 'I've had easier and more successful ones.'

His search for a job hadn't borne fruit then. She went across to sit down beside him and laid a re-assuring hand on his arm. 'There's always tomorrow,' she said optimistically. 'My mother still hasn't returned home, I see. Don't you think I ought to go and report her missing to the police?'

'Your mother is a grown woman. I still don't think they'd do anything.'

Steph nodded. 'You're probably right. She'll come home when she's good and ready. I'd swear, though, that someone has been rummaging around in her room. Her things aren't quite how I left them when we went to fetch her from the hospital.'

Jay looked at her for a moment and then gave a shrug. 'Well, I hope you're not accusing me of poking around in there, because I haven't.'

'No, of course I wasn't,' she protested. 'More than likely no one's been in there at all and it's just my memory playing tricks. I'll go and wash my hands before dinner.'

She made to depart but Jay stopped her.

'Oh, that reminds me, that cook woman gave her notice today, leaving immediately. Got a better paid job. She asked me if she could have her wages up to date. I only had four pounds ten shillings on me after what I spent from the fiver you gave me. She didn't say whether it was enough, just took it, so I assumed it was.'

Steph was gazing at him in surprise. 'Oh! I can't believe she's leaving without giving proper notice. This isn't like Mrs Sanders at all.'

'Well, maybe she's done you a favour. The wages you were paying her could be put to much better use.'

Like saving for a deposit on a place of their own, she presumed he was hinting. But Mrs Sanders had been really good at what she did whereas Steph's cooking was only basic. Still, she supposed Jay was right. It was madness paying someone to do something you could learn to do yourself, albeit not as expertly. She wouldn't have the use of a cook when she and Jay were in their own place, so the quicker she became more competent at producing their meals, the better.

'I was thinking . . .' he was saying to her now.

'Yes?'

He stood up and strolled over to her, sliding his hands around her waist. 'It's really a man's job to take care of the finances. You've got enough to do, keeping up the house, and now you're working as well. It's not fair to burden you on top of that. If you hand over the allowance and your wages to me each week and I put what I earn in with it, I can budget for us. I'll warn you, my aim is to put by as much as I can for our future, so it'll be a tight budget.'

Steph felt she was quite capable of handling the finances, but not having the responsibility would at least spare her from her mother's constant hassle for money and violent temper tantrums when her demands couldn't be met, when she finally decided to return home. And she supposed it was only right that as the man of the house Jay should be in control of their finances.

Her smile gave him his answer.

'What are we having for dinner, I'm starving?' he asked her.

'I'll go and see what's in the pantry.' Hopefully the cookery books in the kitchen would come to Steph's aid. She made to depart then remembered the Situation Vacant card she had spotted that morning in the newsagent's by the bus stop.

'Oh, Jay, I saw an advertisement for a van driver in a shop window this morning. It's for Johnson's factory further down the road. I didn't know whether you'd seen it too?'

He nodded. 'Yes, I did, but I've decided I want to make a complete break from everything to do with the transport business. It's just a constant reminder of what Darren took from me.'

'Oh, doing what?' Steph asked keenly.

He shrugged. 'I don't know yet, but I will when I find it.'

# CHAPTER SIXTEEN

A couple of months later, sitting on a crowded bus which was slowly making its way through heavy traffic while taking her home, Steph suddenly came over all light headed and very tired. Was it surprising, though? It was arduous working full time as well as cooking and cleaning for her husband. It was such a big house to keep on top of. She really needed some help in that department, but the saved wage was swelling their coffers. It was certainly a challenge, managing on the amount of money Jay was allowing her for house-keeping, but he hadn't yet complained about any meal Steph had put in front of him. After paying for their food, household items and bus fares to and from work, there wasn't much left over to fund Steph's personal items, but she was happy to make sacrifices and make do and mend for the foreseeable future.

Jay still hadn't found a job that suited him but was going out every day to check what was on offer, so it was only a matter of time before he would strike lucky. It was her opinion he deserved the highest praise for not wallowing in self-pity, which he could so easily have done after the terrible betrayal and financial loss he had suffered at the hands of his so-called friend.

Steph's temporary job as receptionist for the shoe factory had come to an end last week. Much to her surprise the staff she'd worked alongside all clubbed together and bought her a bunch of flowers, telling her they'd miss her cheery face and pleasant manner in contrast to the miserable old battleaxe who was their permanent receptionist. She was now temporarily handling reception for a firm of solicitors in the centre of Leicester. The work wasn't too taxing for her. Despite finding the three solicitors themselves rather stuffy, humourless individuals, the rest of the staff were as friendly and helpful to Steph as those at the shoe factory had been.

She did know, though, that she had been lucky up to now with her placements as there was a downside to temping. You never knew from one week to the next what type of people you'd be working amongst, but it was up to the temp to fit in or else they'd quickly be dismissed and their pay packet the following week would be short. In her own case that wouldn't do. The less Jay was able to add to their savings, the longer it was going to take for them to fund a place of their own. She wondered how much he'd managed to save up to now, but when she had asked him only last night he'd been very cagey, telling her he wanted to surprise her with the amount when he'd reached the goal he had in mind.

The only thing that blighted her life at the moment was the fact that her mother still hadn't returned home. Steph was suffering mixed feelings over this state of affairs. She was grateful that Ursula's absence meant Jay and herself were left alone to act as they wished behind closed doors. But as more time passed Steph had become increasingly concerned about her mother's whereabouts. No matter what, Ursula would never go anywhere without her personal belongings and by now the money she had taken from her husband's safe must have run out.

The only conclusion Steph could draw was that her mother must have suffered a delayed loss of memory from the bump on her head caused by her fall. God only knew when she would recover it. Meantime, as there had been no reports in any newspaper, local or national, of an unidentified woman answering to her description, Ursula must be being cared for by someone.

Steph's stop was coming up. She made to get to her feet but slumped back in her seat when she came over all peculiar again.

The old dear sitting next to her noticed and worriedly enquired, 'You all right, lovey?'

She flashed the woman a smile. 'Yes, thank you. I just came over a bit faint, but I'm all right now.'

The old dear pulled a knowing face. 'Skipped lunch, did you, 'cos yer on one of those faddy diets, wanting to look like that model . . . whatsername . . . Sticky?'

She meant Twiggy but Steph was too polite to correct her. 'I ate a potted-meat sandwich and an apple for my lunch.'

'Oh, well, only one other reason I knows of to explain a funny turn like you just had.' She then eyed Steph hard and demanded, 'I hope you're married, young lady?'

'I am, actually. Coming up for two months now,' she said proudly, flashing the woman her wedding ring. Then she frowned quizzically. 'But what has me being married got to do with having a peculiar turn?'

The old woman patted her hand. 'Well, it's no fun bringing a baby up on your own. I'm glad to hear you won't be.'

Steph smiled. Lowering her voice so that no eavesdroppers could overhear, she said to the woman, 'I can't possibly be pregnant. We're far too careful.'

'Obviously not careful enough, dear,' she responded matter of factly. 'Mark my words, it's a mother you're going to be. You wanted this stop, didn't yer? Don't forget yer shopping bag,' she said to Steph, pointing to the brown carrier by her feet containing minced beef for the cottage pie she intended to prepare for dinner this evening.

In a daze Steph got off the bus and stared blindly after it as the conductor rang the bell and it continued on its way. She couldn't possibly be pregnant! Jay had never once forgotten to use a condom before he made love to her. Her mind raced as she calculated dates in her head. Her period had always been as regular as clockwork. Twenty-eight days, no more, no less. When had she had her last one? Her brain raced even harder. She couldn't remember. Oh, yes, she could. It was a couple of weeks before she got married. She had been worried she might have to stand Jay up as she was suffering so badly with stomach cramps and backache all day. Whether it had been mind over matter or the pain relief she took she didn't know, but her pains had suddenly ceased and she had enjoyed her night out with Jay after all. And now she had been married just days under two months. She gasped. She hadn't had a period since then! Periods only stopped during pregnancy! Come to think of it, her breasts had been unusually tender of late and she was going to the toilet far more often than she normally did. The old lady on the bus was right in her diagnosis. Steph was expecting a baby.

She dropped her shopping bag in shock. Thankfully there was nothing breakable inside it.

*I'm having a baby.* The words reverberated inside

her head, over and over. She was going to be a mother. She and Jay were going to become parents. Her eyes flew down to her stomach and she placed one hand tenderly over it. A new life was inside her, one that she and Jay had created. Then an overwhelming explosion of joy burst within her. She would make sure she was a damned sight better mother than her own had been. This baby was going to be shown real love. Jay would prove to be a far better father to his child than her own father had been, she just knew. Grabbing her carrier bag, she kicked up her heels and ran for home. She couldn't wait to share her wonderful news. Jay had surprised her with his proposal. Now it was her turn to surprise him.

To her dismay, though, she arrived home to find the house empty. It was after six so did this mean Jay had at last found a job that was to his liking and had started immediately? If this was the case, then tonight was indeed one for celebrating. Her planned cottage pie didn't seem a fitting meal, but it would have to do.

She had prepared it before and it had been a passable effort, Jay had eaten it and thanked her afterwards, but the recipe wasn't yet committed to memory so she still needed to consult it. Having taken the book out and opened it at the page with the recipe on, the ingredients all to hand on the work surface, Steph was just browning the mince while chopping an onion when the back door opened and Jay arrived back.

Dropping what she was doing and taking the pan of mince temporarily off the stove, Steph went across to give him a welcome-home kiss. As she did so, she smelled the waft of beer emanating from him and looked at him expectantly. 'You've celebrated with a drink so you must have got a job?'

He was kicking off his shoes. 'I've had a couple of pints, but not to celebrate getting a job. I'm commiserating with myself that I haven't yet.' Then he eyed her sharply. 'You haven't a problem with me having a drink on my way home, have you?'

Steph looked upset that he could think that. 'No, of course I haven't.' Her excitement at her own news bubbled to the surface then and she blurted out, 'But as it happens, we do have something to celebrate.'

With a jubilant cry he pre-empted her. 'Your mother's returned while I've been out!'

Steph was taken aback by that. From the brief experience he'd had of Ursula, she would not have thought Ursula's possible return would have been welcome news at all.

He made to dash off but she caught his arm. 'No, Mother's not back. Still no word of her whatsoever.' She knew it wasn't her imagination. There had been a definite flash of disappointment in his eyes then. 'Why are you so keen to see her back? Having met her, I would have thought it would be just the opposite.'

Jay looked indignant. 'She's your mother and I know you're worried about her. Her coming back would put your mind at rest, that's all. If you want my opinion, I think she's thoroughly selfish, going off like she has without a word. Anyway, what's this new job you've landed?'

She looked at him, bemused. 'What new job?'

'Oh, isn't that what we're going to be celebrating?'

'No.' Steph took a deep breath, her face lighting up with a brilliant smile. 'I'm having a baby!' Then she continued, 'Well, that's what an old woman on the bus told me after I'd had a funny turn. Of course, I need to have it confirmed by the doctor, but I've realised I've missed two monthlies and there's only one reason they stop, isn't there, so I must be. Oh, Jay, you are pleased, aren't you?'

There was a triumphant expression on his face. It was as if she had just granted his dearest wish. She prepared herself to receive a bear hug, a kiss, a tender embrace. Instead, to her shock, he stepped away from her. Wagging one finger accusingly, he retaliated: 'Why should I be pleased that you're having another man's baby? Well, it's not mine, is it? Every time we've made love, I've used precautions to make sure this didn't happen. If you thought you were going to pass another man's baby off as mine, then you underestimated me.' He glowered darkly at her. 'How could you do this to me? How could you?'

Steph was staring at him, horrified. This was not the response she had expected at all. 'This baby is yours, Jay,' she implored him. 'How could you even think it's not? How could you ever think that I would go with another man behind your back?'

'Well, you must have,' he shouted at her.

'I didn't,' she cried emphatically. 'One of the condoms you used must have been faulty, that's the only explanation.'

He was sneering at her as if she was dirt on his shoe. 'And you'd so like me to accept that explanation, wouldn't you?'

'I haven't been with any other man, Jay. I swear on our child's life, I haven't.'

He glared at her icily. 'And I never thought my friend would do what he did to me.' Then he turned his back on her and yanked open the back door, slamming it shut behind him.

Steph stared blindly after him. She couldn't believe that she had given him any reason to think she would betray him with another man. Fat tears of misery filled her eyes and rolled down her cheeks. Clutching her stomach, she slumped to the floor, rested her elbows on her knees, then cradled her head in her hands and sobbed.

How long she sat hunched in her sorrow she did

not know. Whether it was a sound or sensing his presence that made her lift her head to see Jay looking down at her, she could not decide. It was clear he'd been drinking again.

Wiping her wet face on her sleeve, Steph scrambled up. 'I thought you weren't going to come back,' she said to her husband.

He stared at her for what seemed like an age before announcing in a slurred voice, 'I'm going to bed.'

She heard the clomping of his feet on the stairs as he climbed them, then the sound of a door opening and banging shut.

Steph sank down on a kitchen chair, her mind racing. He had returned which must mean he had realised his own mistake in comparing her to the friend who'd betrayed him, but in his inebriated state he was too stubborn, or felt too ashamed of his own behaviour, to apologise to her. It was the shock, of course, unexpectedly learning he was to become a father, but come morning when he had sobered up and the news had sunk in he would show his delight, she felt positive.

To her surprise Steph realised it was after ten. Neither of them had eaten, but this upset had ruined her appetite. In view of their aim to save every penny they could, she decided the ingredients for the cottage pie would keep until tomorrow. After quickly tidying round and making sure the house was secure, she went up to join her husband.

Jay was not in their bed. The covers hadn't even been disturbed. So where was he? He wasn't in the bathroom and she hadn't passed him on the landing as she had made her way from there to their bedroom. The fact that he had decided not to sleep with her tonight was overridden by her concern for his whereabouts. He must be in the spare room. She went along to check. That room was empty too. The only rooms that remained were her mother's and her father's. He surely wouldn't be so disrespectful as to use her mother's so it must be her father's room he had taken refuge in.

Creeping along, she hesitated outside the closed door for a moment before gingerly turning the knob and pushing the door open just far enough for her to peep through. The room was dark as the curtains were drawn and she knew that they'd been open, the way they'd been left after Gerald's things had been cleared. She could make out a mound under the bedclothes. Whether Jay was asleep or not she could not tell. Hopefully he was awake and trying to work out a way of making right his uncalled-for response to Steph's news. She would leave him alone to do that.

# CHAPTER SEVENTEEN

Steph slept fitfully that night. She had grown used to sharing her bed with Jay and it felt very big and lonely without the comfort of him beside her. She felt sure he was feeling as miserable and lonely as she was, but couldn't bring himself to climb down off his high horse and make the first move towards peace between them.

She had a job to rouse herself when the alarm shrilled at six-thirty the next morning. By the time she left for work at seven-forty, Jay still hadn't shown his face and she didn't want to disturb him in case he'd had as little sleep as she had. She couldn't wait until he got up, though, or she'd risk losing her new job.

She was, however, so consumed by the thought of getting home that night so that they could be reconciled, that at work she made some silly mistakes and would have lost her job if it hadn't been for the head typist. She had taken a shine to Steph. Realising that all was not right with her, she persuaded the office manager that their temp was just having a bad day, like everyone occasionally did, and needed to be given another chance. Steph was very relieved that the office manager agreed but knew she was only remaining under sufferance.

She had never been so eager for a working day to end, and never so glad to get home.

She was hanging up her coat on the hall stand when a footstep on the stairs made her turn round to see Jay coming down. Her heart missed a beat at the sight of him. He looked very attractive, dressed in hip-hugging, flared stone-washed jeans, a red shirt, red, yellow and black striped tank top, black suede jacket and boots. She hadn't seen him in those clothes before, they looked new, but he must have bought them before their marriage as Jay wouldn't be spending a penny on clothes for himself while they were sticking to a tight budget.

Judging by the way he was dressed and groomed, she automatically assumed that he had decided to dip into their savings to take her out by way of apology and to celebrate the news of the imminent arrival of their first child. Steph looked at him expectantly.

To her astonishment, as he walked past her towards the front door, he said matter of factly, 'Don't know what time I'll be back, so don't wait up.'

'You're going out?'

He looked at her as though she was stupid and in a sarcastic tone said, 'Well, I don't dress like this to lounge around the house, do I?'

She felt as though she'd been punched in the stomach. 'Oh, Jay, why are you being like this with me? Surely you must know that I'd never betray you,' she implored.

Icy eyes glared back at her. 'The proof of that will be when *that thing* you're carrying is born, won't it?'

With that he opened the door and went through it, banging it behind him.

*That thing?* And the way Jay had looked at her! As if he had no respect for her whatsoever. Steph appreciated he was disillusioned after what his friend had done to him, but surely he knew he could trust his own wife? What had she ever done to let him down?

Her shoulders slumped. Using the back of her hand, she wiped tears of distress from her eyes. How did she prove to Jay that his accusation was utterly ridiculous? She couldn't. Nor could she bear the thought of him treating her with such mistrust until the baby was born in seven months' time and he could see for himself how unwarranted his accusation was. The man who had just left the house was a virtual stranger to her. It had to be the result of shock that he was going to become a father; that was the only explanation she could come up with to excuse his behaviour.

She tried not to think about her husband, out socially without her. Jay was a good-looking man and she had often witnessed the come-hither looks he received from attractive women. The fact that Steph had been with him herself at the time hadn't deterred them. Jealousy stirred inside her. But then she forced it away, reasoning that it would be hypocritical of Jay to do to her what he had accused her of doing to him. It was bad enough he was acting paranoid without her joining in.

She was far too distressed to eat, so decided to have a bath. Upstairs in her bedroom, while the bath was filling, she was taking off her clothes when the empty space on top of the chest of drawers caught her eye. Jay's personal belongings – his hairbrush and comb, clothes brush, small pottery box he kept loose change in – had disappeared. She wondered what he had done with them. Put them away in a drawer? She went across and pulled out the top drawer where he kept his underwear and socks. To her surprise it was empty. She opened the next drawer down, expecting to see folded tee-shirts and jumpers that she had put neatly away after washing and ironing them for him. That drawer too was empty.

Puzzled, Steph went across to the large double wardrobe and pulled open the door to the side where

Jay's clothes were kept. The hanging shirts, trousers, several jackets and pairs of shoes were all gone.

Her heart pounded painfully and she felt sick. This could mean only one thing. Jay had left her.

Physical pain exploded within her then and she had to clutch hold of the wardrobe door for support as her legs buckled beneath her. This wasn't happening. It couldn't be. If Jay searched his heart, how could he possibly believe she would do anything to betray him? He couldn't go through life convinced that everyone he got involved with was double-crossing him. If only she could make him see reason. But where could he be?

It was then she realised how little she knew about her husband's life before their marriage. They had spent their outings for the most part enjoying each other's company, and hadn't really gone as far as delving deep into each other's lives or introducing each other to friends – albeit she hadn't had any to introduce him to, her mother having seen to that. When he had surprised her with his proposal, all that had seemed important to her at that moment was that Jay loved her enough to want to spend the rest of his life with her, and she loved him enough to agree. They'd had years in front of them to discover everything about one another. But since then there had been too much happening for the closeness she'd expected to develop. He probably wouldn't have a clue where to start looking for her if it was she who had gone off, the same as she hadn't a clue where he could possibly be now.

A lone tear ran down her cheek. All she could hope was that he'd find it within himself to realise what a terrible mistake he had made, and return to make things up with her.

The heat of the bath water did nothing to comfort Steph. In fact, her steady river of tears probably turned it cold. As she automatically cleaned her teeth, she caught sight of herself in the mirror above the sink. Her face looked grotesque, completely blotchy, eyes red and swollen. Part of her even hoped that Jay did not return just now because one look at her would send him straight off again.

With a heavy heart she climbed into bed, pulling the covers around her and his pillow to her. But the scent from it only made her feel worse. Sleep was avoiding her, just like Jay was, and she relentlessly tossed and turned. It was approaching dawn when, through sheer exhaustion, she began to drift into welcome oblivion, but a sudden sound cutting through the stillness of the early morning had her sitting bolt upright.

The noise that had disturbed her was that of a key being inserted into the lock of the front door. Only three people had that key: Steph herself, her mother and Jay. As much as she wanted her mind putting at rest that her mother was all right, she vehemently hoped this was Jay.

She strained her ears. The sound she heard next was of someone obviously falling through the front door. Whether it was Ursula or Jay, they were drunk. Then came the sound of the door being pushed none too gently shut. Then there was silence for a moment before footsteps could be heard stumbling up the stairs.

She held her breath, willing Jay to come through the bedroom door. She didn't care what state he was in, just the fact he'd come back was all-important to her. To her dismay, though, whoever was outside on the landing made their way past her room and she heard a door open and shut further down. The door to her father's room.

Then the truth dawned on her. It was Jay. He hadn't left her, but had moved his belongings into a separate room. She didn't know how she felt about this. She didn't know how she felt about the fact he'd been out until this time, or where he had been, or with whom. She was just so glad he was back.

# CHAPTER EIGHTEEN

It seemed Steph had only slept for a matter of minutes before the alarm shrilled at six-thirty, heralding the start of another working day. She felt a strong urge not to go in today but to stay here instead and sort matters out with Jay, but not to turn up would mean letting the firm down and she had already been warned by them once. Thank God it was Friday. Hopefully over the weekend they could resolve this mess.

Despite her carefully applied make up, Steph knew she still looked dreadful. Considering the time he had come home, she didn't think she would see Jay before she left the house and she was right. All the staff at the solicitor's, even the friendly head typist, were far too busy dealing with their own workload to notice Steph's appearance. Maybe they would have had she been a permanent colleague, but most people's attitude was that there was no point in making much of an effort with a temp.

As it turned out, this day was to be Steph's last working at that particular firm as the permanent member of staff she was covering for was returning on Monday. The agency informed her that her next job was as a filing clerk at an abattoir!

She couldn't wait to get home and begin making amends to Jay. By now surely he had seen that he was being foolish in accusing her of what he had. He would probably want to put things right just as much as she did.

As soon as she entered the front door Jay came out of the lounge to meet her. The stony look on his face sent any hope of a reconciliation from Steph's mind. Regardless, she smiled at him and said, 'Hello, darling.'

'Did you collect the allowance and your wages?' he demanded.

'Oh, er . . . yes, I did, at lunchtime.'

He held out his hand for her to hand the money over to him.

She did.

While she stood looking on, Jay counted the notes and loose change, as though checking it was all there, then handed her back seven pounds.

Steph looked at the notes in her hand.

'You don't need any housekeeping this week then?' he said in a sarcastic tone.

'But this is three pounds less than you've been giving me.'

'Well, you'll be wanting things for . . .' he nodded his head at her stomach '. . . and it all takes money.'

With that he left her standing in the hall.

After taking out his own spending money, he'd gone to stash away the remainder with the rest of what they'd saved, she assumed. By now they must have a tidy sum, well on the way to having enough for a deposit on a rented place, but until Jay secured a regular job they wouldn't be able to keep up the rental. And in a matter of months she'd have to give up work. Maybe he had found something today. He would tell her over dinner. In fact, they had a lot to talk about over dinner. Like him returning to their bed. Surely he had seen how childish he was being by now. Maybe he had already moved his things back.

Then Steph looked at the notes in her hand. It had been challenging enough managing on the money he had given her before. Three pounds less was a substantial drop. She would have to learn to economise further. But at least Jay had acknowledged that their child would need things. That was a step in the right direction. She'd better go and get the dinner on.

The pie was baking in the oven when she heard Jay returning downstairs. She was expecting him to come into the kitchen and turned to face the door. When he didn't, she assumed he'd gone into the dining room to set the table so she went to pop her head around the door and tell him that dinner would be about another half an hour.

It was with surprise that she found him in the hall, putting his coat on. He was dressed for a night out again.

'Oh, you're going out!' she exclaimed.

He looked over at her and snapped, 'You do have a habit of stating the obvious.'

She smarted from his nasty comment but regardless said, 'Well, I didn't know you intended going out. I've cooked dinner.'

'Then you should have asked me whether I'd be home for it or not before you wasted your time.' He flicked back the sleeve of his coat and glanced at his watch. 'I've got to go or I'll be late for my appointment.'

Steph wasn't so naive about the business world that she wasn't aware deals were sealed and interviews given over a drink in a pub, just as much as on a firm's premises. 'I do hope you're successful,' she said in all sincerity.

Jay grinned. 'Oh, I intend to be.'

He was positive he would get this job then. 'I'll wait up so you can tell me all about it.'

'That's up to you, I don't know what time I'll be back,' he called to her as he walked out.

\* \* \*

It was just after eleven. Curled up on the sofa in the lounge, Steph held a mug containing the dregs of some Cadbury's drinking chocolate.

After eating her solitary meal and having tidied the kitchen, she'd gone upstairs to have a bath. To her dismay she'd discovered that Jay still had not returned his belongings to their room. Maybe he felt so ashamed of his behaviour that he was waiting for her to invite him back. She would do it immediately he got home.

While she was up there she thought she may as well collect all the dirty washing together, take it downstairs ready to tackle in the morning. Having emptied the washing basket in the bathroom, she popped her head around the door of her father's old room to check if there was anything else of Jay's that needed washing.

Until she had cleared it of Gerald's belongings after his death, this room had been out of bounds to Steph. On entering it for the first time she had been struck by its difference from her mother's. This room had had dark blue walls and white paintwork; heavy dark furniture; no pictures and not an item out of place – unlike her mother's which always looked like a whirlwind had swept through it.

What her father's reaction would be if he could see the place now Steph didn't like to think. The bed cover was rumpled, wardrobe doors wide open, drawers hanging out of the chest with clothes spilling out of them. A pile of dirty washing was dumped on the floor; a soaking wet bath towel also.

Automatically she went inside, made the bed and collected the dirty clothes and towel to take down with the rest.

After she had taken her bath and made herself look as inviting as she could for her husband when he came home, finishing off with a light spray of the perfume she knew was Jay's favourite, Steph made herself a drink and went into the lounge to await his return while watching television.

Due to her lack of sleep the previous night she was having terrible difficulty keeping her eyes open. The minutes seemed to drag like hours, tonight's viewing on the television was not holding her attention to help her stay awake, so she switched it off and got herself a book. She was determined to be up waiting for Jay when he came home, like a good wife should be.

She suddenly woke with a start at a noise coming from outside. It was the clank of milk bottles. The milkman was delivering already! Through bleary eyes she glanced at the clock on the mantelpiece. It was half-past six! Steph shivered. The fire had burned out and she was freezing cold. Why hadn't Jay woken her when he had come in? Or if he hadn't wanted to disturb her, put a cover over her, like she would have done for him?

She heard the milkman say a cheery good morning. Who was he addressing? Then it became apparent as she heard a key being inserted in the lock and footsteps entering. Jay was just arriving home! This was the second time in two days he had stayed out all night and Steph still had no idea where he had been or with whom. And he was the worse for drink again, by the sound of it. It was one thing going out without her in the evening to discuss a job prospect or meet old friends for a catch-up drink, but he was a married man and it wasn't right he'd stayed out until this hour, acting like he was single again. She didn't want to act the heavy-handed wife, but she needed to let him know that this wasn't acceptable to her unless his excuse was a damned good one.

Before she had time to get up off the settee and go into the hall to greet him, he had already bounded up the stairs and down the landing to his room, slamming shut the door behind him without any consideration for her, asleep in bed for all he knew.

Steph's back ached terribly from the awkward position she had fallen asleep in on the sofa, and she was still very tired. It wasn't likely that Jay would be wanting his breakfast any time soon, so she decided to go upstairs and try to have another couple of hours' sleep herself.

But she couldn't. Reluctantly, just after seven she got up. By nine she had done the weekly wash and hung it out on the line in the garden. Whether it would dry was doubtful as the sky was overcast and a chilly wind blowing. After a cup of tea and slice of toast, she went upstairs to get ready to do the weekend shop. Up until now she and Jay had gone together and she had no reason to think they wouldn't today.

Ready for the off, she sat at the kitchen table with another cup of tea and waited for him to come down. To while away the time, she collected a stack of cookery books that Mrs Sanders and the cooks before her had used, and scoured them for cheap but appetising meals, ones an inexperienced cook like herself could easily prepare. Thankfully she found several she thought would do.

By eleven Jay still hadn't made an appearance. Not daring to leave the shopping any longer in case the shops had sold out, Steph went upstairs to wake him. She found him snoring deeply, sprawled under the covers, his clothes piled in a heap on the floor. She wrinkled her nose at the stench of stale beer filling the room then went across and gave him a gentle shake. He did not stir. She shook him harder. He still did not stir. She shook him even harder and called out his name. He didn't budge.

It seemed she was going to have to manage the shopping by herself this weekend.

Steph was exhausted by the time she had lugged

several heavy bags the half-mile from the shopping parade back home. Jay still wasn't up. After putting away the shopping, she made herself a cheese sandwich and a cup of tea. When she had finished and washed up her dirty dishes, she went to fetch the washing in, folding up what was dry to iron the next morning and putting the still-damp items on the clothes horse in a warm corner of the kitchen. She couldn't do the vacuuming as the noise would wake up Jay, so after putting a duster around she went into the living room and settled herself comfortably in an armchair to while away the time reading a book. She used to look forward to reading a selection of weekly magazines before her marriage, but the budget she had to manage on now didn't stretch to cover those, so like many women who couldn't afford magazines she would have to make do reading back issues when she visited the doctor or dentist.

She only realised she had fallen asleep when she was jolted awake by the overpowering smell of burning. Her immediate thought was that the house was on fire until it registered that what she was smelling was burning bacon. Had she left a pan on the stove and fallen asleep? She couldn't remember doing so. Jumping up, she rushed off to the kitchen to investigate. Just inside the door she stopped short. Jay stood at the stove, poking a fork into a spluttering frying pan.

She rushed over, saying to him, 'The heat is far too high, Jay.'

'I'm cooking it the way I like it,' he snapped.

She looked down into the pan. Crisped almost to a cinder was all of the streaky bacon she had bought that morning. On a plate on the work surface to one side of the stove were four chunky slices of bread that had been hacked off the loaf she had also bought that morning, which was to do them until she bought fresh again on Monday. Half the loaf was gone already.

'What's that look on your face for?' he sneered.

'Pardon? Oh, er . . . well, it's just that you've used all the bacon.'

He gave a nonchalant shrug 'So?'

'Well, it was meant for breakfast tomorrow too.'

'Huh! Well, you'd better go and fetch more then.'

'I can't.'

He looked sharply at her. 'Too lazy to, is that it?'

Steph's face puckered, wounded by his unwarranted remark. 'No, not at all. But after doing the weekend shop this morning, I've worked out I've only just enough money left to buy the rest of the food for the week and put aside the milkman's money. I've none to spare to buy more bacon.'

He gave another nonchalant shrug. 'Well, a man needs a good breakfast inside him and it's up to the woman to provide it, so the problem is yours. Finish off making this sandwich and mash me a cuppa while I hurry up and get ready.'

'Get ready? You mean, you're going out!'

'I'm off to the match and I don't want to miss the kick-off.'

Her face fell. 'Oh, I was hoping we could talk this afternoon. We can tonight, though?'

'Can't.'

'Oh!'

'I've somewhere I need to be.'

'I take it you weren't successful last night then? I am so sorry.' Steph looked awkwardly at him for a moment before she said, 'Look, Jay, the last thing I want to do is come across as the nagging wife, but do these interviews have to be in the evening and in a pub so that you end up drunk and spending money we could put to better use? Can't they be arranged like normal interviews are, during the day?'

He looked at her strangely. 'What interviews?'

It was her turn to look at him strangely. 'The ones you've been attending the last two nights and again tonight.'

'I don't know where you got the idea that I was attending interviews.'

'From you, when you told me you'd be late for your appointment.'

'I didn't say who my appointment was with, though, did I? For your information, it was with

267

friends of mine . . . and a bloody good time we had too.'

She was stunned. Jay had been out enjoying himself, leaving her behind at home, and she had been stupid enough to believe he was attending interviews for work! Anger flared within Steph then and she blurted, 'But this isn't right . . .'

Eyes blazing, he pushed his face into hers and hissed, 'And what you've done is?'

Her face filled with hurt. 'Oh, Jay, why are you doing this? I can't believe you really think I'd betray you like that.'

He retorted harshly, 'I'm trying to come to terms with losing my business, my flat, my car, getting used to being married *and* living in someone else's house. I'm not nearly ready to become a father, and all I know is I made damn' sure I didn't get you pregnant. I never once made a slip. So, as far as I'm concerned, what you're carrying isn't mine and until I've proof to the contrary, I won't be changing my mind.' He tossed back his head and utterly astounded her by continuing, 'Now I think about it, you jumped at my proposal, didn't you? I didn't need to ask you twice. I'm wondering if you were manipulating me into asking all the time, because you knew you were pregnant and needed a father for your baby. It's real one obviously didn't want to know, and you saw me as a likely sucker. Well, now hopefully you'll realise

I'm not the fool you thought me. Forget the sandwich, I'll get something while I'm out.'

This latest accusation had absolutely floored Steph, so much so she didn't hear him leave the house moments later. Slumping down on a kitchen chair, she stared blindly across the room as her mind searched frantically for a way out of this nightmare situation. What could she do or say to Jay to convince him that his accusations were utterly preposterous? She could only be pregnant because he must have used a faulty condom, but she could hardly call that proof. Nor could she prove to him that she hadn't already been expecting a child when she had met him. Presumably once the baby was born at a time consistent with their wedding night, he'd have to believe her.

That was at least another seven months away.

Was Jay proposing they'd exist like this until the baby was born and he could inspect it for its likeness to himself?

Steph's shoulders sagged despairingly and tears of misery welled in her eyes. All her life she had been trapped in a world where she was shown no warmth or affection. Now the man she thought had rescued her from a lifetime of oppression was treating her far worse, and clearly expecting her to put up with it until he decided otherwise. It was going to be bad enough contending with her mother's ways again when she decided to return; Jay treating her like he was on top of that was expecting far too much.

If he still insisted he wouldn't acknowledge the child as his until she gave him concrete proof, then as much as it broke her heart even to consider it, she would have to insist they part company.

It deeply saddened Steph that she was proposing to raise her child without its father, but she vowed she would do her absolute best to make sure it did not suffer by it. She didn't like the thought of raising her child under the same roof as her tempestuous mother either, but if Jay and she did part then she'd have no other choice.

With the confrontation that was facing her, Steph had no enthusiasm to do anything but sit and wait for Jay to come home, which she estimated would be at five-thirty give or take a few minutes. As each minute brought his return nearer, trepidation built within her. She wasn't looking forward at all to what she knew she had to do, didn't know how Jay was going to react, and just wanted to get it over with.

Five-thirty came and went. Six-thirty came and went. At just before seven she finally heard his key. By this time she was a bag of nerves and it took all her strength to stop herself from dashing to her room and shutting herself inside until he had gone out again. It took every ounce of will power for her to raise herself off the chair and go and meet him.

Before she was halfway across the kitchen, though, she heard him shout, 'You can put my dinner on the table now.'

Steph stopped short, anger flaring. Jay may believe that he had a grievance against her, but regardless, it didn't justify him treating her in such a disrespectful manner. She wasn't going to put up with that.

Spinning on her heel, she returned to the table and resumed her seat. He shouted to her again. She still made no response. Seconds later he appeared in the kitchen doorway, glowering crossly at her. 'Are you just ignorant or deaf? I said—'

'I heard what you said, Jay,' she cut in. Taking a deep breath, she calmly announced, 'I haven't made dinner.'

He looked surprised. 'Oh! Well, you'd better hurry up and do it as I'm going out at a quarter to eight. I'm off upstairs to have a wash and shave, so give me a shout when it's on the table.'

He made to depart but she stopped him by telling him, 'I need to talk to you, Jay, then I'll make your dinner.'

'Talk about what?' he snarled. 'As far as I'm concerned, unless you can prove that . . . *thing* you're carrying is mine, we have nothing to talk about.'

'You know that's impossible. Are you seriously expecting me to put up with the way you're treating me until *our* baby is born? And what then, Jay? What if he or she hasn't your eyes or nose? Because they aren't a mirror image of you, are you still going to deny you're their father? This baby is *yours*. I have never so much as looked at another man since we met. Please believe me, Jay. If you're not going to then . . . well, I can't live in this atmosphere. It's best we part.'

He stared at her for several long moments before he said matter of factly, 'Don't let me stand in the way of your packing.'

She stared at him, taken aback. She surely couldn't have heard him right. '*My* packing?'

He shrugged. 'Well, I take it you're not going to leave empty handed. You'd better leave your forwarding address so your mother will know where you are when she comes back and I can send on any mail.'

Steph was looking at him with incredulity. 'But this is my house, Jay. I'm not going anywhere.'

'Oh, so you're expecting me to go!' His face darkened thunderously. 'You cheat on me, try and pass another man's baby off as mine, and then when I see through your game, you think I'm going to be a good little boy and leave you, so you're free to snare some other poor sucker and pass it off as a premature baby. Well, sorry to disappoint you, lady.' He stabbed himself in his chest before continuing, 'I ain't going anywhere, and there's nothing you can do about that.

I'm your husband. You've no grounds to get me out.
I've done nothing wrong. If anything, I could get
*you* out with what you've done to me.'

His grin was cruel and his eyes sparkled maliciously. 'And why should I want to leave? This house
is better than I could ever afford; there's no real
urgency for me to get a job because dear dead daddy-
in-law saw fit to provide my dear wife with a decent
weekly allowance – far more than I could earn – and
as head of the house it's my place to dish out that
allowance in any way I see fit.'

He walked across to Steph and grabbed her
shoulder, gripping it painfully. Then he pushed his
face into hers and hissed, 'After what you've done
to me, do you really expect me to be all lovey-dovey
with you? Well, you were fooling yourself if you did.
I'm treating you how you deserve to be treated for
all the pain and hurt you've caused me. I thought I'd
married the woman of my dreams – only to find she
was nothing more than a lying whore!' He squeeze
his fingers tighter on her shoulder until he saw tears
of pain glint in her eyes. 'Now get me something to
eat,' he ordered.

Steph sat frozen to the spot. There was a look in
his eyes that sent fear through her. It was a challenging, goading look, as if he was just daring her to
refuse him so it gave him an excuse to retaliate.

At her lack of response he smirked and said, 'I

take it that's a yes.' He released his hold on her. Walking out of the kitchen he shot back, 'Give me a shout when it's on the table. And hurry up about it!'

# CHAPTER NINETEEN

Steph jumped as a slab of raw meat, blood dripping from it, was slapped down in front of her on the desk. She looked at it in surprise for a moment, then at the person who had put it there.

Harold Fuller's ruddy face beamed back at her. He wiped bloody hands on a huge apron stretched over the mound of his stomach. It was so caked in blood and slivers of raw meat it was hard to tell if the fabric had actually been white. 'Perk of the job. Let's face it, gel, we all needs some incentive to work in a God-forsaken place like this, don't we?'

Steph couldn't agree with him more. The overpowering stench of dead animal carcasses that met any new arrival well before they had actually entered the premises was enough to turn the most hardened stomach, let alone her own considering the condition she was in. She strongly suspected that the agency had been expecting a telephone call from her as soon as she arrived on Monday morning, informing them that she hadn't the stamina to work in such a place. She couldn't deny that it had been on her mind, but the welcoming reception she had received from the employees and owner of the abattoir had persuaded her to try to stick it out.

The moment she entered the building, she was approached by a huge bull of a man who momentarily put the fear of God in her, looking like he did with a hideous scar across his face – an accident with a meat hook, she learned later – and dressed in bloodied overalls. But the smile of welcome on his face put Steph immediately at her ease. After confirming that she was the office temp they were expecting, he showed her courteously into the owner's office.

Sam Jones was a small, tubby man without a hair on his head. His short-sighted eyes appeared grossly out of proportion behind thick pebble spectacles. After personally making her a cup of tea and not sparing on the sugar, he apologised profusely to her for her being thrown in at the deep end. Marion Yardles, his permanent office assistant, had hurt her back when she had slipped in the factory while handing out the wages last Friday lunchtime. Unable to walk she had had to be wheeled home by two of the slaughtermen, lying flat on top of a metal trolley usually used to transport sides of beef. The doctor had ordered complete bed rest, for how long they did not know.

It took all Steph's inner resources to stop herself from laughing out loud at the comical picture Sam Jones conjured up of the men wheeling the unfortunate Marion Yardles home on the improvised 'stretcher'.

Sam told her that he was aware she didn't possess any typing skills but would be grateful for anything else she could do to keep the office running as smoothly as possible during Marion's absence. Steph assured him she would do her best.

All the men, even the junior slaughterers, were the rough and ready kind who called a spade a spade, but when in her company they acted like perfect gentlemen towards her. She had never in her life felt so appreciated.

How she was being treated at work by relative strangers was in complete contrast to her life at home with her husband.

As the week progressed Steph's memories of their happy times together were rapidly fading as Jay's manner towards her grew steadily nastier. In return, she was finding it extremely difficult to be cordial to him. It seemed he was making it his mission to find new ways of antagonising her. She knew it was not her imagination, he was deriving real pleasure from the fact that he was making her miserable, and she found herself striving hard not to react to his provocation in the hope that if he saw his behaviour was not having the desired effect, he would tire of it and leave her alone.

Jay had been out every night, not returning until the early hours of the morning and always the worse for drink. By now Steph was glad of this as it meant she was left in peace to nurse her misery in private.

She realised that their savings had all gone straight into his pocket. Every time he went out he was wearing something she hadn't seen before. This was hard for her to accept when he was forcing her to scrimp to get by on the housekeeping he allowed her. After paying for groceries she barely had enough over to fund a pair of new tights for work each week. What deeply galled her, though, was the fact that Jay himself wasn't bringing a penny into the house. Her money was funding his extensive social life and nothing was being set aside to buy things for their baby. It would be up to her to provide a layette for their child. How on earth she was going to do this she had no idea, but she was determined to somehow. Bad enough that her baby's father was denying his part in its existence. As its mother she would give it the best that was possible.

Though she felt she was contending with enough at the moment, part of her wished her mother would come back. There was no way Ursula would meekly accept Jay's act of being the head of the house. She'd soon set him straight there.

As she went to thank Harold Fuller for the generous gift, a way of setting aside a few shillings at least for the baby occurred to Steph. The chunk of meat before her was worth ten shillings at least if she had bought it from the butcher's. It would do for at least three meals. A slice cut off to put aside and fry as steak for Saturday, the chunk that was left roasted for Sunday, and the remainder minced for Monday.

Steph opened her mouth to express her gratitude to the slaughterman but stopped short when Sam Jones came bustling in. 'Sorry to interrupt.' He spotted the slab of beef on her desk and eyed it appraisingly. 'Nice bit of topside that.' He looked at Harold. 'You cut it off a beast from Morrison's farm, like I asked you?'

The other man nodded. 'Certainly did, boss.'

Sam gave Harold a slap on the back. 'Good man. Find something to wrap it in. Steph can't take it home like that.'

Harold took his leave and Sam told her, 'Best bit of beef you'll ever taste, lovey. Mick Morrison looks after his cows better than some men do their wives, and a happy cow produces the most succulent beef.' He grinned and smacked his lips. 'Gosh, all this talk is making me hungry.' Then he pulled a quizzical face. 'Now what did I come in for?' he asked himself. 'Oh, it's all right, I remember now. I've had word

Marion has recovered from her fall and is coming back on Monday.'

Steph had mixed feelings about this information. She was genuinely glad the woman was over her fall, and she herself wouldn't miss the smell from this place but she would the people. She hoped the staff at her next assignment were as friendly. 'I'm so pleased to hear that Mrs Yardles is better. I want to say how much I've enjoyed my week here, Mr Jones. I hope the work I did for you was satisfactory?'

He patted her shoulder. 'More than, lovey. And I'm glad to hear you enjoyed yourself with us this week because I was wondering if you'd agree to come back next week as well? There's a backlog of typing Marion will need to concentrate on, and it'd help her if you were around to assist with answering the telephone and taking the filing work off her.'

Steph beamed in delight. 'I'd be glad to.'

He beamed back at her. 'Good, then I'll call the agency and square it with them.'

At just after one-thirty, her wages in her handbag along with next week's time sheet, Steph hurried out of the agency towards the bank. Her visit there had taken longer than it normally did as it appeared two people had gone off sick, leaving a skeleton staff to cope with their busiest day of the week. To her dismay Steph arrived at the bank to find herself joining a long queue of at least fifteen people, and to make matters worse only two counter staff were visible. More than likely the rest were having their own lunch. Why it was that the bank always seemed to have fewer staff on at their busiest times was beyond her.

By a quarter to two, there were still seven people ahead of Steph and she had fifteen minutes left to get back to work. It was a good ten minutes' run away, and she didn't want to let her kindly boss down and be late back. Plus the agency didn't look favourably on temps who were slack time-keepers. It could mean a black mark against her. She would have to come back on Monday to collect the allowance. Her wages would have to cover their needs over the weekend.

She was so concerned about not being late for work and letting her boss down, it never crossed her mind how Jay was going to react to the news.

He was waiting for her as soon as she stepped through the front door. It was obvious he'd been watching for her from the front window. He didn't even bother to greet her verbally, just held out his hand, expecting her to fill it.

'I didn't get the allowance today,' Steph told him as she took off her coat and hung it up.

Before she had a chance to explain why, he snapped, 'I'm not in the mood for games, just hand it over.'

Steph fixed her eyes on him and said quietly, 'I told you, I didn't get the allowance today. When I arrived at the bank there was a long queue and I'd have been late back for work if I'd waited. I'll have to fetch it on Monday. We can manage until then on my wages.'

Jay was glaring at her. 'I had big plans for this weekend,' he snarled. 'Well, hand over what you've got. That'll have to do me. And wait in the queue next time,' he instructed her.

Steph was frowning at him. 'But, Jay, if I give you all my wages, I won't have any money left to pay what we owe for coal and milk or to buy food for the weekend. I need a few personal bits for myself . . . well, I can manage, I suppose, until Monday, but I'll need a new pair of tights then. I've laddered the pair I've got on and I haven't any more.'

He hissed at her, 'Do I look as if I fucking care what you need? Those days were over for you the minute I realised what you were up to.' He had never used strong language in her company before and Steph was shocked by his doing so now. Before she could stop him he'd grabbed her handbag off her, opened it up and tipped the contents out over the floor. He scooped up the brown envelope containing her wages, took out the notes and tipped the change into his palm. Having counted it, he then checked the amount against her wage slip and looked at her accusingly. 'This is ninepence short.'

'I needed it for my bus fare home.' The fact that he had the audacity to accuse her of spending money she had earned herself infuriated Steph nearly as much as his intention of leaving her without any means of buying food over the weekend. Before she could think better of it, she lunged forward and grabbed the notes out of his hand, declaring, 'Earn your own money to go out gallivanting with! You're not having mine any longer.'

Before she had chance to dodge out of the way, Jay had swung back his fist and punched her in the side of the face. The force of the blow caused her to stumble backwards and crash heavily against the front door. The notes flew from her hand and scattered around her.

It felt to Steph as if her brain was bouncing around inside her skull. Excruciating pain from the blow to her cheek was making her feel sick and faint. Then a hand was gripping her throat, she was gasping for breath, and with his face pushed into hers, Jay snarled, 'Next time you won't be able to get up!' He released his grip on her and turned away to gather up the notes. Steph slumped down to the floor and watched him through terrified eyes.

Having stuffed the notes in his pocket he made for the stairs, running up them two at a time, calling out to her, 'Don't bother with dinner for me, I'll be eating out.'

By the time he returned back down, just under an hour later, Steph had managed to crawl to the living room and heave herself on the sofa, where she almost passed out from the pain of her injuries. At this moment she never wanted to set eyes on him again. It wasn't so much terror of him she was experiencing, it was hatred. To think she'd loved him once . . . and he thought so little of her or their child he'd behaved like an animal.

Much to her relief she did not see Jay again that weekend, only heard him arrive home in the early hours of Monday morning, drunk by the sound of it. Thankfully she'd escaped off to work long before he got up. Having no money to buy any fresh food she'd had to make do with what was already in the larder, although she'd no appetite at all, only forcing herself to eat a little for fear of depriving her developing baby. She felt adamantly that Jay did not deserve to benefit from the meat given to her by the kindly slaughtermen so on Saturday lunchtime, just before the milkman usually called to collect his money, she left the wrapped meat on the doorstep with a note explaining that she was ill in bed and would pay him what was owed next week. In the meantime, she hoped he could find a use for the meat, which due to her illness would go to waste otherwise. She felt positive it would be very welcome, knowing the milkman had five school-age children.

The side of her face was swollen and tender; a dark

purple and black bruise tinged with green had appeared just under her eye and only ended halfway down her neck. Jay's attack had also loosened a back tooth which was throbbing relentlessly, not seeming to be eased at all by regular doses of painkillers. Consequently Steph had had little sleep.

On Monday morning she stared at herself in her dressing-table mirror and compared the reflection that looked back at her with Frankenstein's monster. She only went to work because it was preferable to staying at home. Her facial injuries, she knew, would draw immediate attention and she'd be quizzed as to how she had come by them. She hoped her lie was good enough to satisfy their curiosity.

Steph kept her head well down to avoid onlookers on the way, but on arriving for work, as soon as she entered the office, the pleasant-faced, middle-aged woman, sitting behind the desk Steph had occupied last week, exclaimed at the sight of her.

'My goodness! Mrs Connor . . . it is Mrs Connor, isn't it? . . . What on earth have you done to yourself?'

Steph gulped, hating the fact that her first words to this kindly looking woman were going to be a lie to cover up the shame of her husband's attack on her. 'I tripped over the edge of a rug and fell into the coffee table.'

'Well, if that's the damage that was done to you,

I'd not like to think what happened to the table. It looks very painful, dear?'

Steph gave a weak smile. 'It looks worse than it is.' She walked across to the desk and held out her hand to the other woman. Due to her injuries, she spoke as if she had a wad of paper wedged in her cheek. 'I'm very pleased to meet you, Mrs Yardles. I'm glad you're over your own fall.'

Marion accepted her hand and firmly shook it. 'I'm glad I'm over it too. I was in agony for the first couple of days, before it started easing up. My poor husband was run ragged, fetching and carrying for me. Came a right cropper, I did. My own fault. I've worked here long enough to know how slippery the slaughter-house floor gets.

'I want to thank you for keeping this place running for me while I was off. Mr Jones is such a thoughtful man, keeping you on for another week to help me to catch up with the backlog of typing. Working here does have its drawbacks, it took me a long time to get used to the smell, but Mr Jones and the men more than compensate.'

With a twinkle of amusement in her eyes, and lowering her voice for fear of being overheard, Marion continued, 'The slaughtermen all look the sort you'd not want to meet on a dark night in a deserted alley, but none of them would hurt a hair on anyone's head. All got hearts of gold, as I'm sure you've found out for yourself. Well, I'll make us and Mr Jones a nice cup of tea . . . morning ritual when we first arrive is to have a cuppa . . . then we'll get cracking. Oh, there's a packet of digestives in the cupboard in the kitchen, so we'll have a couple of them each to soak up the tea. Of course, that's if the lads didn't find them last week and scoff the lot.'

Steph took an immediate liking to Marion Yardles and knew the week ahead was going to be as pleasant as her last had been.

Pity she was in such pain from her tooth, though. Unlike Marion's back, it didn't seem to be easing at all and by mid-morning Steph was having great difficulty concealing her discomfort. She dare not take any more pain relief yet as she'd had two pills just over an hour before, which didn't seem to be having any effect.

Marion just happened to be looking her way when, above the constant dull throb, a sharp spasm of pain shot through Steph's jaw. She caught Steph wincing and cradling the offending cheek in her hand. Marion eyed the younger woman shrewdly and said, 'That injury to your face is causing you a lot of trouble, lovey, isn't it?'

Hoping the other woman might have some advice to give her on easing the pain, she nodded. 'It is. I think I dislodged a tooth when I fell. The painkillers I've taken don't seem to be doing anything.'

'Maybe you should see your dentist. Give him a call and see if he can fit you in as an emergency. Don't look so worried, Mr Jones won't have a problem with you going out for a while, in the circumstances.'

Like the majority of people, a visit to the dentist's was bottom of Steph's favourite places to go, but on this occasion it was good advice she was receiving and she didn't argue. Looking up the number in the telephone directory, she dialled it. A minute later she replaced the receiver in its cradle and told Marion, 'I don't know whether to laugh or cry, Mrs Yardles. Mr McCorkindale . . . that's my dentist's name . . . is off today because he's having emergency treatment from his own dentist. Apparently he broke a tooth last night playing rugby. I can't be fitted in until tomorrow evening at five to five.'

Marion eyed her knowingly. 'By the looks of you, lovey, there's no way you'll suffer the pain you're in until then. Let me see if my dentist can fit you in. He's a good man.' A few minutes later she said to Steph, 'As you heard, I explained your predicament and Mr Fawkes will see you immediately. If he can't help you, no other dentist can. He's only young but he knows his stuff and actually cares about his patients, unlike others I've had the misfortune to use. Now the surgery is on . . . oh, from here it's going to take you at least half an hour by bus. Hang on a minute.'

She got up from her desk. Leaving a bemused Steph looking after her, she rushed out of the office, returning a moment later to inform her, 'Harold will take you in the van. Hurry up and get your coat on, he's waiting in the yard for you. And, look, don't come back if you're not up to it. I can cope.'

Grateful tears pricked Steph's eyes. How kind these people were being to her, people who hardly knew her. Her own husband must have known he'd hurt her badly yet he hadn't cared enough even to bother coming home over the weekend to enquire after her. She could have been knocked into a coma, could still be lying unconscious where he'd left her. Worse, in Steph's eyes, he could have induced a miscarriage, for all he knew.

# CHAPTER TWENTY

Conscious that his pretty passenger was in extreme discomfort, Harold drove the van swiftly via a short cut he knew to reach Belvoir Street in the centre of town, where Fawkes Dental Practice was situated on the middle floor of a three-storey building.

Steph was too relieved to be there, praying that the wonderful dentist Marion Yardles had described was going to perform a miracle, to notice that the reception area was very inviting, not at all austere like her own dentist's premises. His receptionist did not show any shock at Steph's appearance but actually smiled at her in greeting.

'Mr Fawkes is expecting you, Mrs Connor, so if you'd like to go straight through,' the pleasant young woman said to Steph, pointing her in the direction of the door to the surgery.

A tall, ruggedly handsome man in his early thirties, wearing a white doctor's-style coat over casual slacks and a navy pullover, smiled a welcome to Steph as she walked in.

She was too eager to climb into the chair and have her treatment begin to see the smile on his face fade away, to be replaced by a look of shock. 'Oh, my goodness, was it a train you collided with?' he said.

Now settled in the chair, she was steeling herself for a painful probing to diagnose what was causing her such agony. 'No, I fell against a coffee table. I think I dislodged a back tooth – it feels loose anyway. I've never had pain like this before. I do hope you can do something for me. To be honest, at the moment I'd agree to you chopping off my head if it'd take the pain away.'

She opened her mouth as wide as her injuries would allow her to do and waited expectantly. After a moment, when Mr Fawkes did not approach her to begin his examination, she shut her mouth and looked over at him. To her surprise she saw he was staring at her frozen-faced. Was her appearance so shocking?

Realising his patient was looking over at him, he gave himself a mental shake and said, 'My receptionist announced you as Mrs Connor, but . . . well, you are Gerald's daughter, aren't you?'

Steph stared at him searchingly and recognition struck then. Marion Yardles' wonderful dentist was none other than Paul Fawkes, the man who'd been her late father's lover. But at the moment he could have been Sweeney Todd for all Steph cared, the pain was so bad.

'Are you going to see if you can help me or not?' she urged.

He rushed over to her.

Steph settled back in the chair and opened her mouth again.

A few moments later he said to her, 'There's nothing I can do to save the tooth, I'm afraid. It's going to have to come out. Don't worry, the gap it leaves won't be seen when you smile, it's right at the back. Now, I can put you under with a whiff of gas, but if you brace yourself, one good tug should do it and it'll all be over.'

She'd had gas once before as a child and the after-affects had left her groggy, nauseous and suffering from a dreadful headache for a day afterwards. It wasn't an experience she was willing to repeat unless there was no other option. 'I'll brace myself,' she told him, gripping the arms of the chair so tight her knuckles bulged.

Two minutes later, Paul triumphantly proclaimed, 'That's got it! Now give your mouth a good rinse out, then I'll pack the hole with wadding. You need to bite firmly down on it for at least five minutes for the bleeding to stop. The reason for your pain was that the disturbance of the tooth's root by your fall caused an abscess to form. Don't worry, all the pus came out when I pulled your tooth.'

He paused and studied her while she rinsed out her mouth with some pink liquid. He bent over to insert the wadding, and as he was doing so, said, 'Miss Mortimer . . . sorry, Mrs Connor . . . look, I'm not so daft as to believe the injuries you sustained were caused by a fall. Someone gave you a good right hook is my diagnosis.' Having finished what he was doing he righted himself. 'What kind of monster would want to inflict such damage on a lovely young woman like you?' he said kindly.

She stared up at him blindly, heedless of the throbbing in her inflamed gum, the trickle of blood oozing down her chin that needed to be wiped away before it risked seeping on to the collar of her blouse and staining it. The concern in his eyes was so genuine that she forgot exactly who this man was in her overwhelming need to unburden herself to someone. Tears filling her eyes, she told him, 'My husband.'

A look of pure horror filled his face. Without another word he walked out of the room and into reception. She heard a faint mumbling as he addressed his receptionist. Then he returned and, still without a word, helped her out of the chair.

He guided her out of his surgery and into a small room that more than likely had been used as a store room by previous occupants, but which Paul was obviously using as his private rest area. Two comfortable-looking easy chairs faced each other across a small coffee table. There was a framed print on the wall of a Constable painting.

'Make yourself comfortable,' Paul told her. Steph had no strength left to question why he had brought her in here. 'My receptionist is explaining to my next few patients that I've been called away unexpectedly. They can wait if they want to or rearrange their appointments. We won't be disturbed now.' Then he sat down in the chair opposite and looked sadly at the desolate young woman before him.

Taking a deep breath, he clasped his hands and said to her, 'If anyone came into my surgery with injuries like you have, I'd be showing concern. You're not just another patient, though, you're Gerald's daughter. I know it sickens you for me to remind you of it, I was left in no doubt how you felt about your father and me the night I visited, but he was the love of my life. I miss him dreadfully. For me there'll never be another who'll match up to him. I'm just so sad that Gerald couldn't show you the love and care he showed me.

'I hope, though, you can understand why, as the daughter of the man I felt so much for, I care for you too. It's obvious you're in need of help, and I want to help you. Please allow me to?'

Steph was openly crying now and Paul paused for

a moment, distressed for her. He reached over and laid his hand gently on her knee. 'Nothing you could have done justifies your husband treating you like this. Have you reported him to the police? You must, or else risk him believing he can do it again, any time he feels like it, because you won't do anything.'

'Jay does feel justified for what he's done to me, though. He believes I cheated on him and that the baby I'm having is another man's.'

Paul gasped, 'You're pregnant! And he beat you in your condition? Whether he felt justified or not, the man is an animal.'

Steph felt the need to tell him, 'I never cheated on Jay. I've never so much looked at another man since I met him. I've begged him to believe me, but he won't listen.'

'What reason has he to believe you cheated on him? He must have one.'

Due to the sensitivity of the topic, Steph was unable to met his eyes so lowered her head and said softly, 'We were being careful, using protection every time, so that I wouldn't get pregnant.'

Paul scoffed, 'Many babies have been conceived while their parents were using protection. Nothing is one hundred per cent safe, that's no secret. The manufacturers state as much on the packets. Surely your husband had another reason to be suspicious of whether the baby was his or not?'

Sniffing, she shook her head. 'No, that's it. It isn't quite as simple as that, though. You see, it was a whirlwind relationship we had. We'd only been seeing each other for a few weeks when he asked me to be a witness with him to a friend's wedding – only it was just a ruse to get me there. It was *our* wedding we were attending.'

Her voice lowered to whisper. 'It was so romantic. Jay told me he'd fallen in love with me the first time he'd set eyes on me and knew immediately I was the one for him. He said he wanted to spend the rest of his life with me and begged me to marry him. I was so in love with him, I wanted nothing more than to be his wife. He was everything I'd ever dreamed of in a man, considerate, respectful, liked all the same things . . .'

She sighed heavily before going on to tell Paul everything. How Jay's friends hadn't turned up, and how he'd discovered that his former partner had cheated him, resulting in Jay's losing his business, flat and car.

'We had no choice but for Jay to move in with me and my mother until he got a job and we could get together the money to rent a place of our own. But if he has been offered any jobs, he hasn't accept any, just hasn't had the heart to yet. In all fairness to him, it's a dreadful comedown from having been his own boss to going back to being an ordinary worker;

having his own flat and car to having to live in someone else's house and catch the bus. It's what this has done to him personally, though, that really hurts. The change in him is . . . well, I can only say that he was Dr Jekyll, but now he's Mr Hyde.'

Paul had been listening open mouthed to the awful tale Steph was telling him. 'If someone fleeced me out of my practice after all my efforts to build, it up, I'd be gutted. But if your husband is now going to spend the rest of his life believing everyone is out to betray him, then he's going to end up one lonely man.' Paul's handsome face screwed up in annoyance. 'Any man who resorts to using his fists to get what he wants is a coward, but to use them against a defenceless woman, he has to be the lowest of the low, I don't care how valid he thinks his reason is. You surely can't carrying on living with him, knowing that if you say something in all innocence that he takes amiss, it will give him an excuse to attack you again?'

Steph heaved a deep sigh. 'I have no choice as matters stand. Jay considers himself the injured party, and I can't prove otherwise. I have no grounds to get him out of the house, and can't afford to leave myself.' She saw Paul open his mouth to speak and felt she was guessing correctly what he was about to say to her. 'My father didn't leave me anything. Well, not directly. He provided for my mother. As she's hopeless with money, he knew that if he'd left it to her outright she would have spent it like water and quickly ended up with nothing, so he left the house to me on proviso my mother lives there until she dies. Until then I can't do anything with it. We're paid a weekly allowance to manage on, and anything that's left of the capital when she dies, I receive then. Jay makes me hand over the allowance and my wages to him and decides how much housekeeping I get. You can tell how he reacted when I retaliated against that. So, you see, I'm stuck with my situation until he decides otherwise.'

Paul was looking utterly appalled by this. In a disgusted tone, he said, 'Not many people die without having experienced a devastating blow of some sort, but they don't use it as an excuse to make their loved ones live in terror of them. Oh, if only I hadn't sold the flat and used the proceeds and my legacy from Gerald to expand this business! I've just signed a lease on a much bigger place, bought new equipment and taken on another dentist . . .'

There was a tremor in his voice when he continued, 'You see, I couldn't after all live in the flat without Gerald, too many memories, so I'm back living with Mother full-time. I felt that Gerald would approve of how I was using his legacy.' He looked at her earnestly. 'Believe me, though, I would gladly have let you live there for as long as you needed to, if I hadn't sold it.' He paused and frowned in puzzlement. 'What's your mother saying about all this, though? Surely she has something to say? I mean, I can't imagine any mother turning a blind eye to their child being mistreated, and especially one who's in the condition you are.'

Steph rubbed her hands wearily over her face. 'I don't know where she is. It's not unusual for her to go off without a word, though she never has for this length of time before, and certainly not without taking most of her wardrobe and cosmetics. If anything had happened to her, though, the police would have let us know, so she's got to be staying with a friend somewhere. I contacted all the names listed in her address book but they hadn't a clue where she is. It must be someone else she's with. Knowing how selfish my mother can be, she simply hasn't taken the trouble to let me know where she is or when I can expect her back. To be honest, she isn't the easiest of people to live with. In a way it's a relief I'm not having to deal with her as well as Jay.'

Paul looked genuinely sorry to hear what Steph had just told him. 'My mother is a fusspot and does get on my nerves sometimes, but I cannot imagine her ever behaving that way.' A look of shame filled his face. 'I'm constantly feeling guilty for what I have to keep secret from her. She loves me very much and is so proud of me. I can't bring myself to risk losing her love and respect by telling her I'm not exactly the person she thinks I am.'

He ran his hand distractedly through his hair, looking thoughtful. 'I really wish I could come up with something to help you out.'

Steph gave him a wan smile. 'I haven't had anyone to talk to about this, and I do appreciate your listening to me.'

He pulled a business card out of the top pocket of his white coat and handed it to her. 'Look, I know you might not want to have anything to do with me because of my association with your father, but I just want you to know that if you ever need a friend, at any time, don't hesitate to call here during business hours or else ring me at home. If I'm not there, Mother will take a message.'

Steph had great difficulty stemming tears of gratitude at this. What and who he was hardly seemed important. Just the thought that there was finally someone she could turn to meant everything to her. Choked with emotion, she took the card from him and put it safely in her handbag. 'Thank you.' She got up then. 'I'd better get back to work. And I need to go to the bank.'

Paul got up too. 'Your mouth will be sore for a few days. Try and eat on the other side so as not to irritate the extraction, and rinse your mouth with salt water as much as you can bear to,' he advised her. Normally after such treatment he would have suggested to the patient they take some time off work, but after hearing what was awaiting Steph at home he did not do so.

Jay was waiting for her in the hall when Steph got home. The look he gave her made her quail. If he was trying to make her feel she was the lowest of the low in his eyes, then he was making a good job of it. Wanting to be away from him as quickly as possible, she opened her handbag and placed the envelope containing the allowance into his palm, then walked past him, down the hall and into the kitchen. As she checked the kettle for water before turning on the stove, an icy shiver ran down her spine, making her shudder. She could feel his eyes boring into her back. She knew that Jay was furious that she hadn't asked him for housekeeping money. If he wanted feeding tonight, then he knew he'd have to give it to her or she couldn't buy any food. She felt a small sense of victory.

She heard something being banged down on the table and a grunt of, 'Housekeeping.'

Steph did not turn around until she heard Jay's footfall on the stairs. Going over to the table, she spread the money out and counted it up. She sighed in relief. He'd given her the same amount as last week. She had feared he would cut it down again. But then if he had, he'd have been cutting off his nose to spite his face.

Her jaw was still very tender and the inside of her mouth extremely sore after the extraction; she hadn't been able to eat anything all day and still doubted she could. Anyway, the whole experience of having her tooth removed and opening her heart to the most unexpected of people had taken away her appetite. A lukewarm cup of tea was all she would be able to manage. The last thing she felt like was traipsing down to the nearest late-night shop then returning to cook what she'd bought. She just wanted a hot soak in the bath and to go to bed. But she didn't relish the thought of Jay's reaction should she not place a meal on the table. For the sake of her unborn child, it was best to keep the peace.

She prayed that Jay's trip upstairs was because he was following the same ritual he had been following for the past week: after his wash and shave, he'd eat dinner, return upstairs to dress himself up then go out, not returning until the early hours of the morning. She dearly hoped tonight would be no exception.

She had to find what she could in the nearest late-night shop. Jay didn't hide the fact that he was expecting something more elaborate than sausage, egg and chips. When Steph put it before him, he stared down at the plate for a moment before picking up his fork, stabbing a sausage to inspect it then pushing his plate away.

'I'll eat out,' he said tersely.

It took every ounce of Steph's will-power not to pick up the plate of food and throw it at him. Considering the state she was in, this meal was as good as most other housewives across the country would have served up. It was despicable of him to turn his nose up at good food, and throw money away on drink and enjoyment when she was going without. It wasn't as though he had earned that money himself. She hoped the food he ate out tonight choked him.

# CHAPTER
# TWENTY-ONE

The following evening, at just after five-thirty, Steph walked through the gates of the slaughter house and turned in the direction of the bus stop. She was far too preoccupied with steeling herself for what lay in store for her at home to notice the expensive saloon car with its engine idling, parked at the kerb a little further down the street.

As she passed the car, the blast of a horn alerted her attention. Stepping over, she saw it was Paul Fawkes at the wheel. He motioned her to get into the passenger seat. Intrigued to know what he could be wanting with her, she did.

As soon as she was settled, Paul drove off without a word, weaving down several streets before pulling to a halt before a row of shops. He turned to look at her apologetically.

'Sorry for all the cloak and dagger stuff, but I didn't

want to put you in a compromising situation with the people you work with. Obviously I knew where you were working because of Marion Yardles being my patient.' Then he looked awkwardly at Steph. 'Look, I . . . er . . . well, I just wanted to know how you were? Not in my medical capacity but because I was worried. I haven't been able to get you off my mind. Such a Goddamn' awful situation you're in! I wish I could help you out of it.'

She stared at him. She knew Paul *was* offering her the hand of friendship. She had longed for a friend all her life, it seemed to Steph. Suddenly one had appeared, in the most unexpected fashion. He'd cared enough about her to come and check on her welfare, and that meant everything to her.

'I am honoured to have you as my friend,' she told him.

'I'm so glad,' said Paul softly. 'Oh, and I wanted to know . . . how's the mouth?'

'Getting better by the day, thank you. I've managed to eat a bit.'

He took her hand and squeezed it. 'I just hope you don't have any need of my services again in that capacity.'

Not half as much as she did! 'I'd better be off,' said Steph then. 'Thank you for . . . well, thank you.'

Unexpectedly he asked, 'Come for dinner tonight? You did say your husband goes out and so you'll be on your own. It's nothing special, leftovers from the roast yesterday, but you're welcome to join us ... Mother and me.'

Oh, the thought of being out in congenial company! It sounded just what she needed. Since Jay had turned against her, Steph had not eaten one meal she had actually enjoyed, not because her own cooking wasn't up to standard but because she had been painfully conscious that he had been watching her closely, seeking any opportunity to pass a snide remark or shoot her a look that would make her feel uncomfortable. He was very good at doing both.

'I'd be delighted,' she told Paul.

'Good. Well, I appreciate you won't be comfortable leaving until after your husband's gone out so I'll send a taxi for you at eight. I'll inform them where to bring you.'

What a thoughtful man he was! She could do with one like that in her life.

The single-brick garage at home was set apart from the house. As Steph walked up the steps to the front door a while later, out of the corner of her eye she spotted a red car parked in front of it. She didn't recognise it. Who could be visiting them who owned such a car? She had no idea of the make or model, but did know what was classed as a sporty type of car this one was.

After taking off her coat, she popped her head around the lounge door, expecting Jay to be entertaining whoever the car belonged to. The room was empty but it was evident that someone had eaten in there. A dirty plate, cup and saucer stood on the occasional table to one side of Gerald's armchair, which Jay had now claimed as his. He had obviously eaten his lunch in here and left her to clear up after him.

After collecting the crockery, she made her way to the kitchen. Passing by the door leading into the dining room, she poked her head inside. No one in here either. On the table were some dirty plates Jay had obviously used for his breakfast and not cleared away, as well as the morning paper, still spread out. Again she fought not to let his petty actions annoy her. She sighed as she entered the kitchen. Everything he had got out to make his breakfast and lunch with, he'd left for her to clear away.

She stiffened then as she heard footsteps coming down the stairs. Moments later Jay arrived in the kitchen. Without a word of greeting he told her, 'I want my dinner early tonight, I'm going out at seven.'

Steph was at the sink, filling it with hot water to wash the dirty crockery before she made a start on their evening meal. She was delighted to hear of his early departure as it meant she would be ready in plenty of time for her taxi. Without turning around she evenly responded, 'I'll put it on the table as quick as I can.' Then she did turn round to ask him, 'There's a car parked by the garage. Whose is it?'

He cast a mocking look at her. 'Is there anyone else here besides you and me?'

She frowned and turned her head to look at him. 'Not that I'm aware of.'

'Is the car yours then?'

He knew damned well it wasn't. Despite the warning voice inside telling her otherwise, she snapped at him, 'You know I don't drive so how can it be?'

'Oh, then the car must be mine, mustn't it?'

'Yours!' she exclaimed. 'We can't afford a car.'

He sneered at her, 'There's no *we* any more. You ended that when you tried to pull your stunt on me. *I* can afford a car. Dear Father-in-law made amply sure I can afford the HP payments every week. For your information, what it was costing me in taxis every night more than covers the repayments.'

He told her this as though Steph should be grateful to him for saving money! She hadn't the means to buy herself a new pair of tights this week and so had had to darn her laddered pair. But he was squandering her money on taxis and cars. Coldly, she said, 'The purpose of the allowance is to look after my mother.'

'She isn't here, is she? So I'm using the money as I see fit.' He sneered at her mockingly. 'You obviously can't handle it yourself because you're just a pampered little rich girl who's never had to lift a finger for herself before. Good job I'm here or where would you be, eh?'

It was true, she had never had to handle a household budget before, but Jay was way off the mark labelling her as a pampered little rich girl. She had neither been pampered nor had materially benefited from her father's money while he was alive, other than by having a nice house to live in and people employed to care for her domestically. She wanted to argue with Jay but saw the glint of malice in his eyes. A cold shiver ran through her again. She knew he was out to find himself an excuse to set about her again and was damned if she was going to make it easy for him. Silently, Steph turned her back on him and resumed washing up.

She was sitting at the kitchen table nursing a cup of tea, waiting for Jay to leave so she could go and ready herself for her dinner outing without any questions from him, when she heard his feet pounding down the stairs and, seconds later, the front door slam shut. He didn't even afford her the courtesy now of informing her when he was leaving the house. Still, he was doing her a favour. The less she had to do with him the better, as far as Steph was concerned. After downing the dregs in her cup, she rose and made her way into the hall, intending to go upstairs.

A loud noise stopped her. It was an engine revving. It grew louder and louder. Jay was obviously sitting with his foot pressed hard down on the accelerator. She knew instinctively that he was taunting her with his new car, and prayed the car would let him down by cutting out or, better still, blowing up with him inside it. Her prayer wasn't answered, though. The car's wheels squealed a protest as it was driven off down the drive at speed.

Steph had not been expecting to see such an elderly woman when she arrived at her destination to be greeted by Paul's mother. This had to be his grand-mother, she had thought, until she was informed otherwise. Steph had been expecting his mother to be in her late forties or early fifties, judging Paul to be in his early thirties. He was later to tell her that his mother and father hadn't been too concerned whether they had children or not since they dealt with them every day, in any case, in their work as school teachers. His father had taught maths at an all boys' school, his mother was a primary teacher at an infants' school. When she'd discovered she was expecting her first and only child at the age of forty-seven, the imminent arrival was looked forward to with shock then joy.

The Fawkeses' house was a three-storey Victorian villa cluttered with an odd assortment of old-fashioned furniture and numerous bookcases crammed with more books than Steph had ever seen in one place. Having given her a profuse welcome, Cissy Fawkes led Steph down a brightly lit hall towards a large room at the back of the house overlooking a well-tended garden accessed by French windows. They used it as their daily lounge and dining room.

As they entered this crowded but inviting space, Paul came in from the kitchen to greet Steph. Over his smart casual slacks and jumper he was wearing a flower-patterned apron, obviously his mother's, on which he was wiping his wet hands.

He smiled broadly at her. 'Dinner will be another few minutes. I'm sure Mother will keep you company meantime.'

'You'll join me in a sherry?' Cissie asked Steph, opening a sideboard which held an array of bottles. Steph spotted a bottle of Cinzano; she had always had a liking for that with lemonade, and was about to request one when it struck her that the mere thought was making her stomach turn. It seemed that alcohol was off her drinks list until after the baby was born.

'Could I just have a squash, please?'

Cissie smiled across at her. 'Orange or lemon?'

A few moments later they were seated opposite each other in sagging but comfortable armchairs, toasting themselves by a blazing fire.

'Your good health,' said Cissie to Steph, raising

her schooner glass before taking a sip of the pale sherry inside. Cradling the glass between her gnarled hands, she said then, 'Paul tells me you're the daughter of a patient of his with whom he was on friendly terms. He said you'd recently been bereaved, and as your mother's away at the moment he thought you could do with a bit of home cooking. I am sorry for your loss, dear,' she said sincerely.

Steph flashed her a brief smile. 'Thank you. I appreciate you inviting me for dinner.'

'The pleasure is all ours, dear. Although I can't take any credit for the meal. I never really was a very good cook, and as soon as he was old enough Paul took over. He does love to cook! If he hadn't become a dentist, I expect he would have been a chef.

'I don't get out much these days, my pins aren't what they used to be. Walking further than the end of the road lays me up for the rest of the day so I look forward to a bit of company, especially meeting new friends of my son's. I was very excited when Paul told me we were having a dinner guest tonight.' She then asked Steph keenly, 'Why don't you tell me about yourself?'

The last thing Steph wanted was to make public to this kindly lady the terrible life she was living, but neither did she want to lie.

Thankfully Paul popped his head around the door just then. It was apparent that while busying himself in the kitchen, he was also keeping an ear cocked to the conversation taking place in the room next door. 'Mother?'

Cissie looked across at him innocently. 'Yes, dear?'

He sighed, feigning annoyance with her. 'Now, Mother, Steph has come for a relaxing evening and some good food – not to be interrogated on her private life! I've already told you that our guest is a happily married woman, whose husband is working long hours at the moment, leaving her home alone most nights. We're just friends, nothing more. That right, Steph?'

She smiled gratefully at him for coming to her rescue, and nodded. She also realised that, just in case Cissie was seeing her as a possible candidate for a daughter-in-law, he was putting a stop to that, too.

But Cissie was still eyeing her shrewdly. 'Well, I've a feeling there's more to you than that, my dear, but as I've been warned not to *interrogate* you by my son then *I'd* better do the talking.' She then proceeded to regale Steph with some humorous stories about her teaching career while taking regular sips of sherry. Meanwhile delicious aromas were wafting through from the kitchen, making Steph feel quite hungry.

A short while later, Paul carried through a dish piled high with steaming hot creamy mashed potatoes and ordered them both to sit at the table while he brought through the rest of the food. He'd made a minced meat pie with the lightest of pastry, carrots, peas, and lashings of thick gravy. There was roly-poly pudding and home-made custard for afters. The food tasted as delicious as it smelled. When Steph told Paul as much, he lapped up the praise before ordering them both to return to their armchairs while he went off into the kitchen to make them all a pot of tea. He refused Steph's help with the clearing up.

It was with great reluctance that she finally announced she ought to be making tracks for home at just after ten. She didn't really want to go back, so relaxed did she feel in these lovely people's company, so warm and comfortable in the armchair, but she knew she was in danger of falling asleep which would be rude to her hosts. Paul would not hear of her catching the bus, would have driven her home himself had he not enjoyed several glasses of wine, and insisted on calling her a taxi and paying for it. Before she left both Cissie and Paul made her promise to come back again soon. Out of earshot of his mother, while escorting Steph out to the taxi, Paul made her promise again that if she should ever find herself in need of a friend, she would not hesitate to call him.

As the taxi ferried her home, Steph felt happier than she had for a long time. She had something she'd never had before: friends. She was no longer alone in the world.

Having just come from a house that had enveloped her in its welcoming warmth, she could not fail to notice the difference in her own. Despite the expensive furnishings, thick woollen carpets covering the floors and the warmth supplied by modern central heating, which few houses actually had yet, this house had no welcoming feel to it whatsoever. How could it when everyone who had ever lived here had been unhappy?

Despite checking around to make sure all was secure before she had gone out earlier that evening, Steph did the rounds again, just to double check before she went to bed. She'd gone into the lounge to ascertain that the fire guard was set securely around the fire. Although it had burned low there was still the danger of a stray spark doing some damage. Having done what she'd come in for, she turned around when a space on the wall at the side of the door caught her eye and halted her in her tracks.

She stared over at the wall, stupefied. A picture used to hang there. It hadn't been a masterpiece, just a landscape by a minor artist, but when the contents of the house had been valued as part of her father's estate, the painting had been priced at six hundred pounds, the amount it would cost to buy a small terraced house. It would be a fortune to some people, including Steph herself.

Where had the picture gone? It had been there at the weekend, she could remember dusting it. There didn't appear to be any sign of a break-in so it couldn't have been stolen. Then a thought occurred to her.

Had Jay removed the painting because he had found it offensive to look at? The evidence certainly pointed that way. She was angry at the thought. Pity she couldn't just remove *him*, she thought. She hoped, though, that he had handled the painting carefully when he had removed it, and also stored it properly as paintings were so easy to damage.

It wasn't until the next evening that she got an opportunity to ask him. Having put his dinner before him and sat down opposite, she said to him in a casual manner, 'Do you know what happened to the painting hanging behind the door in the lounge?'

Shovelling food into his mouth as though there was no tomorrow, Jay said shortly, 'Yes.'

'Where is it then?'

He shrugged. 'I've no idea where it is now.'

He was purposely talking in riddles. Taking a deep breath, she said evenly, 'But you said knew what had happened to it?'

Still shovelling in food, he snapped, 'You asked me if I knew what had happened to the painting and I said I did, but I've no idea where it is now.' He laid down his knife and fork and stared at her fixedly. 'Why don't you ask me in plain English what it is you want to know about that painting?'

Steph took another deep breath, forcing down her own deep annoyance. 'Did you remove it from the wall in the lounge?'

'Yes.'

'Why?'

There was a glint of amusement in his eyes when he told her, 'So I could sell it.'

She frowned. 'You did what? You had no right . . .'

'Like you had no right to commit adultery,' he cut her short. 'I told you before, in the eyes of the law what's yours is now mine.' He smirked at her. 'How else do you think I got the deposit for my car?' He rubbed his hands gleefully. 'Fifty smackers I got for that piece of old tat.'

Her jaw dropped. 'Fifty . . . that piece of old tat, as you call it, was valued at six hundred pounds!'

Jay's face screwed up in anger and he banged one fist down heavily on the table. 'That fucking liar at the second-hand shop made me believe he'd be lucky to make a couple of quid profit on it. I shan't use him again.'

His angry response to learning he'd been duped by a second-hand shop-owner made Steph stiffen in her chair, but common sense was screaming at her not to pursue this topic of conversation any further, if she didn't want to risk losing any more teeth. She decided to keep quiet. She was seething at Jay's nerve in selling off her family's valuables, but there was nothing she could do to stop him.

# CHAPTER
# TWENTY-TWO

Friday was an emotional day for Steph, her last working at the slaughter house. As yet she'd no idea where she would be on Monday. When she'd called in at the agency at lunchtime to hand in her time sheet and collect her wages, they'd said nothing suitable had come in for her but that they would contact her either at the abattoir or at home as soon as it did.

At intervals during the day, all the slaughtermen made a point of calling into the office to say their goodbyes to Steph, and before she left that evening Sam Jones presented her not only with a huge parcel containing a whole shoulder of pork and a topside of beef, but also a one-pound box of Cadbury's Dairy Milk that all the staff had contributed towards.

He left her in no doubt that should they ever require the services of an office temp again, he would request it was Steph that the agency sent. She decided not to tell them that very shortly she would be out of commission, due to the fact that she was expecting a baby. The agency still had no idea of her condition, and she felt the longer she could keep it from them, the better for her. Thankfully she wasn't showing any outward signs yet, though she knew it was only a matter of time before she did. What she was going to do when she was forced to give up work and would have to spend more time in Jay's company, she didn't care to think about.

On a Friday evening before catching the bus home, as a way of stretching out her housekeeping, she had taken to visiting the market as she had learned that the traders there sold off their perishables cheaply then.

By the time she arrived, many of the traders had already packed up and left, but thankfully there were still a few and she managed to obtain her supplies for the weekend a few shillings cheaper than she would have done earlier in the day. Weighed down with her heavy load, she was about to depart from the last stall she had visited when she recognised the voice of a customer.

Delighted, Steph proclaimed, 'Mrs Sanders! How lovely to see you.'

The other woman jerked around. She looked at Steph blankly for a moment before recognition struck and she exclaimed, 'Why, it's you, lovey! Oh, it's good to see you too.' Her smiled faded then to be replaced by a look of deep concern. 'I'm so very sorry for the financial mess your father left you and your mother in. I hope you're managing all right? I understood when it wasn't possible for you to keep me on any longer, and actually it's worked out fine for me. The place where I was doing the morning shift gave me evenings too and, to be honest, I doubt I'd have been able to stand working for your mother much longer. The pay's a bit better at my new place as well.'

Embarrassment clouded her face. 'Look, I . . . er . . . well, I'm obviously aware it's not been possible for you to pay me the week's money you owe me or you'd have done it by now. I'm managing all right, so I want you to know you're not to fret about it. At the moment your need for every penny is greater than mine, with all those debts your father left you to pay off.' Mystified, she shook her head. 'Fancy him turning out to be a gambler. I never would have thought it. He came across as such a pillar of society to me.

'Oh, yes, sorry, me duck,' she addressed the stall holder, who was trying to catch her attention and take his money. Having paid, Beryl Sanders turned her attention back to Steph. 'Best get off or I'll miss the next bus.' She patted the girl's arm. 'That husband of yours came across to me as a very nice young man. I'm sure you're going to be very happy together.'

She picked up her bags and was soon lost from Steph's view as she weaved her way through other late shoppers hoping to catch themselves a bargain.

Unaware of the quizzical looks she was receiving, with her brown carriers filled with shopping still stacked by her feet, Steph stared blankly into space, deep in troubled thought. The story Beryl Sanders had just told her certainly didn't match Jay's, though she had absolutely no reason to doubt what Beryl had said. The woman had had no idea she was going to bump into Steph in the market that evening and it would take an expert liar to come up with such an elaborate tale. Steph heaved a deep sigh. Jay had cheated Beryl of money that was rightfully hers, and had also blackened Gerald Mortimer's name. On top of that, he'd asked Steph herself to reimburse him for the wages he'd said he'd paid Beryl. Was there no end to his deception?

Later that evening, having done her chores, Steph was just about to retire into the lounge and watch an hour or so of television before she went to bed when her eyes fell on the calendar pinned to the back of the kitchen door. A bewildered expression settled on her face as she looked at it. It was the middle of December. Her mother had been gone nearly three months. Just where was she holed up? Must be with someone affluent as they'd have had to kit her out with a new wardrobe and toiletries, and that didn't come cheap. It was very remiss of Ursula not to let Steph know where she was, but typical of her as well. She wondered if any of her mother's friends had heard from her yet? They had promised to inform her if they did but maybe they had forgotten. She'd fetch her mother's address book from her room and give them all a call.

Abigail Harvey was the first name in the book. The woman was in the middle of a dinner party and wasn't pleased at being called away from her guests. After Steph had announced who she was and why she was calling, the woman snapped back at her, 'Look, as I told your husband the several times he's called me now, I haven't heard a peep from Ursula. God only knows where she is. If I hear from her, I'll let you know.

'Oh, I can tell you that Geraldine Doubleday is very upset with her. She was supposed to be going on a cruise as Ursula's companion in the New Year, and because no one has heard a word from her, Geraldine isn't sure whether the trip is still on or not and she's been invited to spend the winter on the Riviera with other friends and of course she wants to accept but if she does and Ursula turns up expecting her to be accompanying her . . . well, you can imagine,

I'm sure, that Geraldine will be having strong words with Ursula when she *does* show her face again.

'Now, as I told you, if I hear from her I'll let you know. In the meantime, will you and your husband kindly stop pestering me? Oh, and all Ursula's other friends too – they're constantly complaining about your husband calling them.' With that she hung up.

Steph frowned as she replaced the receiver in its cradle. So Jay had been telephoning around her mother's friends to check if they'd had word from her. But she would have thought it would be in his interests for Ursula to stay away. Surely he realised that once she returned he would find himself with a fight on his hands for control of the allowance. And Ursula wouldn't let him get away with treating this house like a hotel, the way he was doing, or put up with his surly and sarcastic manner.

Then another thought struck Steph. If Jay had been checking up on Ursula in this way, he would have needed her address book to obtain her friends' telephone numbers. So Steph's mind hadn't been playing tricks on her. The book *had* been moved. She couldn't imagine why he was so keen to trace Ursula, but at least he seemed to draw the line at selling *her* possessions, which Steph supposed was something to be grateful for.

\* \* \*

A sudden blare of deafening music had Steph sitting bolt upright in bed, dazed and confused. The music was so loud she was convinced that somehow the radio in her room had come on full blast of its own accord. Her radio stood on top of the chest of drawers. She looked over but no lights were illuminating the tuning strip. The music was not coming from the radio. Then it struck her that it was originating from downstairs, and mingled with it she could also hear a number of raucous voices.

Jay had brought some people home with him and they were having a party!

Fury erupted within Steph then. For him to feel he was at liberty to invite strangers into her home was bad enough, but he'd done so while knowing she was asleep upstairs in bed. He was showing a complete lack of regard for her in allowing this level of noise.

Then, above the music and the voices, the loud crash of breaking glass reverberated.

The revellers were smashing up her home!

Steph scrambled out of bed and hurriedly removed her nightdress. She put on a pair of slacks and jumper, then went downstairs, her aim to put a stop to the revellers breaking anything else.

The hall was thronged with people of about her own age, milling about together, all with drinks in their hands, some entwined around each other, dancing or kissing. By the glazed look in some people's eyes, Steph suspected it wasn't just drink they were high on.

Pushing her way through, she took a look inside the lounge first. The first thing that caught her eye was the fact that the drinks cabinet was open. All the bottles were out, a couple of empty ones lying on their side, dripping their last dregs on to the polished shelf. Then she spotted what else was going on in here and gasped in shock. A couple were lying on the sofa, one on top of the other. The man's hand was kneading the bare breast of the woman underneath him who was groaning in pleasure. Several other couples, also in varying states of undress and very apparently in stages of foreplay, also lay about. Steph stared at them all, appalled. To her, making love was a private matter between two consenting people, not for public display – and certainly not in her lounge. And if this was going on in here, she dreaded to think what was taking place in the other rooms.

Then she saw what had caused the smashing sound she had heard. Someone had knocked over the lamp that had stood on a table beside the sofa. It was in smithereens. Its heavy base was made of crystal and the shade had been in the style of a chandelier. It had been her paternal grandmother's, and was a family heirloom. Did these interlopers have no regard for other people's property!

The blaring music was coming from a Pretty Things LP on the record player. As she went over to it Steph saw that all her father's records, housed in the unit alongside, were scattered higgledy-piggledy over the floor, as though someone had gone through them and chucked each down in disgust on not finding what they were looking for. Reaching inside the cabinet, she lifted the arm of the player off the record. The sudden silence was deafening. She turned and addressed the room. 'All of you ... get out of my house. Now.'

Several of the couples were so engrossed in what they were up to they neither noticed that the music had suddenly stopped nor heard Steph order them to leave, but continued with what they were doing. The rest of them were looking very surprised.

Coming from the hall were loud grumbles of protest at the sudden halting of the music and several people had peered into the lounge to investigate why it had stopped.

'I said, all of you, get out of my house ...'

Before Steph could finish a vice-like grip clamped her arm and yanked her hard. She found herself stumbling along behind the person who was dragging her out of the room and through to the kitchen. People en route stared at her with glazed eyes but did nothing to help. Outside in the garden, she was thrust up against the wall beside the back door.

The fumes of alcohol from Jay's breath almost choked her as, with his face pushed into hers, one hand clamping her neck, he roared, 'What do you think you were doing, ordering my friends out?'

If he was out to frighten her, he was succeeding, but Steph was damned if she would give him the satisfaction of letting him know it. Inwardly she was quaking as she knew what he was capable of doing to her, but outwardly she remained calm. 'Those so-called friends of yours are wrecking the house. A valuable lamp has already been smashed and I'm not about to turn a blind eye to any more breakages. Nor do I like the thought of an orgy going on in my lounge.'

He hissed at her, 'You smug cow! My friends are just having fun. I invited them all back here, and if you dare show me up in front of them I'll give you another taster of what I can do. Only it won't just be a smack in the mouth you get this time, but a broken bone! And that goes for any other time I invite people back in the future. You listening to me?'

Steph gulped. She had no doubt he meant what he'd said. But she wasn't going to show him he was terrifying her.

At her lack of response, his grip on her throat tightened and he harshly reiterated, 'I said, are you listening to me?'

Icily she responded, 'I can hardly fail to as you're

shouting so loud in my ear.' As soon as the words were out of her mouth she stiffened and closed her eyes, waiting for the impact of his fist at her insolent response.

Much to her surprise and relief it did not happen. Instead she felt the sudden relaxing of his grip and heard an unfamiliar voice slurring, 'Ohhh . . . so who's this then, Jay?'

Steph opened her eyes to see that a man had joined them, drink in one hand, cigarette in the other. He was very drunk. His bleary eyes were fixed on her.

Jay smirked at Steph as he grabbed her by the shoulder and pushed her in front of the newcomer, saying, 'She's a slag, that's who she is, mate. If you fancy a shag, she's not fussy who she goes with.' He gave Steph a push on the shoulder that made her topple on to the man. He automatically put his cigarette in his mouth and caught hold of her arm. Jay was continuing, 'Be my guest, mate. And enjoy yourself.'

Then he turned away from them and disappeared inside the house.

Steph couldn't believe that her own husband, no matter how little he felt for her now, was actually offering her to his friend to have sex with!

Before she could stop him, the man knocked back the remains of the drink in his glass, lobbed the glass into a shrub close by, along with the stub of his cigarette, and pushed her back against the wall. He started rubbing himself against her while wrenching up her jumper.

Steph fought to push him away from her, bellowing, 'Get off me, you beast!'

He took no notice.

It was apparent that drastic measures were required. Lifting her knee, she brought it up forcefully into his groin.

He yelped out in shock and excruciating pain, letting go of her while stumbling backwards.

Seizing her chance, she was already through the back door and into the house and did not hear him yell out, 'You fucking whore!'

The music was blaring out again. With her head down, Steph weaved her way through the revellers and back up to her room. Thankfully she did not see Jay. In the safety of her room, she shut the door and pulled off her slacks and jumper. She was just about to take off her bra and pants and put her nightdress back on when she jumped in shock as the bedroom door burst open and a young man and woman stumbled in. They froze on spotting Steph, then the woman burst into giggles and said, 'Oh, sorry, we thought this room was free.'

Both snorting with mirth, they stumbled back out, leaving the door wide open.

Steph shot over to the door and shut it, then dashed

to the chair by her dressing table. She tilted it so she could wedge the back underneath the door knob, to stop any more intruders invading her room. Thankfully there was a good distance between the houses on the street, but she still worried that the neighbours would hear the noise and call the police. Though at least if they did, Jay would be forced to send everyone home. After putting on her nightdress, she crawled back under the covers and pulled them over her head, trying to block out the noise coming from below. She failed miserably and lay there sobbing.

The neighbours were obviously turning a blind eye or were miraculously managing to sleep through it, because it wasn't until after five in the morning that the music ceased. Steph suspected that it was only because everyone downstairs had either gone home or fallen into a drink-induced slumber and there'd been no one left to replace the record. It was only then that the relief of sleep engulfed her.

# CHAPTER
# TWENTY-THREE

When she dragged herself out of bed the next morning, threw on her slacks and jumper and ventured down the stairs, she wasn't surprised to find the chaos that greeted her.

She was staring around at the mess, not knowing where to make a start on clearing it up, when a faint tap sounded on the front door.

She went to open it and to her pleasant surprise found Paul on her doorstep. He looked at her in concern. 'You look . . . well, did you not sleep last night, Steph?'

She sighed as she stood aside to allow him entry. 'No, I didn't. It's lovely to see you, though. You will excuse the mess?'

'Since you're asking me in, I trust the coast is clear? Only I wouldn't like to be the cause of any trouble between you and your husband. I just wanted to check how you were, that's why I've called by.'

Then Paul stopped short as he saw the state of the hall, littered with plates where people had helped themselves from the fridge and pantry. Dropped food had been carelessly trampled into the carpet, and discarded glasses filled the air with the stench of stale drink.

'You weren't joking when you asked me to excuse the mess, were you? If this is the state of the hall, I dread to think what the rest of the rooms look like. Had a party in here last night?'

She was having to fight back tears.

'Jay invited a few friends of his back.'

Paul raised his eyebrows. 'Very disrespectful friends, judging by the state they've left this place in. I won't say what I think of your husband for allowing his friends to treat your house this way. Still in bed, is he?'

She shrugged. 'I presume so. I haven't seen him this morning, but then I've only just got up myself as the music was blaring until after five and I didn't get any sleep until then.'

Paul's eyes narrowed. 'And you in your condition! The man is beneath contempt. He should be treating you like glass now you're carrying his baby.'

She sighed heavily and reminded him, 'That's the trouble, though, Jay still doesn't accept that he *is* the father of the baby I'm carrying. That's why he's being like he is with me.'

Paul looked sadly at her and laid a sympathetic hand on her arm. 'Let's hope he soon finds someone who can offer him more than he's getting here. Hopefully he'll move out then and leave you in peace to raise your child.'

Steph dearly hoped so too. The trouble was that she couldn't see Jay meeting anyone in a hurry who could match or better what he was getting here . . . a weekly allowance, a lovely home from which he came and went as he pleased, and Steph herself to do his washing, cook his meals and clean up after him.

'I've an hour or so to kill. Allow me to lend you a hand cleaning up. Don't worry, if His Nibs comes down and catches me here, I shall tell him I was one of the guests partying last night and felt it only right to stay and help clear up the mess we all made. I should think it's most unlikely he'll remember everyone who was here. I shall be a friend of a friend.'

Steph was so fatigued from her own terrible night and the scale of the clean-up operation she could have fallen on Paul and hugged him to death in gratitude.

'I'll gladly accept, on one condition.'

'Oh?'

'The boss of the abattoir where I was temping the last two weeks presented me with a whole shoulder of pork and a huge joint of beef when I left yesterday. Pick one of the joints to take home with you. That's fair exchange, isn't it?'

He grinned. 'Only if you'll come and join me and Mother in eating it?'

She smiled appreciatively. 'I'd really like that.'

'Right, I'll make a start in the lounge. I trust you keep the cleaning materials under the sink in the kitchen?' He headed off there then a thought seemed to occur to him. 'Er . . . I won't be offended if you turn me down, but I've two tickets that I bought months ago for a performance of *Madam Butterfly* at the De Montfort Hall next Thursday evening. Mother isn't fond of opera and I . . . er . . . wondered if you'd like to accompany me, save the ticket going to waste?'

Steph realised the tickets had originally been bought for himself and her father. 'I've never been to an opera before so I'm not sure if I like it either, but I'd like to find out.'

Paul smiled in delight. 'That's a date then.'

Jay finally came down, naked under his striped towelling dressing gown, at just after five o'clock. He was in a foul mood. Finding Steph in the kitchen peeling potatoes for chips, he snarled at her, 'Think it was funny putting the vacuum around while I was trying to sleep, did you?'

He was standing just inside the kitchen door, several yards from her, but even at that distance he made her skin crawl, she hated him so much. He was obviously spoiling for a fight and Steph felt it wise not to annoy him further.

'I apologise. I didn't realise the noise would carry upstairs. I won't do it again while you're in bed. Are you hungry? I'm doing chips and pork chops for dinner. I hope that's all right for you?'

She inwardly sighed with relief that her ploy to thwart him had worked when he issued a grunt then turned and walked out. She heard him return upstairs and slam shut the bathroom door, then the rumble of the hot water tank, so she knew he was running a bath.

# CHAPTER
# TWENTY-FOUR

I t was just like normal for Steph.
Christmas Day and she was alone.

Well, not entirely, she supposed. Jay must be up in bed, sleeping off the effects of his night out. Unusually, he hadn't roused her when he'd come in. She had been up early to prepare the Christmas dinner, working as quietly as she could so as not to wake him.

Sitting at the kitchen table, nursing a cup of tea, she glanced over at the clock on the wall. It was now a quarter to two. She then looked worriedly over at the pans on the cooker, their lids tightly in place in an effort to keep the contents hot. Jay had informed her that he expected his Christmas dinner to be put on the table at one as that had always been the tradition when his mother had been alive and he intended to keep it up.

Her parents had never believed in decorating the

house to make it look festive. Well, why would they bother as neither of them was usually at home to enjoy it. But when she was of age, Steph had always put up a small tree in the lounge. The tinsel tree itself was about as old as she was and very much the worse for wear, as were the decorations that adorned it, but it brought cheer to Steph and she would sit in the evening with the lamps off, delighting in the twinkling fairy lights on its silver branches.

At least her parents had marked the occasion by giving her small tokens, usually jewellery and money to buy herself something with, but her husband hadn't bothered. Well, what did you buy a wife you were convinced had cheated on you and tried to pass the result of her affair off as yours? In turn, what did a wife buy a husband she had once adored but now despised after his vicious treatment of her?

Steph's thoughts turned to her mother then. Was she now in Scotland as she had planned to be with her friends, celebrating the festive season in style, or with her new benefactor? She certainly must have one or she'd have been back home weeks ago, claiming her share of the allowance. Wherever she was and whoever she was with, Ursula obviously had had no thought at all for her daughter or she would at least have sent her a card or given her a telephone call, to let her know all was well with her.

Another thought occurred to Steph. Maybe her

mother's close brush with death had resulted in her realising her own mortality, and therefore she was grabbing at any opportunity that came her way now. Though Steph wondered what opportunity could have presented itself between her mother checking herself out of the hospital and arriving back here. Well, she would have to show up one day as her private documents and passport were in a drawer of her dressing table and she'd need those if she were to marry again or go abroad.

Steph took a sip of her lukewarm tea and a picture of Paul rose in her mind. She smiled at the thought of him. No one would believe it if she told them how their friendship had come about.

In contrast to her husband's behaviour. Paul was ever kind and thoughtful. Because of his sexuality she knew his friendship to be of the genuine kind, he'd no hidden agenda, and so she felt safe with him and relaxed in his company.

She had immensely enjoyed their outing to the opera two weeks ago. It wasn't really her cup of tea but Paul had proved the perfect escort. Since then she had been out with him several times, for a drink, a meal, and to the cinema. He had a passion for visiting stately homes, apparently, and had asked Steph if she'd like to go with him on a coach trip in the New Year. She had told him she'd be delighted to, and very much looked forward to it now. She'd never been on a coach trip before, never had anyone to go on one with, and it would be a new experience for her.

Paul and his mother would be eating their dinner now, packed like sardines around a table in his aunt's house, along with all her family, fifteen of them, give or take. Since Paul's father had died some years back, Cissie's sister had insisted they both come to her for the day. Paul had managed to escape to be with Gerald, celebrating the day together quietly in their flat, but not this year. His aunt insisted they all wear paper hats and Steph chuckled at a vision this conjured up of Paul in his. He had told her that as usual he'd be quizzed unmercifully on whether he'd met a woman yet, and as usual would tell them that they'd be the first to know when he did.

Steph was very aware that it would be a difficult day for him, so soon after the death of the man he had thought to see out his days with. She sincerely hoped that he had managed to push his hurt to the back of his mind and that he and his mother were having fun. She was envious of them, really. How wonderful it must be to belong to a loving family who shared high days and holidays together; were there for each other all year round, in fact. Steph felt she would give anything to live like that, especially now with a child to consider.

She looked down at her stomach and rested her hand gently on it. She was over three months pregnant, still not showing enough to broadcast her condition to the outside world and thankfully able to wear her normal clothes, albeit they were getting tighter on her. But soon she would be showing and that was when she had to hope that Jay would allow her some money for maternity clothes. She would also find out what the agency's policies were on employing pregnant women.

Since she had left the slaughter house she'd had two different placements, none of them as enjoyable. Christmas Eve had seen her coming to the end of a week of filing for an insurance company. The permanent staff had all been in a festive mood and had brought in mince pies and sweets to share out. She hadn't been included in the present-giving, though, and it was at times like that it was brought home to her that she was more of a permanent outsider.

She did wish she could get to know another pregnant woman; she wasn't fussy about their age, just someone she could discuss her condition with and share her worries. Hopefully they'd be wiser in these matters than she was and could put her mind at rest that her pregnancy fears and what she was experiencing physically were normal.

Steph lifted her eyes to the clock again. It was now two-thirty. A worried frown creased her face. There was only so long food could be kept hot before it began to deteriorate. She was still honing her cooking skills and, having tasted the turkey, was dismayed to find it was rather dry against what Beryl Sanders used to produce. Steph hadn't a clue why. She just hoped Jay didn't notice.

Despite voicing to her his expectation of the full festive fare, he had refused to give her extra house-keeping, telling her his own mother had managed to put on a spread by saving for weeks beforehand and that was what he was expecting her to do. But he didn't give her enough to have any spare towards Christmas extras so she hadn't the means to buy such luxury items as cranberry sauce and Christmas crackers. But through her newly acquired bargaining skills, Steph had managed to buy a small turkey at a knockdown price as it only had one leg, plus the stuffing, and a small ready-made Peek Frean Christmas pudding that the Home & Colonial were selling off cheap just before closing on Christmas Eve. To accompany the turkey she had cooked sprouts and carrots, roast and mashed potatoes, and thick gravy using the turkey juices and some cornflour to thicken it with. She proposed to make sandwiches with some of the leftover turkey, and a pie with the remains for tomorrow.

There was nothing else for it. She would have to go and wake Jay or the vegetables at least would be un-eatable and she had no spare to do fresh.

Outside his room she pressed her ear to the door and listened. She could hear no movement from within. Taking a deep breath, she tapped lightly on the door.

She received no response and tapped again, louder this time. Still no response. Taking a deep breath, she knocked, opened the door and stepped inside.

To her utter surprise she saw Jay's bed was empty. It hadn't even been slept in. No wonder she hadn't heard him come in. What an idiot she had been. If only she'd thought to check if his car was outside, she'd have known long ago he hadn't come back last night.

Anger swamped Steph. She didn't care where he had stayed, but couldn't he at least have had the decency to be back in time for the dinner he'd insisted she prepare?

The sound of the front door slamming shut made her jump. So he'd finally come home! She retreated out of the room and had just shut the door behind her when she spotted him advancing down the landing.

'Caught you snooping in my room! Find what you were looking for?' he hissed at her.

She raised her chin defiantly and looked him in the eye. He stank of stale beer and cigarette smoke and had the pallor and heavy eyes of someone who'd had little sleep. His clothes were not crumpled, though, so he clearly hadn't slept in them.

'No, you did not catch me snooping. You said you wanted dinner on the table at one and it's now after two-thirty. I thought you were still sleeping so came to wake you up before the food ruins completely.'

He smirked at her. 'As you saw, then, I didn't sleep here last night.'

The look he was giving her told her he was willing her to ask just where he had slept, but she didn't care. Whoever it was with, they were welcome to him as far as she was concerned. 'I'll go and serve the dinner,' she told him, moving past him to head for the stairs.

'Don't bother for me,' she heard him say. 'I've not long had a big breakfast. You can make me something when I get up later, before I go out again.'

The next afternoon Steph answered a summons on the front door and to her delight found Paul on her doorstep. He whispered to her, 'I saw His nibs's car wasn't parked by the garage, so I take it the coast is clear?'

She stood aside to allow him entry. 'I'm glad to say it is. He could come home at any time, though.'

As Paul took off his coat and hung it on the stand, he said to her, 'Oh, taken to staying out at night, has he?'

'It's a relief to me, if you want the truth. When he doesn't come home he doesn't disturb my sleep. And knowing he's out, I don't have to creep around the house in case I should make a noise that wakes him.'

She could tell by the look Paul was giving her that he wished he could do something to ease her situation, but it wouldn't ever get better unless Jay decided to go.

'Well, don't worry if he comes back while I'm here and accuses me of being the father of your baby. I'll tell him I'm the new vicar, visiting my parishioners to introduce myself.'

It was the first time Steph had laughed for weeks.

They both sat down with some tea in the lounge and he entertained her with details of his Christmas Day. He didn't mention what a trial it had been to him, how every moment he'd missed the man he had loved so dearly, but he knew he didn't have to. Steph understood. When he'd finished Paul automatically asked her, 'So how did your day go? No trouble from *him*, I hope?'

She knew Paul would be distressed for her if he learned how abysmally Jay had treated her. But, in fact, she had had a better day without him around than she would have had in his company. 'It was a pleasant enough day for me,' Steph replied evasively.

Paul looked relieved to hear it. Reaching inside his trouser pocket, he pulled out a folded piece of newspaper. 'I spotted this in the *Mercury* on Christmas Eve,' he said, handing it to her. 'Straw's Coaches are taking bookings for a trip to Chatsworth on January the twelfth, a Saturday. It's a house I've wanted to visit for a while. Great historic interest. It's also got beautiful gardens even at this time of year. Do you fancy going?'

Oh, anything other than the mundane for Steph to look forward to. She very much wanted to say yes, but due to Jay's tight grip on their finances she had no money to spare. She couldn't let Paul pay for her again.

He could see what was going through her mind. 'You can treat us both to a cup of tea and sticky bun in the cafeteria.'

How could she refuse an offer like that? Steph smiled. 'Then I'd love to come,' she told him.

He beamed in delight. 'I'll book two seats.' He looked a bit awkward when he added, 'You'll probably be able to tell your condition by then so if you don't think it's impertinent of me, I shall book the tickets in the names of Mr and Mrs ... what do you think ... Smith?'

Oh, he was such a thoughtful man! Jay had been like him before he'd turned against her. Steph chuckled. 'And what if we forget, and we're being called out by the tour guide, and she thinks we're ignoring her?'

'Mmm,' Paul mused. 'Well, I suppose we'd better go with Connor and then it's just me to remember I have a new name for the day. I'm really looking forward to this trip. I shall pack us a picnic. Anything Baby Connor is giving you a passion for?'

'Not at the moment, but I'll let you know if he or she is by then.'

# CHAPTER
# TWENTY-FIVE

Steph raised her glass of lemonade in the air and said aloud, 'Happy New Year', simultaneously with Kenneth McKellar and his Scottish compatriots who were helping the English welcome in the New Year, courtesy of the BBC. She then lowered her glass and took a sip, wondering what 1966 was going to bring her. Whatever it did, could it be any worse than what she had endured during the latter months of 1965? It couldn't be. Could it?

She wondered how Paul was feeling. After putting on a brave face at Christmas he couldn't face partying at New Year, even though he'd been invited to several dos by family and friends. His mother was going to her neighbour's for a knees-up but he'd opted to sit quietly at home and reflect on his time with Gerald. He hoped by doing so he could begin to lay his lover's ghost to rest and start to build a future without him. Steph sincerely hoped his plan worked for him. Part of her still felt guilty that she was not grieving for the loss of her father like Paul was. The truth was, she wasn't missing him at all.

It had crossed her mind that she just might receive a drunken telephone call from her mother but as the minutes ticked by and a quarter past midnight struck, she gave up on that hope.

Steph gave a yawn. She'd stayed up to see the New Year in, hoping her toasting of it would bring her some luck for a change. Now she had, she was going to bed in the hope she'd be so deep in sleep that for once Jay would not disturb her when he came home. Getting up, she automatically went over to the table to switch off the lamp. She was surprised by the empty space where it used to stand. Of course, Jay's friends had broken it. Besides that, he had sold several ornaments, some pieces of porcelain and a silver tray, saying it was only right as she wouldn't be bringing in any money over Christmas, since no one took on temps then.

In a very short time she wasn't going to be bringing a wage into this house at all. What was he going to do to make up the difference then? Force her to get a job where she could take the baby with her or systematically go through the house selling everything off until there was nothing left?

She couldn't turn a blind eye to what he was doing.

Jay would laugh at her if she politely asked him to stop, but she would try to save as many of the family belongings as she could by asking Paul, the next time she saw him, if he could store some of them for her for the foreseeable future. If it was at all possible, she felt sure he would agree.

The screech of tyres on gravel and then a car roaring at speed down the drive had her running to the window to see what was going on. What she saw made Steph's heart sink.

Jay was falling out of his car. Spilling out of it too were five other people, all very inebriated by the looks of them. A couple of scantily clad young women were wearing silly hats on their head and blowing paper horns. One of the young men grabbed hold of one of the girls and she willingly allowed him to take her round the back of the garage, it was obvious what for. Then another car hurtled up the drive, coming to a squealing halt behind Jay's. Several more people spilled out of that, all clearly in a party mood.

Steph wasn't going to get much sleep tonight.

# CHAPTER
# TWENTY-SIX

Steph smiled down at her stomach as she gently rested a hand on it, giving it a tender rub. Over the past week her condition had started to become obvious. Her once flat stomach had a roundness to it, her thickening waist making it difficult for her to fasten up her skirts. Her breasts were swelling, too, starting to overspill her bras. Like it or not, Jay was soon going to have to give her the money to buy a couple of maternity outfits. Also she would have to tell the agency of her pregnancy before they heard via the firms she was temping for.

At lunchtime today a woman she had been working beside doing a week of clerical duties for a shoe importer had been eating an egg and cress sandwich. The smell wafting from it had caused a wave of nausea to wash over Steph and sent her dashing for the lavatory where she had been violently sick. On returning to her desk, her working companion, a mother herself, had looked at her knowingly but thankfully hadn't said anything.

Her next placement was at the Royal Infirmary as an appointments clerk in the Eye Clinic, filling in for the permanent person who'd gone off sick. This could be her chance. It was past time that she went to a doctor and had her pregnancy officially confirmed so she could start her ante-natal care.

Up to now she'd experienced no evidence that there was a baby growing inside her apart from the fact that her periods had stopped, but her expanding body, coupled with the incident at work yesterday, had made her realise that soon she would be responsible for another human life. To her amazement, she found she already had feelings of love towards the child growing inside her, not caring what sex her baby was, just desperate for it to be healthy. She felt sure that although Jay was denying his part in bringing life to this child, once he saw it, he would understand how wrong he had been and want to be a father to it. For the child's sake, Steph would have to be willing to forgive his vile treatment of her.

As soon as she'd arrived home she had found Jay waiting for her in the hall as usual, his hand outstretched, that glint in his eye warning her not to resist. The sight of him had disgusted her. Dressed in rumpled pyjama bottoms, hair all tousled, smelling of stale sweat, it was apparent he'd been in bed most of the day while she had been toiling. As soon as she had done his bidding and been handed back the paltry amount he allowed her for housekeeping, he returned to his room. Not a word passed between them.

Steph had gone into the kitchen and found he'd left his usual mess for her to clear up after making himself his breakfast and lunch. It was more annoying than ever today as she wanted to get through dinner as quickly as possible, so she could do the washing tonight before her coach trip with Paul the next day.

She prepared to make a start when she heard footsteps coming down the stairs. Jay would know she hadn't had time to do the meal yet so she hoped his destination was the lounge, to watch television and leave her in peace to get on with it. She was about to turn on the tap when she felt a presence behind her. Turning round, her jaw dropped in astonishment at the sight of the young woman who'd just entered. Her hair was all tousled, smudged make up smearing her very attractive face, and over her otherwise naked body she was wearing the rumpled shirt Steph had seen on Jay when he had gone out last night.

Spotting Steph, the young woman shot her a superior look. 'You must be the woman who does for Jay? Well, I take it you are because he just told me to tell the woman downstairs to get the dinner sharpish. Oh, and he said for me to tell you to book me a taxi as I need to get home so I'm ready for when he comes calling for me at eight. You're to pay for it too.' Then she saw the clock on the wall and pulled a worried face. 'Oh, God, is that the time! The clock on Jay's bedside table says it's only a quarter to four. He obviously hasn't wound it up. I need to be home before my mam because if she sees I'm still dressed in the clothes I went out in last night . . . God, will I be for it!'

She gave a little grin then. 'Mind you, what sensible girl would turn down the chance of getting together with a man like Jay? Obviously does well for himself, judging by the money he was splashing about last night and this place he lives in.' When Steph didn't respond she snapped, 'Well, chop-chop. Tell that taxi to get here double quick.'

With that she turned and rushed back up the stairs, leaving Steph staring after her.

She couldn't believe that Jay was taking his revenge to new heights. Not only bringing that woman back to Steph's own house to have sex with her, but leading her to believe that his wife was his char lady!

And she had thought he couldn't hurt and degrade her any more than he had already. How wrong she'd been.

The walls of the house suddenly seemed to be closing in on Steph. She felt like a caged animal, unable to open the trap and make her escape. Her legs began to buckle beneath her. She turned around and clutched the sink for support. It was then that she spotted the bread knife. Her eyes fixed on it. All she had to do was go upstairs and plunge it into Jay, then she'd be rid of him for good. The next thing she knew she had the knife in her hand, gripping the handle ready for action. Then realisation of what she was about to do hit her and she dropped the knife as if it had scalded her hand, sending it clattering on the floor. She knew she needed to distance herself. Spinning on her heel, she made for the back door, yanked it open and fled out into the dark garden, not stopping until she'd run out of breath.

When she realised where she was, she was not surprised. The well had always been her place of sanctuary. She sank down on the edge of it, not caring for once that the stones were crumbling in places, and cradled her head in her hands. A few months ago she had thought she'd have her work cut out marrying spoiled, egotistical William. In fact, life with him would have proved a joy compared to life with Jay.

'Oh, William,' she uttered. 'Why did you have to go and die?'

Lowering her arms, she peered down into the inky depths of the well. How easy it would be for her to join William and her father by throwing herself down it. Trouble was, it wasn't just her own life she had to consider any longer. She was responsible for another . . . the child she was carrying. When she was a child, she used to come here and ask the fairies to help her. Too late for that now, she thought in despair.

She jerked up her head as she heard an angry voice shouting from a distance. It belonged to Jay. 'Where's that taxi you were supposed to be ordering? Why is the dinner not on? Where are you, you stupid bitch? Fucking showing me up in front of my friend . . . well, you're going to regret that.'

If she returned to the house now she couldn't trust herself not to pick up the knife and do her worst with it. Jay knew about her place of sanctuary and might guess she was here. He'd just warned her what to expect when she next came face to face with him. Either way she needed to get away from him for a while, to calm herself down, steel herself for what he would dish out to her when they met up again.

Heedless of the fact that a bitter wind was whipping up, the clouds above threatening rain and that she had no coat on, Steph found her way to the tradesmen's entrance and slipped through it. Hugging her arms around her, she put down her head and walked along the mud path that split the house from the boundary wall of the one next door, until she arrived in the street.

Then on and on she went, with no idea where she

was going, just knowing she wasn't yet ready to face what she knew awaited her back at the house.

She had no idea she had entered a park or was sitting on a bench, was so cold she couldn't feel her own hands or feet, until she jumped in shock at the touch of a hand on her shoulder and heard a deep voice saying, 'It's time to leave now, lovey. It's just coming up to eight and I'm locking the gates in a couple of minutes. I'd hurry if I was you. It's not very well lit in here as it is, but it'll be as black as a coal hole when the lights automatically go out at five past eight.'

Steph managed a brief smile of acknowledgement. It was eight o'clock, was it? She had no idea just where she was exactly, but by the time she got back Jay would hopefully have given up on her and gone out. No doubt he'd be planning to punish her later. Well, he would have to wait because she was going to make sure he couldn't enter her room when he came home. She would wedge the back of the chair under the knob to prevent him from doing so, and she was going to be out all day tomorrow on her coach trip with Paul which she was still determined to enjoy. Hopefully by the time she arrived home afterwards Jay would have gone out for the night again. With a bit of luck she might not see him now until she got home from work on Monday evening.

She rose, preparing to take her leave, then froze

rigid. The park-keeper was over at the bench opposite hers, addressing what looked to Steph to be a tramp lying on it with a ragged blanket covering their body. She couldn't see their face as the park-keeper was blocking her view, but she certainly recognised the voice of that tramp.

'Please, just turn a blind eye to me tonight. I've nowhere else to go.'

The keeper turned and shot a look at Steph, giving a shrug. 'Bloody winos think they can use my park as a place to bed down for the night. Well, I run a respectable place for people like yerself to enjoy, not a doss house. As this dirty devil is about to find out.'

He turned back to face the ragged creature on the bench and made to forcibly drag it away but was stopped short by Steph crying out, 'Leave her alone!'

Next thing he knew Steph was elbowing him out of the way so she could crouch down to address the figure on the bench. 'Mother?' she said tentatively.

The park-keeper stared down at her, astounded. Had he really heard that respectably dressed young woman, albeit she wasn't exactly dressed for this bitter weather, addressing the vile creature on the bench as *Mother*?

Steph, though, was oblivious to the fact that she had shocked the park-keeper and to the stomach-churning smell wafting up from the figure on the bench. She was far too intent on confirming that underneath the grime ingrained into her skin from lack of washing, under the mass of matted hair, it was most definitely her own mother looking wildly back at her. Had Steph not recognised her voice or seen through the caked dirt, though, she would have known the coat Ursula was wearing. It might be filthy but it was definitely the one she had taken to the hospital for her mother to wear home.

Before she could stop her, though, and much to Steph's surprise, Ursula had pushed her hard on the shoulder, toppling her backwards to land awkwardly on the path. She hurried away, still clutching the ragged piece of blanket and her battered handbag, heading for the park gates.

With the bewildered park-keeper looking on, Steph jumped up and rushed after Ursula, calling out, 'Mother, it's me, Stephanie! Don't you recognise me? Mother! Mother!'

She caught up with Ursula just as she passed through the gates. Grabbing her arm, she pulled her to a halt, crying out, 'Mother, it's me, your daughter Stephanie.'

To her absolute shock, Ursula responded frenziedly, 'I'm not stupid, of course I know who you are, but you mustn't tell him you've seen me! You *mustn't*. He'll not stop until he's killed me. Now leave me alone!' she cried, desperately fighting to shake herself free of Steph's grip.

But Steph wouldn't let go. What was her mother babbling on about? Who did she think was trying to kill her? Then the truth dawned. The doctor at the hospital had been wrong in his diagnosis. That knock to her mother's head had caused much more than mild concussion, it had somehow disturbed her mind. She obviously believed her husband was still alive and out to do away with her, and that was why she had signed herself out of the hospital, choosing to live rough rather than with the man she still believed to be alive and for some reason out to kill her.

Steph grabbed both of her mother's arms and fixed her with her eyes. 'He's dead, Mother, don't you remember?'

Ursula gazed back in confusion. 'Dead! He's dead? Really dead? But how could I remember when I couldn't possibly have known? How could I when I haven't been around?' Her relief was plain to see, then her face contorted in fear again as she asked Steph, 'Did he ... did he say anything to you before he died?'

She shook her head. 'I wasn't there when it happened. Such as what, though?'

'Nothing, nothing.' Ursula's relief was again very apparent. 'How did he die then? Accident, was it, him being so young? I expect it was.'

Her father had been in his mid-forties, not so young to Steph, but she supposed it was to someone of her mother's age. Ursula was well aware of how her husband had met his end, but nevertheless Steph told her. 'He was flagging down a passing car to get help to fix a puncture. The police told us he was killed by a hit-and-run driver.'

Ursula's filthy face lit up. 'He's dead! He's really dead. So I can come home now. Oh, you don't know how relieved I am that this nightmare is over!'

Her mother was displaying such strange behaviour, Steph felt it best to humour her. She'd get her home, scrubbed free of the filth caking her, some hot food inside her and into bed. In the morning she'd get the doctor in to see her and decide what treatment she needed. As she put her arm around her, Steph realised that her mother had lost a good deal of weight. Through the coat, she could feel Ursula's ribs. It greatly distressed her to picture how her mother had been surviving all this time. At this moment, those things could wait, however. She needed to get her mother home. What was surprising to Steph, though, knowing her mother's past fondness for drink, was that of the many nasty smells emanating from her person, none was of alcohol.

# CHAPTER
# TWENTY-SEVEN

Steph shot bolt upright when she heard the slam of the front door heralding Jay's arrival home. Although she'd been asleep, her subconscious had been listening out for him, not from fear of his threat to make her regret disobeying his orders earlier, but because she didn't want him to disturb her sleeping mother.

Steph had been grateful to find that he had left the house when she got back with Ursula. Hopefully, once she'd recovered, Ursula would prove herself a far stronger opponent than Steph had ever been. She very much doubted Jay was going to get away with taking charge of the household finances any longer. Now he'd have to get a job and stop living off their money. One thing was certain: he wouldn't be at liberty to keep selling off the family heirlooms when her mother was around to put a stop to it.

As soon as they began their journey home, much to Steph's bewilderment, Ursula's confusing behaviour ceased and she seemed almost her old self. She was eager to get home and talked non-stop about her desire to resume her old life. Immediately she walked through the front door, she ordered Steph to get her a drink – which to her chagrin Steph was unable to oblige her with, as Jay and his friends had finished every drop they had at New Year.

Desperate to shed her filthy clothes and scour the months of accumulated grime from her body, Ursula then commanded Steph to run her a hot bath and to lay out her nightclothes. And then she could prepare a hot meal.

For Steph it was like old times. But she decided that, starting tomorrow, she wasn't going to revert to being at her mother's beck and call. Steph was going to start standing up to her. It was going to be hard, Ursula was not an easy woman to say no to, but there was Jay to drudge for, too, and the baby's health to consider. Steph couldn't take on any additional burdens.

Now, hearing her husband's feet pounding up the stairs, Steph was scrambling out of bed, pulling on her dressing gown to go and intercept him.

If he had brought that woman back with him again it was just too bad. He would have to explain to her who Steph really was. Ursula didn't take kindly to having her sleep disturbed, and Steph suspected this would be the first decent night's sleep in a proper bed she'd had in quite a while. She arrived at the top of the stairs at the same time as Jay.

When he spotted her, he smiled wickedly. 'Ah, you've done me a favour, saving me coming to you.' He put his hands on his hips and hurled at her, 'So, wife dear, make me look an idiot in front of my friend, would you? Well, you won't do that again.' He made a grab for Steph's hair but she jumped back out of his reach, snapping at him, 'Save what you've got in mind for me for another time. I don't want you waking my mother. This is the first decent—'

He stared at her in astonishment before cutting her short. 'Your mother's back!' he exclaimed.

The gleam of delight that sparked in his eyes puzzled her. What he said then utterly confounded her.

'At last! I knew she'd turn up eventually. Everything comes to those who wait. Seems *my* wait is over.'

Baffled by his remark, Steph asked him, 'What do you mean?'

Jay stared at her for a moment. 'Eh? Oh, well, I knew how worried you'd been, not knowing where your mother was. It was just a waiting game until she came back and put your mind at rest. Anyway, I'm off to bed. You sleep well, Steph.'

He stepped by her and jauntily made his way to his own room. She couldn't believe the change in him. Since he'd accused her of having an affair and trying to pass off another man's child as his, he had said not a single kind word. Now he was proclaiming that he was glad her mother was back and her mind had been put at rest. He'd even wished her a good night's sleep. This sudden change in Jay didn't make sense at all. But Steph was too tired after her eventful time tonight to try to fathom her husband's behaviour.

She was dreaming about her mother, although in the dream she couldn't actually see her, just hear her muffled voice, as if it was coming from a distance. Ursula was obviously trying to fend off an attacker. She was crying out frenziedly, 'Don't do this! Please, don't. No, no . . . don't!'

Then a shrill cry of fright rent the air and Steph sat bolt upright. It was no dream she was having, her mother really was crying out. Ursula must be having a nightmare.

Opening the door to her room, Steph ran inside, prepared to soothe her mother, only to stop short and stare uncomprehendingly at the scene that met her eyes.

There were two windows in the room. Her mother stood on the sill of one of them, hands pushing back against either side of the frame. Jay had both his hands on her shoulder blades.

'What on earth . . .' Steph blurted.

Jay's head jerked around. For a moment a look of horror crossed his face before it changed to one of relief. Grabbing hold of Ursula's arms, he gave a heave, pulling her backwards, and they both tumbled on to the floor with a thud. Scrambling upright, an incensed Jay exclaimed, 'I just stopped your drunken mother trying to throw herself out of the window again.'

Steph's eyes went to her mother, lying crumpled on the floor where she'd just fallen. 'What! Oh, my God. Why, Mother? What on earth made you want to kill yourself?'

Ursula jerked her head up to look at her. Eyes darting wildly, she cried out, 'You told me he was dead! You told me he was dead! Why did you lie to me? I'd never have come back if I known he was still alive.'

Steph was staring at her, astonished. Her mother's behaviour really was very worrying. She'd been acting irrationally when Steph had found her. On her return here she'd seemed more composed, but now . . . this.

Steph decided she would arrange for a doctor to come and see her mother first thing in the morning.

'I didn't lie to you, Mother. He *is* dead. You went to his funeral, remember?' Then a thought struck her and she looked at Jay in surprise. 'But . . . Mother isn't drunk. It was the first thing she ordered me to do when I got her home, fetch her up a bottle of vodka. I couldn't oblige because you and your friends finished off every drop of drink we had at New Year. So it's not drink that's made her do this again,' she told him adamantly, at the same time wondering just what had.

He gave a shrug. 'Oh, well, if she didn't do it through drink then it's probably that blow to the head she got when she tried the last time.'

'I just thank God you managed to stop her,' Steph sighed in relief. Then another thought struck her. 'But how did you happen to be in here, just when Mother was trying to jump out of the window?'

'I couldn't sleep. I was on my way down to get a drink when I heard the sound of a window opening coming from this room. Because of what had happened before, I was immediately worried so I popped my head around, just to check, and couldn't believe it when I saw what she was up to.'

Steph stared at her mother and implored her, 'Please, tell me, why are you trying to do away with yourself? Do you really see your life as so bad now you have to manage on a set amount each week? It's not a fortune, I grant you, but you could live well enough on it. It's a lot more than many families have to live on.'

Ursula refused to meet her daughter's eyes. Looking down, she gave a shrug.

Steph said to Jay, 'We'll have to get the doctor in, to see what he says about this.'

'Well, we can't leave her on her own tonight. I'm not really that tired. I'll stay in here and keep an eye on her.'

Ursula was staring at Jay, backing away all the time he spoke. 'There's no need for that really. I won't try anything to hurt myself again, you have my word. You don't need to stay in here and keep an eye on me.'

But Jay shook his head at her. 'Best be on the safe side. Now, you won't even know I'm here. I'll sit in that corner in a chair. Oh, has Steph told you our good news? We're having a baby. You're going to be a grandmother in a few short months. Now isn't that something to live for?'

At this news Ursula's face turned a deathly white and she moaned, 'No! Please tell me this isn't true?'

'Afraid it is,' he affirmed. Then, seeing the look of horror on her face, his own filled with disappointment and he said to her, 'Oh, I thought you'd be really pleased you're going to become a granny.'

Groaning in despair, Ursula doubled over. 'Oh, my God. Oh, my God,' she muttered.

Jay then addressed a shocked Steph, smiling at her. 'It's all right, darling, I've realised what an idiot I've been and just hope you can forgive me. We'll talk about it tomorrow, I can see you're dead on your feet now. Back off to bed with you and leave me to deal with your mother.'

But Steph wasn't listening to him. Her mother's reaction to this news didn't shock her. Ursula refused to admit in public that she was old enough to have a daughter of Steph's age, so becoming a grandmother was hardly going to be good news. What had really shocked Steph was Jay's sudden about-face. He'd told Ursula he was the father of her grandchild, when so far he'd steadfastly refused to accept he was, and even accused Steph of committing adultery. What was going on?

Jay cut into her thoughts, urging, 'Didn't you hear me, Steph? Come on, back to bed with you.'

'What? Oh, yes.' But she was worried for Ursula, lying crumpled on the floor, her head bowed. 'I'll just have a couple of hours then come and relieve you,' Steph suggested.

Jay nodded. 'If that's what you want to do.'

She made to depart but stopped short as a sudden vision of what she'd actually *seen* on first entering the room rose before her. He mother had had her feet firmly planted on the window sill, her hands pressed against each side of the frame. Jay had had his hands flat on each of her shoulders.

He was looking closely at Steph now. 'What's the matter?' he asked warily.

She stared at him blankly for a moment then her face turned a deathly shade of grey as the real truth of the situation dawned on her. 'You weren't trying to stop my mother from jumping out of the window, you were trying to push her out!' she blurted.

He glared at her. 'What? Don't be ridiculous, of course I wasn't.'

But she was adamant. 'I know what I saw.'

'What you saw was your mother trying to jump out of the window and me trying to pull her back in.'

Steph frenziedly shook her head. 'That's *not* what I saw. I saw that Mother had her feet on the sill and her hands pressed to either side of the frame. You had your hands flat on her shoulders blades. If she'd been trying to jump out of the window, she wouldn't have been trying to push herself backwards, would she? If you'd been trying to pull her back inside, you would have been grabbing her shoulders, not with your hands flat against them. You only grabbed her shoulders when I came in. What woke me up wasn't a nightmare, it was Mother pleading with you to stop doing what you were trying to do. You meant to kill her.' She saw him about to deny her claim and cried, 'I know what I saw. Why, Jay? For what reason do you want my mother dead?'

Then she knew, saw it all as clear as day. 'Oh, but of course. With her out of the way, I come fully into my inheritance, don't I? Was your plan to bully me into handing it all over to you, like you have been with the allowance and my wages? My mother was right all along about you, wasn't she? She said you'd only turned your attention to me because I'd told you she wasn't coming into Father's money, as you thought when you first made your play for her. Only you didn't know at the time that my father had left his affairs in such a way I would only come into the house and what was left of his money after my mother died.'

She recoiled from him in horror. 'She wasn't lying about that night you met, was she? It was *you* who was chatting her up in that club, and *you* who'd arranged to go out with her that night you called here. If I hadn't told you then that she wasn't the beneficiary of my father's Will, how far would you have gone to get your hands on the money, eh?

'We didn't bump into each other accidentally the next day, did we? Knowing you were wasting your time with my mother, you went after me, aiming to seduce me with your charm. And you succeeded there, didn't you? God, I was taken in by you! How stupid of me. You never loved me, did you? Everything you said to me was just lies. I can't believe I'm having the baby of a man who'd prey on vulnerable women to fill his own pockets. My child will turn out nothing like its father, I shall see to that.'

Eyes brimming with devastation, Steph continued, 'Mrs Sanders didn't leave of her own accord. You got rid of her, didn't you? Was that to save on her wages so there was more for you to spend or were you just getting her out of the way so no outsider would see what I was too stupid to?

'You were never defrauded out of your business by your friend, were you? That was just a scheme to get me to hand over my father's money to you, on the pretext I was saving my husband's business. Oh, God, and my heart was broken for you then. How stupid I was not to query why the figure you came up with to salvage the business was just about the same as my father had left. Of course, you'd have heard my mother bragging in the club to anyone who would listen about just how much her husband had left her, that's how you knew how much there was. As soon as I'd handed it over, I'd never have seen you again, would I? Oh, how bad you must have felt when I told you I couldn't get my hands on it! All that wasted acting talent.

'Was that when you planned to kill my mother? That very night. You obviously didn't realise when you succeeded in pushing her out of the window that there was a big shrub below that would break her fall, and that's why you were using the other window tonight.'

She scraped her hands through her hair, distraught.

'Now I realise why you were so upset when we arrived at the hospital to find Mother had signed herself out, and so anxious for her to come home. You couldn't try to get rid of her again if she wasn't around, could you? You weren't ringing round all her friends because you were worried about her whereabouts, but because you were hoping that one of them had heard from her and knew where she was hiding and you could get to her there. *That's* why you were so against me reporting her as a missing person to the police, just in case they should find her before you did and she decided to tell them the truth.'

Then she addressed her mother. 'But why didn't you report him?' she implored. 'You covered up what he'd tried to do to you by telling the hospital staff you fell out of the window. Instead of living here, you chose to go into hiding from him, living rough when your money ran out. It doesn't make sense to me. Well, I'm not going to turn a blind eye to this.' She looked hard at her mother who was staring back at her without saying a word. 'I'm fetching the police and you are going to tell them the truth about what *he* tried to do to you. And hopefully . . .' she swung round to face Jay and hissed '. . . *you* will rot in jail.'

To her shock, her mother frantically shook her head and cried out, 'No, you mustn't fetch the police! Look, you've got it all wrong . . . Jay didn't try to kill me either time, it was me that tried to kill myself.'

Steph stared at her in astonishment and cried out, 'You're lying, Mother. I keep telling you, I know what I saw. He was trying to push you out of that window and you were trying to stop him. Why are you shielding him? Well, whatever hold he's got on you, he's not got one on me.'

She made to carry out her threat to fetch the police when she felt a hand gripping her arm like a vice. She was being yanked backwards and thrown down on the bed. Gathering her wits, she looked up to see Jay glaring down at her. 'You've had your say, now I'm having mine. Then we'll see if you still want to get the police involved in this.'

That familiar nasty expression was back. 'You're right about all of it, my darling wife. I'm out to relieve you of everything you have, but not because I'm a con man, seeing a way to make himself some easy money. No, I'm doing it for revenge.'

'Revenge!' Steph exclaimed mystified. 'For what?'

His eyes slitted dangerously, he thrust a finger at Ursula. 'Why don't you ask *her*?'

Steph looked in confusion at her mother, still huddled on the floor.

'Mother? What's going on? What did you do to Jay that was so bad he's seeking revenge? Mother, answer me,' she demanded.

Ursula was opening and closing her mouth. Finally she stuttered, 'I . . . I . . .'

Jay leaped across to her. Before Ursula could stop him, he had clamped his hands under her arms, lifted her bodily off the ground and was hissing at her, 'Tell her.'

A look of pure horror on her face, Ursula beseeched him, 'No, please don't make me do this? I beg you. I'll do anything, anything you want, but not this, please, not this . . .'

'I said, tell her,' boomed Jay, squeezing her arms tighter, making her cry out in pain.

Fear of the unknown nearly shifted Steph. Just what was it Jay was demanding her mother tell her?

Putting his lips against her ear, he ordered Ursula, 'Either you tell her or I will.'

Ursula lifted her eyes to meet her daughter's fearful ones. Gulping hard, she muttered something so low it was inaudible to Steph.

Jay poked her hard in her shoulder. 'Louder, so we can all hear.'

She gulped again and hung her head so low her chin was touching her chest. But the words that came out of her mouth struck Steph with horror.

'Your husband . . . he's . . . Oh, God, he's my son!

# CHAPTER TWENTY-EIGHT

Steph felt the walls closing in on her. Her mother's words were reverberating inside her head. *Your husband is my son. Your husband is my son.* It was a sick joke. It had to be. Were it not then the situation she found herself in was too horrific to contemplate. That she was married to her own brother and having his baby . . .

'This . . . this is some sort of cruel joke, isn't it?' she pleaded.

It was Jay who answered. 'Afraid not. I am your elder brother. Half-brother actually, but still your brother.'

'I didn't know who he was, I promise you I didn't, until you were already married!' Ursula cried. 'He came up to see me in my room while you were busy getting him something to eat, and that's when he told me who he was. He said he wanted me to know who he was and why he was killing me. Then he pushed me out of the window.'

'And you never thought to tell me I had married my brother before you disappeared from hospital?' Steph cried, incensed.

Ursula implored her, 'He'd tried to kill me once and I knew he wouldn't stop until he had. I had to sign myself out of the hospital before you came to fetch me home or I knew I'd be done for the next chance he got.'

Her mother's selfishness had reached new depths. Her only thought had been to save her own skin, not a care for getting Steph out of an incestuous marriage before she got pregnant! The room swam before her. She felt that her life's blood was draining away.

Jay was smiling in ghoulish amusement. 'I thought she was selfish, abandoning me as a baby to give herself a better life. But skulking off like she did to save her own skin, sooner than risk it informing her daughter just who she'd married . . . well, it beggars belief, doesn't it, Steph?' He sounded quite kindly.

Then he addressed Ursula. 'Look at me.' His barked order had her head jerking up, terrified eyes meeting his. Sneering at her, he continued, 'Have you any idea what it was like for me to find out, at the age of twenty-five, that the woman I thought was my mother, the woman I adored, was not even related to me? That my own mother abandoned me just to get a better life for herself.

'My mother . . . or the woman I always believed to be my mother . . . told me it all on her death bed. She said she couldn't go to her grave carrying such a terrible secret. I was the son she couldn't love more, she was my mother in every way . . . but she never actually gave birth to me. The woman who did went off one day and left me behind when I was nine months old. She said she'd meant to tell me one day, knew she'd have to when I needed my birth certificate for anything, but she realised I'd be hurt by all this . . . hah! That's an understatement . . . so left it until she had no choice but to tell me, hoping I'd take it better the older I was.'

The icy expression in his eyes turned to blind hatred for the woman at whom he was glaring. 'My mother found you sheltering in a shop doorway one night when she was on her way home from work. You were crying, and because she was a kind person she stopped to ask you if you needed any help. You told her you were pregnant, that your family had thrown you out with not a penny to your name and nowhere to go, so she took pity on you and offered to share her home with you.

'You were being sick all the time so you couldn't work. She kept you, and then, of course, after I was born you still couldn't work, so then she supported both of us. Then, when I was nine months old, you went out one day to fetch the weekly groceries while she stayed home with me. Only you never came back. It wasn't until afterwards that she realised not only had you gone off with the grocery money, you'd also cleared out the tin where she kept her money to pay the bills and give us all a good Christmas. She never heard a word from you after that. Not one word. She didn't know whether you were dead or alive. Years later she found out you were very much alive, though.

'She saw a picture in the *Mercury*, of you and your husband when he was being honoured for something by the hospital. She didn't recognise you, all glammed up, but she recognised your name. "Gerald Mortimer with his wife of twelve years, Ursula Mortimer *née* Turnbull", it said under the photograph of you both. It was obvious then to my mother that you'd abandoned me to get yourself a better life. Because that's what you did, didn't you? Admit it, you selfish bitch!' he bellowed furiously.

Gulping, Ursula admitted, 'Yes . . . I did. But . . .'

'Was my father married, was that it, or were you just a slut who slept around and found yourself pregnant without knowing who the father was? Was that why your family threw you out?' he demanded.

A shaking Ursula, wringing her hands, blurted out, 'No, it was nothing like that. I was adopted as a child of three by a family who had a son a year or so older than me. Alan and I always got on, and when we grew older it turned to love. We secretly planned to marry when we were of age. He wasn't my real brother so we were doing nothing wrong. We only went together once, we never meant it to happen, we just got carried away. I was just sixteen at the time and had no idea I was pregnant, but my adoptive mother knew I was.

'She tackled me and it all came out, about Alan and myself. It was just so awful . . . My adoptive father was staring at me as if I were a whore, and my mother was screaming that we'd committed incest. We were brother and sister . . . if this became public they'd never hold their heads up again. The next thing I knew my bags were packed and I was out in the street, told never to darken their door again. I was also told that Alan was being sent immediately to Ireland, to stay with an uncle there and put the greatest distance possible between us. I was at my wit's end when Nancy found me that night. I was so grateful to her for taking me in . . .'

'. . . that you repaid her by walking out with her money and leaving me behind,' Jay screamed at her. 'Had you met Mortimer by then, realised what type of life he could give you, but knew he wouldn't marry you if he learned you had an illegitimate child?' He saw the look on her face and knew he had hit the nail on the head. 'You make me sick!'

Ursula implored him to understand. 'But I wasn't only getting a better life for myself, I was giving you a far better one than ever I could while I lived with you. I knew Nancy loved you. It was obvious by the way she always looked at you, the way she held you. She desperately wished you were hers, the son she would have had if her husband had not been killed in the war. By leaving you with her, I was giving her what she wanted, wasn't I? I was fulfilling her dreams. She had so much more to offer you than I had. She had a home to live in, a well-paid job as a supervisor for the GPO . . .'

'Which she had to give up when you left,' Jay savagely cut in. 'She couldn't look after me and go out to work as well, and she'd no family other than a sister who lives in Scotland to help her. She couldn't afford to live in her house any more so we had to move to a tiny terrace house with no hot running water and only an outside lavatory shared with the family next-door.

'I asked Mum why she never handed me over to the authorities, like she easily could have done when she realised you weren't coming back for me, and she said she couldn't do it because she loved me too much by then, couldn't bear to live the rest of her life thinking of me in a kid's home or being adopted by people who might not treat me well.

'You called me Robert. She wasn't fond of that

name so she called me Jason and changed my surname to hers to stop questions being asked.' His face was filled with contempt for Ursula. 'My own mother didn't care a damn about me, yet a woman with no blood connection was prepared to go to the lengths she did to see me right.'

A ghostly faced Ursula couldn't meet his eye. 'I never knew any of this . . .'

'No, because from the day you left, you forgot about us. We no longer existed for you, did we? There were you, living the life of Riley, in your lovely big house, wearing your fancy clothes, lavishing money and attention on your legitimate child . . . while another woman was having to slog her guts out to support your illegitimate brat. If you'd even thought to send her a few pounds now and again, it would have made things so much easier for her. But, no, that would have meant less to spend on yourself, wouldn't it? Mother did machining at home, working from the crack of dawn until well after I'd gone to bed at night, and what she earned from all her hard work just about kept us in rent and food, with damn all left over. But she chose to do that so she was always home for me, especially when I came home from school. She didn't want me being a latch-key kid. The first holiday we ever had was after I'd started work. We went on the train to Mablethorpe for the day. It took me weeks to save for it.

'How she did it I'll never know, but I always had shoes on my feet and clothes on my back and good food in my stomach. I passed my eleven plus and was told I was bright enough to go to grammar school. It broke Mum's heart because she couldn't afford to send me there, had no choice but for me to attend the secondary modern. I could have been someone, had a well-paid job, if I'd been educated at the grammar. Instead I ended up in a dead-end job in a factory as a loader, then driver, for a delivery firm, but at least I was able to ease my mother's burden by handing over a good bit of my wages every week. And, let me tell you, she felt guilty for taking it off me. I had to insist she did.

'I was twenty when she was first taken ill. She collapsed over her machine and blacked out for well over ten minutes. She told me the doctor said it was nothing to worry about, but I think he told her she was working too hard and needed to rest more. Doing that would have meant she'd need to take more money off me, and she wouldn't, so she continued working as hard as ever. Then one day she was rushing to catch a bus home after being in town for some shopping, needing to get back as she had an order to fill that the bloke who supplied her outwork was coming to collect later that afternoon. She couldn't get her breath and collapsed in the street. Someone called an ambulance and she was taken to hospital.

They kept her in to do some tests on her and found she had a disease of the lungs. There was no cure for it. Naturally I said I would look after her then. She was my mother, after all.

'I was engaged at the time to the woman who was the love of my life. I idolised her. At first she was great about the fact that our wedding would have to wait because I couldn't put anything by when I was keeping my mother as best I could. Then Mother started getting worse. It got to the state where she couldn't be left on her own because she couldn't even make herself a cup of tea, the exertion tired her so much. Thankfully the old biddy who lived next door kept an eye on her while I was out at work, and I stayed in with her every night. That was when my fiancée dropped her bombshell on me.

'This state of affairs could go on for years, she said, and she wanted to get married, have a family. She wasn't prepared to wait for me indefinitely so she was ending it between us. She gave me back my ring. I was devastated . . . I loved that woman with all my heart. She was everything to me. I couldn't even tell my mother the real reason for our break-up as she would have felt so guilty. I had to bear my misery in silence.

'Mum had been ill for over four years by now. It was awful for me watching her slowly get worse, knowing there was nothing anyone could do for her. At times the pain was so terrible she couldn't bear it. The hospital were useless. Some nights I'd hear her crying with it, from my room next door. Then five months ago, in the middle of the night, I heard her banging on the wall to summon me.

'I found her in a dreadful state, struggling to breathe. I insisted I call the doctor, she insisted I didn't. She knew her time had come and wanted to die in her own bed, not surrounded by strangers in a hospital. But she couldn't die carrying the burden of her secret. That's when she told me she wasn't really my mother and how I came to be with her. She held no bitterness towards you for the hard life your selfishness brought her. She said the joy I'd given her more than compensated for what she'd had to go without. Five minutes after she finished telling me all this, she died. I was holding her in my arms. She was forty-five years old.'

He glared at Ursula then with pure loathing. 'My mother might not have had any bitterness towards you, but I certainly did. I vowed that I'd make you pay for the years of struggle she went through to raise me and for your responsibility for her early death. I know that had she not been so worn out from working her guts out to raise me single-handed, that disease might never have taken hold in the first place. It was obvious to me that all you cared about was money, so that was where I decided to hurt you most. I was going to bleed you dry of every penny you had, then I would be living the life you'd been enjoying and you'd know exactly what it had been like for me and Mum, living the life we had to. And while I was at it, I was going to hurt you in any other way I could find.

'When I was going through Mum's personal papers after she died, I found the newspaper cutting she had saved of you and your husband. Finding out where you lived was easy enough. Mum had been paying for an insurance policy to cover her funeral. After paying out for that there was just over sixty pounds left over. I had my fighting fund.

'I used most of it to rent the furnished flat I told my dear sister I owned, and to buy an old banger that came in handy. The rest of the money I used to pursue Steph.

'Oh, but before that, I knew Gerald Mortimer worked at the hospital so I chatted one of the porters up and found out which was his car. I followed him home one night and for several days after that. Sitting in my car, I watched the comings and goings from this house to get a feel for things while I worked out how to ruin you. That's when I found out I had a sister.

'I wondered who the young blond woman was who kept coming and going from the house. So one night, when she'd come out of the end of the drive and was going off down the street, I asked a woman walking her dog who she was, making up a story that I was looking for a long-lost friend and could she tell me if that was her. She told me that the young woman was Professor Mortimer's daughter, Stephanie.'

He looked at Steph, huddled on the bed, her face the colour of parchment from the shock of his story. 'I'd never met you but I hated you. *She* never abandoned you, did she? Look at the life she gave you and the one she gave me. It wasn't fair. But I was going to make it my business to remedy that.'

His flashed his eyes back to Ursula. 'First, though, I knew I had to get Mortimer out of the way. It would be him controlling the purse strings. I needed you in sole control for me to get my hands on the money.' Then he looked at Steph again. 'I was intrigued to know what you got up to when you went out at night, so I followed you and saw you were involved with a bloke. Asking around, I found out you were engaged to him. Well, I'd lost the woman I loved, why shouldn't my sister find out what a romantic disappointment felt like? He was going to have to go, too. Only you weren't in love with your fiancé, were you? I found that out later. His death didn't affect you like I wanted it to.'

The fact that Steph had been engaged to be married was news to Ursula, but she was too traumatised by everything else that was going on for it to register properly.

Steph, though, was looking wildly at Jay as the

significance of what he'd just said cut through the mist in her mind.

'What exactly do you mean by saying you had to get my father *out of the way*? That William *had to go*?'

The grin on Jay's face was one of pure evil.

Steph gasped in horror. 'Neither death was an accident, was it?'

The grin widened. 'Well, the police were happy, weren't they?' He proudly puffed out his chest. 'Your fiancé was easy. It took a couple of nights of lurking in his garden, but it was worth it. It was obvious to me he was drunk by the way he drove his car up the drive. He was so drunk he fell out of it. While he was struggling to get up, he never saw me creeping out of the shadows at the side of the garage. Didn't even cry out when I whacked him on his forehead with a piece of lead pipe. Went down like a stone. The only hard part was heaving that fat body of his over to the rockery and making it look like he fell over and bashed his head on a stone.

'Mortimer wasn't so easy. I was watching from my car when you all drove out in his car one night, dressed up to the nines, so it was obvious it was some posh do you were going to. I decided to follow in case I saw my chance. I was parked a little way down the street from the house you'd all gone into when I saw a taxi turning into the drive. When it drove out again you and her . . .' he flashed a dark look over at Ursula, '. . . were in the back of it. That meant Mortimer was by himself and hopefully driving home in his car. An idea to get him to an isolated spot so I could carry out my plan to get rid of him came to me then. I put a note under his wiper, telling him I had important information about his wife that he ought to know and, if he wanted to find out what it was, I'd be waiting in the lay-by on the A47 just after the Red Cow pub.

'It was a country road and unlit. I began to worry he wasn't coming, it was after two and I was about to go home. Thankfully I didn't. When he finally turned up, he just sat in his car waiting for me to go to him. Well I wasn't going to; the jumped-up little shit could come to me. Besides, I hadn't quite decided how I was going to finish him. It wasn't until he finally got out of his car to come over that I knew. Before he had time to reach me, I revved up my car and headed straight for him. What an impact!' Jay smiled at the memory. 'Mortimer flew at least three feet from the ground. I could see his face so clearly in my headlights. My car was a bit of a mess afterwards, the bonnet was completely caved in, but the engine was still working so I could still make my getaway. The only thing left to do was burst one of the tyres on Mortimer's car, so it looked like he'd had to stop because of a puncture. Oh, and drag the body into the road so people would think it was a hit and run.'

Steph felt faint with horror. 'You murdered my father *and* William?'

Stabbing a finger towards Ursula, Jay spat, 'My mother died before her time through what *she* did to her. That's murder, too, in my book.'

Steph screamed at him, 'What Mother did to you was very selfish, and maybe it did play a part in your adoptive mother's early death, but she never physically took a life! You're mad ... insane! You won't get away with this.'

Jay smiled maliciously at her. 'But I already have. You've no proof I'd anything to do with those deaths. You may be right about me being mad, though.' He glared over at Ursula. 'I was mad as hell, after I'd spent all that money on buying drinks for my own mother and pretending I was head over heels for you that night in the club, to be told by your daughter that all the bragging you had done about coming into a fortune from your dead husband was just lies, because he'd left it to *her*.'

He gave a digusted snort. 'It wasn't hard for me to charm you, though, was it – Mother? I've never met a woman so full of herself, totally convinced she's irresistible to any man. You lapped up the attention I was giving you. Couldn't wait to parade me in front of your friends. It sickened me to know the trash I was descended from. I couldn't wait for the moment I could tell you just who I was. After I'd got what I wanted, of course.'

Ursula was doubled over by now, arms wrapped around herself, rocking backwards and forwards, mumbling softly.

Jay continued, 'Anyway I was fucking mad with rage again when after all the trouble I'd gone to, I learned that my dear little *wife* here wasn't able to get her hands on anything expect a paltry few pounds a week until . . .' he jabbed a finger in Ursula's direction again '. . . *that bitch died*. Well, I wasn't going to wait indefinitely, playing the dutiful husband. You're right, Steph, that was the night I decided my dear mother was going to join her husband and your fiancé, and then you'd come into your inheritance which I was going to relieve you of. If that shrub hadn't have saved her neck, this would all have been over by now and I'd have fulfilled my vow and been living it up.

'Oh, and by the way, those condoms I used to stop you getting pregnant . . . well, before I used them, I pricked holes in all of them. I wanted to let you see what it was like to be left with a baby, like my mother was. And once you were pregnant, by claiming it wasn't mine, I didn't have to pretend any longer that I was your dutiful loving husband. I could have some fun playing the injured party instead. The fact I got

394

my sister pregnant was a bonus. Before I went off to live my new life on your money, I was going to let you in on the joke, naturally.'

There were no words strong enough for Steph to describe how she felt about this man before her. He had to be deranged to go to such lengths to seek his revenge against Ursula. But just because he had been sussed by them, she didn't feel it was likely he would give up on fulfilling his vow. Now his plan was all out in the open she saw only one way he could fulfil his ambition. Get rid of herself as well as her mother, and as her husband he would be the sole beneficiary of the full inheritance. Could he get away with throwing them both out of the window or would he concoct another diabolical *accident*? But like hell would she sit here meekly and wait for him to do his worst. She and her mother would both put up a fight.

Her eyes darted, searching for something she could use as a weapon to launch a surprise attack on Jay. Whether she could immobilise him for long enough to get downstairs and summon the police was debatable as she was no match for him physically, but anything was worth a try. Her eyes caught the heavy-based lamp on the bedside cabinet. Could she distract him long enough to reach over and grab it?

Before she had time to think any further, she jumped in shock as an unexpected shrill scream rent the air, to be followed by a dull thud. Simultaneously

Jay let out a cry of 'Fucking hell!' as he fell to his knees, clutching the side of his head.

Steph could see her mother on her feet, arm raised as if she had just thrown something. Steph's eyes darted to the floor beside Jay. Lying there on its side was a heavy glass ashtray, fresh blood smeared on an edge of it. Her mother had done what Steph herself had been intending to.

Without further ado, Steph seized her own chance. She made a dash for the door and down the stairs. In her haste to arrive at the bottom, she nearly slipped on the edge of a step, only just managing to save herself from tumbling head over heels the rest of the way down by grabbing the banister. She ran for the table beside the stairs on which stood the telephone. She was just about to dial the last nine when she froze.

'Put down that phone,' a familiar voice ordered her. She jerked up her head to see Jay glaring down at her from the top of the stairs. There was a trickle of blood oozing from a wound on his temple where the ashtray her mother had thrown had made contact. Her mother! Where was she? What had he done to her?

There was no time to think about that now, though, as Jay was racing down the stairs. Steph's eyes darted to the front door. It was doubtful she could make it. The only other way for her to escape was out of the back of the house. Dropping the receiver which thudded dully as it landed on the carpet, she kicked up her heels and dashed to the kitchen. The back door was unlocked. She shot through it and on into the garden. Intent on putting distance between them, she ran. The sensible course would be to head for the tradesmen's entrance again but a bright moon was hanging over the garden, illuminating the boundary wall. Steph stuck to the shadows. She was heading in the direction of the well.

She had no idea how far behind her Jay was but if she changed direction now she would have to run back across an exposed length of lawn and he would see her. But a few feet behind the well was a small dense copse of trees and thick undergrowth. If she could reach that, she could hide herself in it until he tired of looking then she'd be at liberty to make her way to the tradesmen's entrance and fetch help. By now she had a stitch in her side and was panting for breath but she was not far from the well . . .

She was only a few feet or so from it when, without warning, a hand grabbed her ankle and down she went. Rolling over, she jerked up her head to see Jay scrambling to right himself after his dive to stop her flight. She jumped upright, meaning to turn around and resume her escape, but Jay was on his feet too by now and within reach of her.

They stood staring at each other: Steph tremulous

with fear; Jay triumphant. He took a step towards her. Instinctively, she took a step back. He took another step forward. She took one back. She knew he only had to stretch out an arm and he could grab her. Why wasn't he? He was tormenting her, that was why. He was squeezing out every last drop of revenge he could. The light from the moon lit his face grotesquely. Any minute now she knew he was going to make his final move on her. She had nothing to fend him off with.

He took another step forward, she took one back. And froze. Her heel had hit a solid mass. The wall of the well. No more stalling for time, hoping for a miracle. This was it then. Before she met her end, though, there was something she needed to put him straight on.

'You said your mother loved you more than life itself, went without herself to provide for you, was always there for you whenever you needed her? Well, I had none of that with our mother. You've just had a taste of how selfish she can be. I've had a lifetime of experiencing it, day in, day out. If I'd had the choice of swapping my life for yours, I'd have grabbed that chance.'

But she could see her words had bounced off him. His need for revenge was all that mattered to Jay. He was standing over her, smiling menacingly down. Powerless, she watched as he slowly raised his right arm, caught the glint of moonlight on a metal object clutched in his hand. To brace herself for what was to come, she smacked down both hands to steady herself on the stone sides of the well, knowing that behind her loomed the inky blackness of the shaft.

A stone under her right hand wobbled. Her heart thudded, a sliver of hope invading her. She clutched at the stone and gave it a tug. The remains of the crumbling cement still holding it in place fell away. Clutching the weapon tightly, she thrust back her arm and swung it forward with all the force she could summon, to land against the side of his head, mechanically jumping sideways to avoid the weapon in his hand.

The meat mallet he'd been in the process of clubbing her with arced away in the air, to land by Steph's feet. Blood pouring from a fresh gash on his temple where the stone she had struck him with had made its impact, Jay stood staring at her in utter shock for what seemed to Steph like hours before slowly he started falling forward. As she watched in horror he doubled over the edge of the well then slid head first down it, several sickening thuds resounding as his body hit the sides. Then came a final dull report as it landed heavily at the bottom, twenty or so feet below. How long Steph stood staring blindly down into the darkness she wasn't aware. It was the screaming that jolted her out of her stupor, and then she realised it was her own screams she was hearing.

When Steph had calmed herself a little she realised she had killed her husband . . . brother. Was she now a murderer, the same as him? Her whole body began to shake violently. She had no idea what to do first. Call the police or an ambulance? A picture of Paul rose before her then. He had made her promise that if ever she was in need of help, she must not hesitate to call him, day or night. He would tell her what she needed to do.

The phone seemed to ring for hours before she heard a sleepy voice announce, 'Hello, Paul Fawkes.'

Steph blurted hysterically, 'You said I could call you if I needed you! I *do* need you to tell me what to do. I don't know whether I killed him or not. I . . .'

'Is that you, Steph? But it's three o'clock in the . . . Oh, God, has he done something to you? Has he attacked you again? Are you injured?'

'No, I'm not. But he did attack me . . .' The tears came then and she cried out, 'He tried to kill my mother! Then he tried to murder me, but I think it's me that's killed him. Oh, Paul . . .'

'Steph,' he commanded her, 'you can't possibly know what you're saying. Stay where you are, I'm on my way.'

She heard the receiver being slammed down and then the piercing sound of the dialling tone.

# CHAPTER
# TWENTY-NINE

She couldn't remember making her way back to the well but that was where Paul found her a while later, sitting with her back against it, knees drawn up, head buried between her arms, sobbing her heart out. As she sensed his arrival, her head jerked up.

'Oh, thank God you're here! I'm so sorry to disturb you but I didn't know what to do for the best. I just couldn't seem to think straight . . .'

As Paul dropped down beside her, frantically scanning his eyes over her, expecting to find physical injuries and relieved to see none, he told her, 'I'd have been here sooner only I couldn't make you hear at the front door and had to find my way around the back. I was on my way to try the door, hoping I could get in that way, when I heard you crying. What the hell's happened, Steph? What is it that your husband has done?'

'He's not just my husband though, Paul.'

He screwed up his face in incomprehension. 'What do you mean?'

'Jay's my brother too.'

Steph took a shuddering breath and related her horrific tale to him. When she had finally finished, Paul was so astounded by it all he could not speak for several minutes. All he could do was gather the poor young woman into his arms and cradle her to him, muttering over and over, 'Oh, Steph. Oh, Steph.'

It was she who finally pulled him out of his state of shock. 'We need to do something, don't we? Fetch help. He could still be alive down there, and if he is, we can't leave him to die, can we?'

Can't we? thought Paul. There was indeed a chance that Jay had survived and was lying down there, injured and unconscious. With medical help he could well pull through, and then he could prosecute Steph for trying to murder him, and she'd be imprisoned. Even if he didn't go to that length, for the rest of their days Steph and her mother would constantly be in fear of him. Blind hatred swamped Paul then. Two could seek revenge. After all, the man at the bottom of the well had senselessly murdered the love of Paul's life, for his own vengeful madness.

He unwrapped his arms from around Steph and spoke firmly to her. 'Listen to me, there is no way that . . .' he couldn't bring himself to say Jay's name

'. . . that vile monster down there is still breathing, believe me. Now if I had my way we'd just leave him there, but we can't, it wouldn't be right. What you did was in self-defence, but for the police to reach that conclusion you'd need to tell them everything that led up to this. The newspapers would have a field day. Do you really want to live the rest of your life with fingers pointed at you? Do you want your child to have it known that its father was also its uncle? Sensations such as this are never forgotten. But there is a way no one need know any of this. So I'll tell you what you should do next.'

He could see she was struggling with her conscience. 'If you can't do this for yourself, do it for your child,' he urged then.

Steph eyed her swelling stomach. Placed one hand gently on it. This new life developing inside her was the innocent product of one man's insane lust for revenge. It wasn't right that a child's whole life should be blighted because of the misdeeds of its father. She would see to that.

'What do I need to do to keep it all a secret?' she asked Paul.

# CHAPTER THIRTY

The smells wafting through from the kitchen were mouth-watering.

Steph took a last appraising look around the room, to satisfy herself that all was in place for the arrival of the guests she had invited to help celebrate the first birthday of her daughter Mira, named because it was the nearest she could get to 'miracle' without actually naming her that. It was what her daughter was to Steph.

After discovering the close relationship between Mira's father and herself, throughout the rest of her pregnancy Steph was never without the fear that her baby could arrive in the world suffering from abnormalities, but those fears had miraculously proved to be unfounded. She had arrived perfect in every way. Mira was the image of Steph herself. When she was old enough to ask questions about why she hadn't a father, she was going to be told by her mother that he'd been a wonderful man who had been looking forward to becoming a father, but had died in a tragic accident before she'd been born.

Death due to Misadventure was the official conclusion drawn by the Coroner when he'd been presented with the facts of Jay's death by the police. Steph herself had related them, just as she'd been rehearsed by Paul, when she had called them in the next morning. The police were told by his distraught wife that Jay had gone out the previous evening, saying it was for a drink with his friends. She'd been in bed when he'd come home, and only knew he'd come back because his car was in the drive. He hadn't joined her in bed that night, and on checking around the next morning for his whereabouts she had found the back door wide open and no sign of him anywhere except for a packet of his cigarettes lying on the grass by the well. Fearing the worst, she had summoned the police.

It was a grave-faced PC who had confirmed her fears. They had found her husband's lifeless body, crumpled at the bottom of the well. The police surgeon had established he'd been drinking. In fact, the smashed remains of a bottle of rum had been found around his body. (In truth, Paul's doing, having returned home to fetch it that night to add weight to the tale they were about to weave.) It was concluded that on arriving back that night, Jay had taken the bottle and his cigarettes and gone down to the well, for reasons known only to himself. The worse for drink, he must have toppled backwards off the wall and fallen down inside. It wasn't possible to determine whether the injuries he'd suffered had been the cause of death or whether the icy cold down there had been responsible. Or perhaps both.

With the help of Paul, Steph had locked all memories of that night away, along with the rest of her time with Jay. For the sake of her daughter she had turned him in her mind from the vile man he was into a thoroughly decent, loving person whose loss to her would forever be deeply felt.

Steph had resigned herself to the fact that she would never again take another man into her life romantically. To have a full, lasting relationship, of the type she had truly believed she had found with Jay before she'd fallen pregnant, would involve being honest about her past. For her daughter's sake, that was something she could never be.

Towards her mother, Steph would always carry mixed emotions. Part of her could never forgive Ursula for choosing to allow her daughter to remain in a relationship with her own brother. But had Ursula for once in her life chosen to act unselfishly, then Steph would not be about to celebrate her precious daughter's first birthday, or had the last year of joy with her to look back on, the years of joy stretching ahead of her too.

Her daughter apart, some further good had come

from Jay's disruption of their lives. Ursula was now a changed woman. After agreeing with Paul their plan of action, Steph had discovered her locked in the wardrobe by Jay, waiting in terror for him to return after dealing with Steph and revenge himself on her. No one had been more relieved than she to learn that her son no longer posed any threat to her. In her gratitude she had announced that from then on she would become the mother she had never been to Steph, and would be a doting grandmother to the baby when it came.

On hearing this, Steph had felt it best not to hold her breath. This new Ursula would probably be short lived, judging by her past behaviour. But in this she was to be proved wrong. It appeared that her behaviour of the past had come back to haunt her, and her two brushes with death had made Ursula take stock of herself. She went to bed one woman and got up the next day as someone completely different. She always put others before herself now, did more than her fair share of looking after the house, and never went out socialising unless it was to attend something with her daughter and granddaughter. Any spare money she had was lavished on Mira, never herself. The delicious smells drifting in from the kitchen had been created by Ursula, her granddaughter sitting in her high chair beside her for company.

The allowance was providing them with a decent lifestyle for the moment, but prices were rising and in time Steph would probably return to work while Ursula stayed home to look after Mira.

The house that for all but a year and a few months of her life had been Steph's prison, was now her sanctuary.

The cheerful chime of the doorbell alerted her to the fact that the first of their guests had arrived. She knew without checking who it would be.

It had been decided by Paul and Steph jointly that Gerald had already hurt his wife enough with his homosexuality. There was no need for her to know Paul's significance to him. To Ursula, Paul was a man her daughter had become friendly with in one of her temporary jobs. The friendship had developed into the close one it was now. He was also Mira's proud godfather and, as long as he was alive, the child would never lack for a father figure. Paul doted on his godchild. At Mira's christening he had vowed to be there for her at every stage of her life, whenever she needed him, and Steph never doubted he always would be, no matter what.

She hoped that one day Paul would fall in love again, even if society would not let him display his love for his partner in public, but as matters stood right this minute he was content. He felt Gerald would have been very happy for him to use his legacy to expand the dental business, which was going from strength to strength and keeping him very busy and well provided for; he'd two wonderful friends in Steph and Ursula; and in Mira he had a child he could love.

The doorbell chimed again and continued chiming. Steph laughed. Paul was obviously standing with his finger pressed to it and wouldn't release it until his summons had been answered.

She cast one last look around the room. At the table groaning with children's party food, a pink iced cake centre-stage; the bunches of balloons hanging from the ceiling, creating a riot of colour; the birthday banner hanging across the back wall; the toys laid out to keep all the invited children and the birthday girl herself amused.

Nodding in satisfaction that nothing had been forgotten that could make her treasured daughter's first birthday a memorable occasion, Steph hurried to let Paul in.